The Last Sunset

The Last Sunset

Daniel Jay Paul

To order additional copies of this book, contact:
Xlibris
1-888-795-4274
www.Xlibris.com
Orders@Xlibris.com
554343

Is it the wisdom of the ages or the knowledge of the aged that we revere? And in the end is it death or undying love that prevails?

ONE

On the outskirts of the small city of Evergreen, thirty miles from where the White Pine River empties into Lake Michigan at Farehaven, the river gently meanders past the Pioneer Manor Nursing Home. It was a sultry June morning, as Steve Hadley eased his car through the gently winding curves along the riverbank, out past the city limits. An anxiousness gnawed at his stomach in nervous anticipation. What did community service really mean? How bad could it be? Emptying patient bedpans? Peeling potatoes in the kitchen? Scrubbing toilets? It was an old fear, at least as old as a nineteen year-old can have, the fear of the unknown.

Steve cracked the side window of his Ford Mustang in response to the beads of sweat ponding on the curly blond hair at the back of his neck. He swallowed hard, his throat dry, as he pulled up the drive.

One thousand hours of community service, he couldn't really believe it. Obviously, the judge had no sense of humor when it came to college pranks. This prank had involved too much alcohol, too much spray paint, and, as luck would have it, a sculpture donated to the university by Judge Granby's family. He was sure now, in objective reflection, that losing his temper in the courtroom hadn't helped his situation either.

Steve wheeled into a parking spot, ignoring the 'employee of the month' sign, listened to the end of "The Horizontal Bop" on his tape player, and turned off the car.

He walked slowly, his amble showing neither arrogance nor fear; he was determined to not let it show. He was tall, and broad at the shoulder, but narrow at the hip. The arms extending from his short sleeve, green polo shirt, were muscular and sculpted. His blue eyes flashed over the landscape, taking in a facility that he had passed a hundred times before, perhaps a thousand, but had never noticed.

Unkempt arbors surrounded the building, white paint from the wood trim carelessly splattered on the chocolate brown brick. Nurse Hackett met him ten steps inside the door, sized him up instantly, and looked at her watch, "You're late!"

"You know who I am?" Steve wondered aloud.

"You're the jailbird, right?" She didn't wait for an answer, "come with me."

Nancy Hackett had the shape of a mushroom turned upside down. She was a shade over five foot, her pudgy, round face, which bore a small mole by her lip, was still pleasant despite the abundance of her excess weight. She waddled down the corridor, the floor of tan tiles flecked with white bordered by tan concrete block walls glistening under the florescent glow, her enormous buttocks bouncing with every step. Steve followed along like a lost puppy examining his new surroundings. If death had a color, he was sure that the Pioneer Manor Nursing Home was decorated in that grim hue.

Nancy Hackett had once been a good nurse, there was a time not so long ago when she actually cared about her job, and the people that she cared for. In fact, she did not even realize that she had stopped caring, but she had, suffering under the dominance of her husband Barton Hackett, the nursing home administrator. His unrelenting pursuit of the dollar bill had worn her down, for when he wasn't talking about money directly, he was talking about discipline, staff discipline and fiscal discipline, and productivity, always productivity. Some days she would like to take his productivity and tell him just where he could stick it.

She led Steve to an office marked 'Barton Hackett, Executive Director', "Wait here," she commanded, and entered the room unceremoniously.

"Steve Hadley is here from Judge Granby," she announced without emotion.

Barton Hackett looked up at his wife, her hair short, red, and tidy. He was eight years her senior, but he was sure she was well on her way to catching up. He wasn't a medical person by training, he was a certified numbers cruncher, but he was sure, nevertheless, that the extra load she struggled with continuously was aging her rapidly. He looked up at her blue eyes behind the wire-rimmed spectacles, and then down to her hips, which had a circumference that equaled her height. When he thought of the girl he had married ten short years before, it hurt him just to look at her. At twenty-three she had possessed an athletic body. How could he have known that she didn't have the fortitude or constitution to maintain it? He no longer made any public reference to her as his wife, and spent the private moments, when visions of her and her obesity forced their way into his thoughts, assuring himself that he had no part in the blame for her condition. He sighed.

"Show him in, Nurse Hackett."

Steve felt as though he were being either ushered into the inner sanctum of a holy shrine, or let in the private, behind the scenes area of a funeral parlor, he didn't know which.

"Mr. Hackett, Judge Granby sent me over." Steve extended his hand, offering a folded letter from the court.

Barton Hackett looked up from his desk. He was immaculately groomed, and dressed in the finest executive manner, a starched white shirt with gold collar pin securing a blue and gray striped tie with gold tie clasp, all neatly framed by a Brooks Brothers suit. He had grown stocky and had developed a touch of silver at his temples, but now, at forty-one, it was not unattractive for someone of the executive persuasion.

When Barton looked at Steve, he saw a child of privilege, a class, a condition, which invoked his intense and immediate dislike. Of course, Steve did not see himself in that light. After all, the Mustang convertible his parents had given him wasn't new, and it wasn't like he had a monogram sweater for every day of the week, every other day at most. For every gift or opportunity that you could point out that Steve had, he could point to two that he didn't.

Barton did not extend his hand to take the paper. "I would invite you to sit down, Mr. Hadley, if this were a social visit," Barton spoke softly, a snarl in his undertone, "but it's not and you will not be staying that long."

"Won't I?" Steve was letting optimism get the best of him, thinking that the whole thing might really be a sham, that they really had no use for him in a place like this, that maybe somebody somewhere had realized the whole matter would be better resolved with turpentine and elbow grease.

"No, I'll be handing you back over to Nurse Hackett for your work assignment as soon as I'm sure you know the lay of the land around here, and especially clear up any misconceptions you might have concerning who's the boss."

"I think I'm fairly clear on that, Mr. Hackett," said Steve, "those big gold letters on your door makes that kind of hard to miss."

"Do I note a hint of sarcasm in your voice, Mr. Hadley?"

Steve was not much on trying to read other people, but there was no mistaking that when senses of humor were being handed out, Barton Hackett was standing in another line. "I'm just a poor college kid, Mr. Hackett, I don't even own any sarcasm."

"Are you a fool, Mr. Hadley?"

"Well, sir, I guess that depends on who you ask." What was this asshole getting at? Steve thought. "I'm sure Judge Granby believes I'm a fool."

"Do you believe I'm a fool, Mr. Hadley?"

"No, sir, I don't believe you're anybody's fool."

"Do you believe you're here to make a fool of me?"

"I'm not here to make anything of you, sir."

"Do you know what I believe, Mr. Hadley?"

"I truthfully don't have a clue."

"I believe that those of us who find ourselves in positions of authority are obligated to encourage, extol, and coerce, if necessary, those who are in our charge toward a higher purpose. Don't you?"

Steve stood perplexed, the backs of his calves were beginning to tighten up from standing in one spot for so long. Had he stumbled into the kingdom of some religious zealot or what? "I certainly believe you believe it," he said.

"And what is it you believe in, Mr. Hadley?"

Was this a trick question? Did he dare answer sunny days, beautiful girls, and driving ninety miles an hour with the top down with "When I Learn to Fly" by the Foo Fighters blasting on the stereo? Did he dare, was he really a fool? Steve stood silent for a moment.

"Well?" Barton's impatience was showing.

"Happiness," Steve said finally.

"Happiness?" chuckled Barton, "well you see where that belief has gotten you, don't you?" He shook his head as if staring into the face of sheer ignorance. "What in the world has ever been learned by happiness?"

"Is that a rhetorical question, Mr. Hackett?"

"Nothing!" Barton shouted. "That's what's been learned by happiness, absolutely nothing. Learning and growth, indeed the whole progress of human civilization is advanced only by anguish and hardship."

"Is there a point in you telling me this, Mr. Hackett? I'm just here to do some community service, I'm not out to advance civilization."

"Atonement." Barton said somberly.

"Atonement, sir?"

"You've been sent here to atone for your indiscretions," he took a deep breath, puffing out his chest," and it's my obligation, my duty, and my responsibility to see that you do."

Moses Bailey, "Old Man Moses" they called him, sat precariously perched in his wheelchair, leaning on his forearm, stretching, straining to see out the window. He watched Steve arrive in his Mustang convertible, the wind blowing through the young man's curly blond hair.

He remembered what it was like, the feeling of the wind rushing through his hair, of sunny afternoons such as these, spent astride his motorcycle, the throttle thrown wide open, or more often, out on the open water, his small boat under full sail, riding the wind across the waves.

In Moses' wry smile you could see the boy trapped in the old man's body. A body that was failing him now, his skin dry and as fragile as that of an onion, his legs unable to support his weight for any but the shortest periods of time. His thick glasses magnified his soft, green eyes, which all too often failed him now as well, his vision coming and going with a will of its own, some days better than others. Remarkably, he had still kept his hair, although it was now silver, and he wore it well trimmed and combed back from the temples.

He never thought he would end up like this, confined in a wheelchair, housed by strangers, spending the last of his days and long lonely nights in a body that was past usefulness, yet somehow refused to die. Moses was all alone, in the loneliness of waiting for the end to come.

Moses spent many of his hours, many of his days, thinking back and wondering. If he had known it would turn out this way, would he have done anything any different? Over and over he asked himself that question, and over and over he came to the same conclusion. No. If he had it to do over again, he would still make all the same choices.

He did not know if he had had a choice of where he was born, he was sure he would find out the answer to that one in the not too distant future, but if he had, he thought he had made a pretty good one. A vision returned of his 8-year-old self, running down to the water's edge in the northern Michigan village of Northport. As a child Moses would stand, watching the sailboats come in on a breezy summer day. Northport harbor with the train puffing furiously along the waterside tracks, the docks, and fishermen's shanties made for a thrilling and adventurous playground for a child, and he would stand in awe as the white boats would silently carve their way through the rolling water. Inevitably, he would get too close and a wave would crash upon the shore soaking his shoes. He would return home barefoot, carrying his shoes with his wet socks stuffed into them. His mother would first scold him, and then fix him a bowl of tomato soup, and if he was especially lucky a homemade cinnamon roll. She never stayed cross with him for long, as if she knew from the beginning, that he was in love with the water and all the magic that carried with it, and there was nothing anyone was going to be able to do about it. Nobody save one, and it would be fourteen more years before he met her.

When he was twelve, he sent away for a plan for a small sailboat out of the back of a sailing magazine, and set about that winter to build one. It was a cold winter, but a passion burned deep within him. And after the plans had come, he took over the family garage, and using his father's carpentry tools, he planed and mortised and sanded and clamped, and soaked and bent and clamped and planed and mortised and sanded every piece with his own hands. With his own hands, he was very particular about that, and very proud.

He worked every night after school and on the weekends from the early morning light, in the evening darkness he sewed the sail by the glow of a lantern. He worked in the cold of the garage. He would cut and sand and mortise and plane until his hands and cheeks turned pink with the cold, then he would cut and sand and mortise and plane some more. Until finally, his mother would come and order him into the house out of fear that he would lose his hands to frostbite. Then after a bowl of soup and a crust of bread, back out into the cold he went. To work, to build a dream, his dream.

And work he did, until it was done, lacquered and waiting for spring. He called it "Slap Shot," and stenciled the name across the stern. He stood back, brush in hand, a smudge of blue paint still wet on his freckled nose. He looked at it, it was done, and it was good and he knew that it was good. Before it ever touched the water he knew. It was a replica of a "Beetle Cat", a small, twelve-foot (twelve foot three, the young Moses would correct you) day sailer designed by John Beetle in 1920 and produced for the weekend boating enthusiasts by the Concordia Company for years afterward.

With his hand on the tiller, she would give him the sensation of a much bigger boat, with a wide deck forward, the bulky mast, and the boom stretching out astern. He would have to look back over his shoulder to see that there was nothing there. Like magic, her tail had disappeared. Like a cat, she would be quick and agile, sailing like a witch. And from that moment on he owned his dream, both physically and spiritually.

In summers he learned all there was to know about sailing, from his first tentative ventures going from Northport to Suttons Bay, gradually, as he became older and more experienced, working his way up to long excursions out of Grand Traverse Bay to the islands of Lake Michigan, equipped with nothing more than a compass, a picnic basket and a sleeping bag. He was one with the boat, and the boat was at home on the water. Moses became one with the water, sailing with an instinct, an inborn knowledge, that made family and neighbors alike believe that this was something God must have intended.

While he was waiting for the summers to come back around, there was hockey. He perfected his slap shot. Hour after hour at the ice rink, there was no cold, there was no tiredness, there was only the physics of the slap shot. Hockey was his sport; a sport played on ice, a sport where he could fly across the frozen water. The people of Northport took notice of Moses Bailey when he came on the ice. Some said he was good enough to turn pro. And when as a senior in high school, he scored back-to-back hat tricks against Manistee and Sutton's Bay on successive nights, his loyal fans were sure of it. They were convinced it was only a matter of time before the Red Wings or the Blackhawks would come calling.

But it wasn't just the hockey fans that took notice of the young Moses Bailey. The girls of Northport referred to him as the one with the lonely, sad eyes. There were those who remarked about how they liked the way he looked lean and tan as he sailed out of the breakwater. They saw him as detached, and in his own way he was. They believed he was arrogant, but quite the opposite was true, fearing judgment, he stayed to himself. Shyness and introspection are often mistaken for arrogance.

The young Moses had wondered about those girls, those girls who one day would become women, and who one day would make men of the boys such as he. He wondered what it would be like to hold the nakedness of a woman, to touch and be touched. Would he know what to do? He wondered about how and when he would find that one for him, and if she would find pleasure in him.

It was such a long time ago, or was it just yesterday?

Dawn McNally, a student nurse, entered his room, "What do you see out there Moses?"

Moses hated the bars on the windows; it made it look more like a loony bin or a prison than a nursing home. "By the way he's walking across the parking lot, I reckon we're getting some fresh meat, the judge must be at it again."

"Today would be the right day for it, wouldn't it?" she replied stripping his bed.

Moses admired the trim figure of the young girl as she stood up arching her back, rubbing her sore hip, and for a moment forgot the infirmities of his own eighty-three year-old body.

Dawn's dark hair, pulled back with a blue ribbon, flowed in waves down her back, and her brown eyes reminded you of a fawn, she was beautiful. Yet Dawn was completely unaware of her own beauty, and in fact, was quite convinced to the contrary. And because of this, she spent little time with makeup, grooming, and dress, as other girls of her age might. But rather, it was the welfare of others that occupied her mind, and topped her priority list. Serving others, looking after those too old or too young to care for themselves, was her attraction to nursing. And as a student nurse, all who came into contact with her knew that she was a natural fit for it.

Dawn was in the second year of a two-year nursing program at the community college. The spring term had ended, and she was going to complete her clinical hours over the summer. Pioneer Manor had not been her first choice of where she wanted to get her clinical training, but she had grown to love the residents she cared for, a practice she was frequently and forcefully admonished for by her supervisor, Nurse Hackett, her older sister by nine years.

"Is it?" asked Moses, "one day seems pretty much like any other, they all seem to run together."

Dawn looked up from the bed, hearing the despondent tone in his voice, "Are you OK, Moses?"

Moses sighed, "I don't know how to answer that, child, without sounding like a smartass."

Moses wondered often, why he had been chosen by God to go on, what was the purpose in outliving everyone he had ever loved, and outliving, to a large extent, his own body. Moses had been an artist, until crippling arthritis in his hands had prematurely ended his career. He was known, to the extent he was known at all, for his waterscapes, and particularly for works featuring three-masted schooners slicing their way through the rolling water. It had been years since he had considered his life rich and full, but until two years ago, when he was incarcerated in the Pioneer Manor Nursing Home, he had at least been able to handle the fact that he had outlived his purpose. When his freedom was taken away, that was the last straw.

Outside his window, a hummingbird hovered around a small lilac tree. Moses thought of his wife Sarah, long since departed, and her affection for birds, and all manner of creatures for that matter. He thought of her twinkling gray eyes, and the softness of her cheek under the roughness of his fingers. How he missed her that morning, and all mornings, if the truth be known. There was little wonder why Moses spent more time in the past than he did in the present.

TWO

Sarah was 24 when she first met Moses in the summer of 1939. Moses was twenty-two then, in a northern place called Sutton's Bay, and the wind was warm and fresh as it blew off Grand Traverse Bay.

Moses squinted in the bright sunlight, as he slouched against his front porch post, the last of a cigarette smoldering between his fingers. Up the dirt drive of the orchard, between the cherry trees, he saw the sun reflecting off the windshield of a shiny, black Lincoln Zephyr. It came to a halt before him, the door swung open, and he saw a slender ankle and a petite foot in a heeled, summer sandal lightly touch the ground. How does love begin? Who knows? And why? Destiny perhaps? Perhaps something more. So it happened, a car door opened in a cherry orchard outside Sutton's Bay and so did Moses Bailey's heart.

A head popped above the door, a wide-brimmed hat, oversized sunglasses, and bright red lipstick. "You Moses Bailey?" she asked.

"For anybody but the bill collectors." He grinned, flicking his cigarette into the grass.

"I bought one of your paintings in town," she closed the door and pulled off her glasses, revealing gray eyes with more than a hint of mischief. Her beige suit with fitted jacket and calf-length skirt was expensive, sophisticated, and subtle, but not subtle enough. Not for Moses. He watched her alluring curves move toward him, her golden curls cascading down around her shoulders as she removed her hat. This was a woman the boys down at the tavern would come to blows over.

"Thank you, I appreciate the business," he said.

She moved with an easy confidence, riveting him with those gray eyes, he stood motionless until she stopped directly in front of him. "Got anymore?"

It was as if he didn't hear her. He studied her skin, how would he paint a texture like that, so wondrously smooth? Had she come so close purposely to let him smell the fragrance of her perfume? He studied her hair, wondering if it was really as soft as it appeared to be, wondering how it would feel if he took a handful of it and bent her over the hood of that big black car right then and there. Somehow he had the feeling that she would laugh and bend willingly if he did. "Yep," he finally answered.

"Could I see them?"

"Not out here."

"Could I come in then?"

"Girls from around here aren't so forward as to invite themselves into a man's house."

"I'm not from around here." She stepped up onto the wooden planks of the porch and made her way past him. His gaze followed her hips as she sauntered through the barn door. "You live here?"

"Yep."

"With a barn door to your living room?

"It makes it easier to bring my sailboat inside for the winter."

"You have a sailboat in your living room all winter?"

"I don't have a davenport."

She smiled and looked around appraising his home, then did the same to him. He was tall and thin with intense green eyes that held just a hint of gold, and hair and skin that reflected hours spent in the sun. His home was one that revealed a man who lived alone, and for the most part kept his own company. There were streaks on the windows, crumpled clothes on the floor and dishes in the sink. In a corner near the kitchen area was the table where he took his meals. It appeared to be thrown together from building scraps, two by four studs ganged together for the top, with individual studs acting as table legs. He pulled out one of the three unmatched chairs that surrounded it, and gestured with an open palm in invitation.

"Could I offer you something cold to drink?" He at last noticed the large diamond and the wedding band on her left hand. "It's a free offer I have for my first customer of the day. Iced tea?" He owned only three glasses, and all three were dirty in the sink, he quickly washed two up while she continued to wander.

"You have any sugar?"

"You are forward aren't you?" He chided, "helping yourself to a man's sugar during times like these." He shook his head in mock disapproval, taking ice and a pitcher from the refrigerator and filling two glasses. He opened the cupboard above the sink and took down the sugar bowl; he spooned a teaspoonful of sugar into her glass and handed it to her.

"More sugar Mo." She grinned, "Can I call you Mo?"

"Sure." He spooned in another teaspoonful.

"Mo sugar Mo, mo sugar, Sugar Mo" she said, her voice almost singing, suddenly affecting a southern drawl, "Sugar Mo, I like that. Can I call you that?"

You can call me anything you like, he thought. "Sure," he answered again.

It was a simple life. He painted, a small shop across the street from the Park Place Hotel in Traverse City sold his paintings to rich tourists, earning him enough to buy his groceries and other necessities. He worked at his paintings all winter, except for an occasional diversion of playing hockey. And in summer he sailed.

The converted barn was nearly all weather-beaten gray, only a faint residue of the barn-red paint remained. It was small as barns went, but larger than most cottages. Moses had left it almost completely open inside when he converted it, with one space spilling over into another. His art studio mixed with his bedroom, his bedroom mingled with his living room, and his living room blended with the kitchen. And somehow it seemed as though this was the way it was supposed to be. His father had been a carpenter and with the knowledge he had gained from watching his father work, and on occasion working at his side, he had converted that barn into his home. He, indeed, had left the barn door so he could bring his sailboat into his living room in the winter, giving it a new coat of lacquer or two whenever he was waiting for the muse to move him again, demanding he splash waves and a glowing sun onto another canvas.

The center of the big open room was his work area, his studio, a large easel stood in the light from the window, a brick and board bookcase beside it. At the back was a low four-post bed with the comforter pulled across it. A record player stood on a makeshift stand beside it, record albums stacked under it.

"Are you anyone's sugar, Mo?"

"The paintings are over here." He led her to a stack of canvases leaning in a corner beside the bed.

"Do you always ignore a lady's questions?" She asked, slowly paging through the paintings, occasionally pulling one up and holding it in the light of the window.

"Just the ones I don't want to answer."

"These are really good," she said, "where did you study?"

"Northport Public School."

"I mean seriously."

"Seriously."

"You've never had formal training?"

"No."

"Have you ever had a show?"

"For a lady who hasn't even told me her name, you're asking an awful lot of questions."

"I'm sorry, that is rude isn't it? I'm Sarah Conner."

"Mrs. Sarah Conner," he added.

"Yes." She agreed and lowered her eyes.

"And who is Mister Sarah Conner?"

"Doyle Bradley Conner."

"And what does Doyle do?" he asked.

"You're an artist and you don't recognize the name?"

"Should I?"

"The Conner Gallery in Chicago? Does that ring any bells? Set off any whistles?" Her husband, Chicago art dealer Doyle Bradley

Conner, was fourteen years her senior. She was his trophy wife, the only kind of wife he had ever wanted.

"I've never been to Chicago. I thought I was going to get a try out with the Blackhawks a couple of years ago, but it didn't work out."

"The hockey team?"

"Yeah."

"Sugar Mo, you're a mystery," she sighed. He loved the way she sighed, he thought. He would like to find other ways to make her sigh. He revised his fantasy, it now involved unbuttoning her clothes with his teeth and stripping her naked. "Can I bring him to see your work?"

"If he brings his own sugar." He grinned.

After giving Steve the orientation tour, it was time for Nurse Hackett to give him his first assignment. He was confident it would be something good, not too demeaning, and not too taxing. Even though she hadn't smiled at him, he was sure she liked him, was there anyone who didn't? Except Judge Granby, of course.

"Here's a mop, there's the pail, and there's the floor," said Nurse Hackett, "training over." Before he could utter a sound, she was moving down the corridor away from him and out of earshot.

He knew it would not be all that bad if he could only get his mind around it, if he could come up with the right attitude, maybe make a game of it like when he was a kid and had to clean the garage for punishment. It shouldn't be so hard. Mop in the water, swish it all around, twirl in the hall, and watch the fuzz balls drown. He was admittedly getting a bit sloppy as he energetically swished and swirled in the corridor, but there didn't seem to be anyone around to notice.

"Oh, oh, oh, my!" Steve was startled by a voice from behind him and turned just in time to see Moses lose his footing and crash to the floor landing on his derriere. "Ugh . . ." came a gasp from somewhere deep inside the old man.

A flash of blue and white stripes came whirling around the corner, "Mr. Bailey, Mr. Bailey are you all right?" Then, "Oh my," as Dawn McNally also lost her footing on the wet floor, and with a resounding thud, ended up sitting on the floor beside Moses.

"I was just trying to walk a little," said Moses.

"Are you all right, Moses?" The initial panic faded from Dawn's voice, now it was dripping with compassion and concern.

"I'm fine, dear, all that's hurt is my pride." He put an arm down to prop himself off the floor, "and I don't have much of that left."

Dawn's attention turned to Steve, and all the kindness fled from her tone, "and what the hell do you think you're doing?"

"Excuse me?" was all Steve could manage. Her lustrous, dark hair pulled back with a blue ribbon intrigued him. He studied the creamy softness of her face, the smoothness of her cheek He could pay attention to little more than her beauty.

"These people have a hard enough time getting around, without someone coming in and sabotaging them." Dawn continued. "Are you totally brainless or did you do this on purpose?" She pointed to the water all over the hallway. Her nostrils narrowed. She glared at him. Their eyes met and locked, his steel blue, hers brown and on fire.

"I'm sorry, I didn't think . . ." She was possibly the most beautiful girl he had ever seen, he thought.

Dawn was having a great deal of trouble getting up off the floor, it was her hip again. At it's best it was unreliable, and at it's worst, times like now, it was as if it belonged to someone else, going it's own way despite whatever commands Dawn's brain gave it to the contrary. It refused to push up her weight, and it was aching again. At times like these, she could relate to her patients only too well. She rocked forward, but could not catch her balance and fell back again onto the wet floor. She felt the color flow up her neck and onto her face and wished for a moment she had learned how to curse.

Steve extended a hand, "May I help you?"

She slapped it away and with the adrenaline that added humiliation brought to her fury, she sprang to her feet powered by her good leg.

"Are you hurt?"

"Not really, just get Mr. Bailey into a wheelchair."

"But you're limping."

"It's nothing, will you please just go about your own business."

Nurse Hackett arrived with a growl. "Mr. Hadley! Would you prefer to be working for the judge or for me?"

"You ma'am."

"Well your work so far is totally unacceptable. Do you understand that?"

"Yes ma'am." He could feel his temper begin to flare, he did not take criticism well, and coming from a blimp with a butt the size of New Jersey, made it all the harder to handle. He managed to keep his tongue and silently counted backward from ten.

"If you don't get it together, I'll send you back to the judge. Do I make myself clear?"

"Yes ma'am." His face reddened. He didn't like being berated in public, but to have it done in front of this beautiful girl made it nearly intolerable.

"Clean up this mess, and report to the kitchen, maybe they'll have better luck with you."

"Yes ma'am. I'll try harder."

She began to walk away. "And don't poison anybody," she shot back over her shoulder.

Dawn lived in a one-bedroom apartment, two blocks from the main downtown street of Evergreen. From the second floor of a two-story brick building, her front window over-looked a well-manicured lawn shaded by two large Elms. Although the furnishings were sparse and inexpensive, her little home was immaculately kept, with a few tenderly chosen reminders of her mother back home in Indiana, and a representation or two of her philosophy and spirit.

She took the stairs up to her apartment as she always did, two feet on each step, two straining hands upon the rail. Stairs were the worst, and she stopped halfway up trying to remember why she had ever said yes to a second floor apartment. She was breathing heavy by the time she got to the top of the stairs. Any other girl would have allowed herself to cry after what she'd been through that day, but she just sighed, then stood erect rekindling her anger, and let herself in the door.

Later her anger subsided, leaving her empty and forlorn. Dusk had fallen and a melancholy light washed across the apartment from the living room window. On an end table next to the pale blue couch was a small statue of a nurse with angel's wings. As she gazed at it and let her finger trace its form, a sad expression covered her face. How old had she been when her mother had given her that little statue? Seven or eight? It had been before the accident, without a doubt. She had wanted to be a nurse her whole life, there wasn't a moment she could remember where there had ever been a question as to what direction her career would take.

She remembered the day when her mother had given her the gift; she remembered how she had been so happy, back when she was whole and thought all things were possible.

She remembered the night she made that fateful trip down the stairs. She had not known then, that the pain of a broken hip meant the end of the possibility of having a daughter of her own or a husband to give one to her. She had not known then, that she would be forever a cripple, and that no man would want a cripple.

She poured herself a cup of tea and went and sat down on the bench of her upright piano. It had always been her one consolation, the piano, and the soothing music she had learned to coax from it. It was not much to look at, as it was many times older than she was, and it had more than its share of nicks, bruises, and blemishes, but the comfort she had received from it over the years was worth a thousand times the pittance she had paid the little widow lady for it, indeed a thousand times a thousand. But that night there was no comfort to be found, at the piano or any place else.

It was early, but Dawn was exhausted. In the gloom of her lonely apartment, she turned from the little statue and began to get ready for bed. She pulled down the shade, and unbuttoned her uniform and hung it up. She pulled off the pad she wore on her hip that gave the world the illusion of symmetry and set it on the dresser. She put on her nightgown and checked the lock at the front door, as was her ritual. She set her alarm clock, and crossed off another day on her bedside calendar. Night after night she went to bed, marking off the days of her lonely life.

She lay in bed and stared up at the ceiling. There were so many things she wanted, a real house and a yard, a garden and a kitchen, where she could make suppers. Suppers for her children and her husband, that special someone who'd worked all day and had come home hungry to share the stories of his day and laugh with his children. That someone who, after the children were tucked in for the night, would lie beside her, holding her, breathing as one, and sigh off to sleep.

She turned her face to the window, none of it would happen, she thought, as she wiped away her tears on the pillow.

THREE

It seemed to Moses in that distant summer, that Sarah Conner had brought the whole cherry orchard to blossom. And when Sarah arrived the next morning with her husband, Moses could barely take his eyes from her. She was even more beautiful than he had remembered, if that was possible. She wore a blue and white striped top over a pair of white short shorts, exposing a mile and a half of the most exquisite legs he had ever seen.

"Hey, hey, Sugar Mo," she called entering his studio. Doyle Bradley Conner entered behind her. His expensive business suit of navy blue was in stark contrast to her summer vacation image. His face was full and expressionless under a receding hairline, his hair cropped short in military fashion.

"Sugar Mo meet Sugar Daddy." Doyle shot her an angry glance. "Just kidding, Doyle," she said sternly. "Moses Bailey, the one and only Doyle Bradley Conner."

They shook hands without comment, then "I liked the piece of your work that Sarah brought home last night, very impressive," said Doyle. "I'd like to see more."

"I've gathered them together over there by the kitchen table, help yourself. There's ice tea if you're thirsty. Sarah knows where the sugar is," a slight smile crept onto Moses' face, "I'll be on the front porch having a smoke, if you need me."

Moses sat down on the front step looked out across the orchard, over to the bay where a blue and white sloop was out under full sail, making its way toward the waters of Lake Michigan.

He took the pack of Lucky's from his pocket. "You got one of those for me?" asked Sarah, joining him on the step.

He tapped the pack and turned it to her, she slowly withdrew one from the pack, her eyes silently connecting to his. He lit a match. There was something totally delightful in having her light her cigarette from his offered flame, something that brought a secret smile to him that he did not dare let creep onto his face.

"You're totally unimpressed that I've brought Doyle Bradley Conner to see your work, aren't you?"

"Totally."

He watched her exhale the smoke, then lit a cigarette for himself from the match he was still holding.

"He's much older than you," Moses observed.

"Fourteen years."

"How'd you meet?"

"I went to Chicago on vacation and fell in love with the city, the night life, the parties, the dancing, the music. So I bluffed my way into a job as a secretary in the Tribune's advertising department. Doyle would stop in once a week or so with ads announcing the 'flavor of the week' as he called them, the artist whose work he was displaying, and he asked me out. He was always polite, took me to the best places, wore expensive suits, so when he asked me to marry him, I couldn't think of any reason not to."

"Sounds like true romance to me."

"More like a little girl's fairy tale."

"Why a little girl?"

"Stories for little girls don't have sex in them." She sent an unspoken message with her gray eyes and lightly chewed her lower lip.

"Oh, I see. And how long ago was this, that he rescued you from the doldrums of the advertising department?"

"Three years, but it seems like a lifetime already."

"Is that good or bad?"

"It just is."

Doyle emerged from the house, "I like them very much," he said, "I'd like to discuss representation with your lawyer."

"Representation?" questioned Moses.

"Doyle would like to make you 'flavor of the week' at the gallery," explained Sarah, "that's why I brought him here, it's actually quite an honor."

"And can be quite economically rewarding as well," added Doyle.

"Mr. McKinney is not doing too bad for me down at Traverse Treasures, he sold one to Sarah, now I'll give him another one to put on display. It pays for the groceries, and buys the sugar," he smiled toward Sarah.

Doyle appraised the converted barn, as if he were picking apart a Picasso forgery, "I'm not talking about eking out an existence, I'm talking about a show of your own in a major metropolitan market, having your work reviewed in the Tribune and national magazines, and with good reviews, creating an international demand for your work."

"Mr. McKinney lets me dock my boat at his place on the West Bay," said Moses.

"Come along Sarah," Doyle commanded and stormed toward the car.

"He has no sense of humor," she said putting her hand on Moses' arm. "Now don't get mad, Doyle," Sarah called after him, making her way across the grass. "Sleep on it, Sugar Mo, and join us for lunch tomorrow. OK?"

He did not answer, but merely took the pleasure of watching her hips move as she walked.

As she reached the car, she turned back to him. "Lunch tomorrow, OK?" she repeated.

He nodded. He would not pass up any chance to see her again, even if she did belong to somebody else.

"We're staying at the Park Place, we'll expect you around one."

He waved as she closed the car door behind her, and they backed out between the cherry trees.

The Park Place Hotel towered over State Street and downtown Traverse City. Constructed in the 1870's, it offered an incredible view of Grand Travers Bay from the upper floors, true turn-of-the-century opulence, and in its confines one could find no hint of the desperate times that still enveloped much of the country in 1939. Everything was elevated in the brown brick structure, even the dining room was high enough to see across the two blocks that separated it from the shoreline.

Moses entered the dining room wearing his only tie on his only clean denim work shirt; he carried his unseasonably warm corduroy jacket over his arm, insuring against the event that a dress code of some sort might be imposed upon him.

Sarah stood as he approached. He swallowed hard, awestruck by the elegance and beauty of her in her simple black dress.

Doyle rose as he reached the table, smiled and extended his hand. "I'm sorry I lost my temper yesterday," he said. "I'm usually much more composed in business matters."

"I'm sorry I made light of your offer," said Moses, talking to Doyle but still looking at Sarah, then finally shifting his eyes to Doyle, "I don't know you well enough to poke fun, but you were talking money, and money doesn't mean a whole lot to me. I paint, I sail, and in the winter time I play a little hockey, I really don't lack for much." He looked back to Sarah. And what he did lack, he wasn't about to confess to that company, at that time.

"I guess I should have realized that," said Doyle, "it's just in this era when so many artists are on the government dole through the WPA, I thought you were being ungrateful for my offer." Doyle spooned himself a plateful of scrambled eggs, shook on the pepper, and generously administered the salt. "But you really don't care if the world gives you any recognition, do you?"

"No, Mr. Conner, I don't." Moses put a scoop of sugar into his coffee and looked to Sarah, "I live the way that pleases me, and I let the world do the same. Whether it goes to heaven or to hell is of no concern to me."

"Do you ever plan to have children?" asked Doyle.

Moses was taken aback by the question. "I'd have to find the right woman first." He began to blush for reasons he couldn't fathom, and looked away from Sarah and back to Doyle.

"Well the way you're living now is fine for a young single man, I can see that," Doyle said between bites, "but you would never be able to support a wife and children like this. What I'm talking about here is securing your future, making it possible to dream of a wife and children and a home of your own."

"What exactly did you have in mind, Mr. Conner?"

Doyle explained in painstaking detail, the ins and outs of putting on a debut exhibition of an artist's work in the Conner method. From putting the show together through the selection of work, to the hanging, to the lighting, through the promotion, the press, and working the gallery at the opening. Moses sat silently listening. Once Doyle had made it clear that his whole proposition would give Moses multiple opportunities to see and be with Sarah, he could have saved his breath. Moses only needed to be shown where to sign on the dotted line. "So what do you think?" concluded Doyle.

"Sounds wonderful," said Sarah.

"Yeah, just fine," said Moses.

Doyle beamed like a used car salesman who had just made a deal. "So we'll give you the rest of the summer to finish off any work you have in progress, all the time we'll be priming the promotion pump with tidbits to the press. Then in say, October, I'll send Sarah back up here to help you with final selections of your work to be sent to Chicago, she's got a great eye, as you can see." He had done this a hundred times, but each new artist, each new show, pumped him full of adrenaline. "Then you'll come to Chicago in November and we'll turn the art world on its ear."

"You're the boss," said Moses.

"That means you'll be ours for Thanksgiving, Sugar Mo," Sarah did not try to hide the excitement in her voice, "so put that on your social calendar."

"I'll bring my best tie."

A week in the kitchen for Steve could not stop him from thinking about Dawn. When he looked into a bucket of potatoes to be peeled he thought of Dawn, he saw the reflection of her face in a sink of dishwater, and he imagined the touch of her skin when he closed his eyes in bed at night.

Dawn had not been affected in nearly the same way, in fact, Steve had not entered her thoughts at all after the outrage of the moment had passed, and she had been assured that Moses Bailey had not been seriously injured.

Steve was standing at the dishwasher, looking past One-eyed George, the kitchen supervisor, who was standing at the pass-through opening from the nursing home kitchen to the cafeteria. He surveyed the sea of white laminate and brushed aluminum tables surrounded by melon-colored concrete block walls.

He had been waiting to see her again, and then there she was, shuffling into his new domain, the cafeteria. "Something's wrong, George. Look."

"What?"

"Is she still limping?"

"Who?"

"That girl, that beautiful girl."

"Yes she is."

"My god, did I do that?" The guilt rose in Steve's voice.

"Is that the one you knocked on the floor?"

"I didn't, I just, oh, never mind that. Yes, it was my fault. Is she limping because of that fall?"

"I thought that was the first you met."

"The only time."

"Then it couldn't a been you, son, that did that to her, cause she's limped ever since she's worked here. By the way she moves with it, I'd say a long time."

He watched her move across the room, she was coming toward him, her limp very pronounced. He frowned, once more watching her fall to the floor in his mind's eye. He noticed the snugness of her uniform, and what it revealed about her shape. She was small at the rib, her arms thin. Her shoulders were narrow, her neck long.

"I'll have the Salisbury steak with corn, if you don't mind, George," she said.

George served up a tray and Steve handed him two dollar bills, George looked up at him and Steve gestured toward the girl, enough to communicate that he was paying for her lunch. Dawn put the plate of food on her tray and stretched her hand toward George with a five-dollar bill. "Your meal's already paid for, Dawn," he said.

"Paid for? It can't . . ."

"By Mr. Steve here, our helping hand from the judge."

She turned to see Steve standing in the back of the kitchen grinning, his blue eyes riveted to her. They stared at each other and then he nodded his head.

"I'm quite capable of paying for my own lunch, George," she announced loud enough for Steve to hear. "And even if I wasn't, I wouldn't accept charity from a mop bucket assassin like him, I'd starve first." With that she threw the bill at the cash register, and shuffled toward the door. Steve watched her leave, holding her head high, staring straight ahead as if she were a racehorse with blinders.

FOUR

Summer had always been his favorite season, but the summer of 1939 was torture as the young Moses waited, days seeming like years, for another chance to see Sarah. He thought a lot about Sarah Conner, he hadn't ever reacted so strongly to a woman before, and she was definitely all woman, he wondered how long it had been since anyone described her as a girl. There was a physical attraction there, but something else, something higher as well. He spent more than one night awake, wrestling with it with no conclusion. He spent long afternoons out on the water, wondering what all this anguish was about over a woman he hadn't even kissed, a woman who belonged to someone else.

Finally, autumn had arrived. A soft knock at the door and he was looking into Sarah's gray eyes. Form-fitting white slacks and a red sweater cut low enough at the neck to get his imagination going in high gear. "Hey there, Sugar Mo," she grinned, "you miss me?"

He didn't quite know what to make of the question, "Were you gone?"

Sarah had returned to the studio to help Moses pick paintings for his Chicago debut, and he knew she was there on business, no matter how much he wanted to fantasize otherwise. He had arranged his paintings, leaning them all around the outside walls of the studio. He had completed a couple in her absence and those stood propped against the kitchen table. "Where have you been hiding these?" she asked walking over to them.

"I've just finished them, in fact the one on the left is still wet."

"They look, eh, truly inspired," she said, not sure if that were really the right word, "they're wonderful, I've got to take these new ones for sure."

"Fine." Was all he managed, absorbed in the thought of painting her, painting her without the red sweater, painting her without the tight fitting slacks.

"I've got a bottle of Chardonnay cold," he said recovering, "can I offer you a glass?"

"I don't drink alone."

"Well then, I'll have one too." They laughed.

He poured the wine and handed her a glass, "How does your husband feel about you drinking wine with another man out in the middle of a cherry orchard?"

"He doesn't pay attention to that kind of thing, I don't think he has a jealous bone in his body. Besides, when he's at work, he's totally focused on work, he won't even think of me again until I'm standing in front of him back in Chicago, then his first word will be, 'did you bring the paintings?' That's just how he is, sometimes I don't know if I'm a wife or a gallery ornament."

Moses lit a cigarette, leaned against the kitchen counter, his thumbs looped into the front pockets of his denims, and stood admiring her. He watched the sun from the kitchen window wash over her. She glowed. Her breasts moved freely beneath her sweater and her slacks stretched tight across her hips and thighs as she sat, straddling a kitchen chair. He could not quite decide if this vision was his personal torment, or a private entertainment, but something was happening inside him.

When they had finished their first glass of wine, Sarah backed up the trailer she was towing behind the Zephyr to Moses' barn door with a practiced touch. They finished selecting and loading the paintings. Then they went back in and finished the wine. And a perfect autumn afternoon ended all too quickly.

"You driving back tonight?" He wanted desperately to find the magic words that would extend the day, but had no clue where to look for them.

"I'll stop for the night in St. Joe," she said, "it probably would have been a better idea to plan a couple of days for this, then it wouldn't seem so rushed."

"Next time," he said, forcing a smile.

"Yeah, next time, Sugar Mo."

He thought she seemed as reluctant to leave as he was to let her go, but neither of them put the thought to words.

She looked around for a topic of conversation, but finding none she opened the door a last time. Then she suddenly turned and said, "You've got Thanksgiving with me, uh . . . , Thanksgiving with us on your calendar, right?"

"In big bold letters," the corners of his lips turned up slightly at the thought.

"I'm counting on it," she flashed him a smile that struck him like a bolt of lightning, and then she closed the door. He stood motionless, wondering if he should laugh or cry.

At Pioneer Manor, Steve had volunteered for tray pick-up duty, for the residents who, for one reason or another, were unable to take their meals in the cafeteria. He had volunteered in part to escape the constant scrutiny of "One-eyed George", but mostly in hopes of once again running into Dawn, perhaps this time on a friendlier basis. He didn't know exactly how he would overcome her poor first impression of him, but nonetheless he held high hopes that providence, or destiny, or luck, would find a way.

"You call that shit food?" yelled Martha Campbell, room 204, "of course I'm done with it."

"I'm sorry you didn't like," apologized Steve.

"Like it? Do I look like a hog?"

"Of course not, in fact you're looking very nice today," he said, attempting a friendly overture.

"They feed slop to the hogs, you know?"

"I know, I'll take it away." He picked up the tray and began backing out of the room.

"And stick it where the sun don't shine," Martha yelled after him.

This job wasn't going to be as easy as he had first thought if all the residents of the nursing home reacted this way to the menu. Nevertheless, if he could meet that dark-haired beauty, if he could just see her again, suffering any abuse these old codgers were going to heap upon him would be well worth it, he was sure.

But every patient wasn't like Martha, for some, Steve entering the room was like a visitor come to call, somebody new to talk to, and someone to chase away the loneliness, even if it were only for a short while.

Steve entered room 305, and then stopped dead, as if his shoes had suddenly glued themselves to the floor. There she was, with her dark hair rolling down her back, as she helped the old man who had slipped on his floor-washing job back into bed.

She glanced at the door as he entered. Dawn recognized him instantly. "Killed any little old men lately?" she quipped.

"Mr. Bailey, I'm really sorry you almost got hurt." He directed his comment to Moses, momentarily taking his attention away from Dawn.

"No harm," said Moses raising a palm.

"Moses, you've got to rest now," interjected Dawn.

"See the way she takes care of me?" Moses grinned. "How lucky am I having a beautiful woman like this taking care of me?"

Dawn blushed. "Are you flirting with me again?"

"I ask her to marry me once a week," said Moses smiling and turning back to Steve.

"And what does she say?" smiled Steve. Dawn ignored him.

"What do you think she says?" asked Moses, abruptly, "she says, 'no', of course."

"Then why do you keep asking?" inquired Steve.

"It let's her know what I think of her."

"Are you through with your lunch?" interrupted Dawn.

"As through as I'm gonna get," said Moses.

"Then I think you've told this stranger enough of our secrets," said Dawn, "I'm sure he has better things to do than listen to this," she took Moses' food tray from the bedside stand and handed it to

Steve with a jab, looking him straight in the eye, "like finishing up an assassination plot or something."

"I'm not usually so irresponsible," Steve continued his apology, "I'm really sorry."

Moses was more forgiving than Dawn; he had once been young, and more than a little wild. Young and invincible, never knowing, never dreaming, he would turn out like this.

"Don't waste your time worrying about it, I was young once too." Moses told a tale from his youth, his eyes glazing over as he looked out the window, embracing some vision from the past. Steve heard the words, but they did not register, his attention had once again focused on Dawn. What was this feeling she had awoken inside him? He was engulfed by the mystery of it. He had no answers; but merely cherished this moment, to look at her and savor that vision for as long as it would last.

He looked back to Moses, into those glistening, weary eyes, as the old man ended his story. There was wisdom in his eyes that was beyond knowing, Dawn had seen it when she first came to work at Pioneer Manor, and now Steve had seen it too. This could be me in another sixty years, Steve thought. A cold shiver went up his backbone.

"You're new around here, aren't you?" asked Moses. "I saw you coming in for your first day."

"Yes sir. I'm here doing community service."

"Sir? What's this 'sir'? Everybody around here calls me Moses. Moses to my face, 'Old Man Moses' when they think I'm not listening."

"Yes sir, er, yes Moses." Steve recounted the story of the prank that had landed him there.

Moses smiled and then, "destiny brought you here, you know."

"I thought it was an old judge who had no sense of humor."

"No, seriously, there is a reason you are here, and now I see that it is more than one reason."

"Is that reason called 'penance', or do you prefer 'atonement' like Mr. Hackett?"

"I prayed for you to come," said Moses softly.

"You prayed for me?" asked Steve.

Dawn looked at Moses, then to Steve, then back to Moses.

"I told the Lord I needed someone with a disregard for authority, and he sent me you?"

Steve smiled. "What for? Has the kitchen been overcooking your eggs, or what?"

"I want to see the sun set over Lake Michigan, one more time before I die," said Moses, the faraway look returning to his eyes.

"That doesn't sound like such a tall order, why is that something you have to pray . . ."

"Mr. Hadley!" Nurse Hackett interrupted, storming into the room, "by my watch you've been in this room all of twenty minutes, how long does it take you to pick up a food tray?"

"I didn't know I was being paid by the piece," said Steve, "oh, that's right, I'm not being paid at all."

"Mr. Hadley! Do I have to remind you . . ."

"Judge Granby," he interrupted, "no, you don't have to remind me, the judge is constantly on my mind."

"Well, then I suggest . . ."

"I'm on my way," he looked to the old man, "I'll see you tomorrow, Moses, I promise." And he was out the door faster than Nurse Hackett could waddle after him.

Brady Park sprawled on the edge of Evergreen with hills rolling out into flat fields of manicured green. Steve had grown up there playing his little league games, flying kites, and hunting frogs in the winding creek. Behind the park, was Walnut Acres the subdivision where Steve lived with his parents in a thirty year-old ranch house. A yellowish brick decorated the bottom half of the front exposure with olive green siding rising above it. Around all four sides grew mature junipers and various evergreens.

Steve entered the house after work distracted. His mother was in the kitchen, but he did not notice. He grabbed a glass from the cupboard and went to the refrigerator, pouring himself a glass of milk. He grabbed a sandwich cookie from a plate on top of the breadbox and began to pace the floor of the kitchen, glass of milk in one hand, cookie in the other. When one cookie was finished he replaced it, and continued to pace.

Finally, his mother spoke, "what's bothering you, Steve?" She was a good-natured plump lady in her mid-fifties whose sole purpose in life seemed to revolve around being Steve's mother.

"Why should you ask that?" He replied, "I haven't said anything about something bothering me."

"I didn't just meet you yesterday," she smiled. "When you start pacing the floor eating cookie after cookie, you've got something on your mind."

"You know me too well."

"You make it sound like a bad thing," she grimaced. "It's no sin to tell your old mother what's on your mind."

"I know."

"So spill it."

"Well, there's this girl at the nursing home . . ."

"I've been wondering when we were going to have this talk."

"What do you mean?"

"All through high school, they're was worries over making the basketball team, teachers you thought hated you because they made your homework so hard, there was nervousness over getting up in front of everybody in the school play, but never any girl trouble."

"I never liked anybody like that before . . ."

"Before now.

"Yes."

"So tell me about her."

"I don't know where to begin. Probably with the fact that she hates my guts, or else that she's the most beautiful girl I've ever seen. I don't know."

"If she hates you, it simply means she doesn't know you."

"Why do you say that?"

"Just call it a mother's instinct."

"Well there's something else."

"Yes?"

"She's got a limp."

"And?"

"I don't know if she was born that way or if it's because of something very bad that happened to her in her past."

"And that disturbs you?"

"I don't know."

"We all have wounds, Steven. You were wounded when the teacher called attention to the fact you wet your pants in class in the first grade. You were wounded when you let Jocko off his leash and he was hit by a car."

"And I never really got over the fact that they asked me to leave the choir, I love music so much."

"That's exactly what I'm talking about. And you've had other, deeper wounds that I won't even talk about because I love you too much. As for me, I don't think I've ever been the same since the day my mother died in my arms. We all have wounds, it just sounds like one of this girl's wounds is visible on the outside."

He silently nodded and set down his empty milk glass.

"Is this something you somehow hold against her? Like it was her fault or something?"

"No, no, nothing like that. I just don't know how to treat a girl, not a girl like this. She's been hurt so badly, I'm scared to death of hurting her."

"Like when you knocked her down in the hallway?"

"Does everybody in town know about that?"

"There's not much that gets past the beauty shop."

"Mom, you just don't know how that made me feel. I saw her limp and I thought that I had caused it by my carelessness, I swear my stomach turned itself upside down."

"Good thing you weren't home, you would have eaten me out of two bags of cookies for that one."

FIVE

When Steve entered Moses room, Nurse Hackett was yelling at Moses, "When you got to go, damn it, ring the bell, don't try to do it yourself, now somebody's got to clean up your shit."

"What's wrong?" said Steve, steadying Moses by the elbow as the old man took off his pants at the doorway to the bathroom.

"I, I, I just didn't make it," said Moses, looking at the floor, "I just didn't make it to the bathroom, and I've messed my pants."

"You're just in time Mr. Hadley," said Nancy, "you can clean this crap up."

Dawn entered the room, "It's my fault, I wasn't here, Moses always has to go right after breakfast, and he relies on me to be here, but Irene down the hall needed me . . ."

"All he has to do is ring the damn bell," scowled Nancy, "I don't need any crap about it from anybody, it's simple enough for even somebody with 'old timers' disease to understand."

Steve tried to butt in, in defense of the girl and Moses. "You're going to get old too, Nurse Hackett," he interjected.

"You may think you have a right to your opinion in the outside world, but you're not in the outside world, so don't cross me," Nancy was snarling now, "I won't hesitate a minute to call Judge Granby and get you jerked right out of here. You jump when I tell you to jump and clean shit when I tell you to clean shit, other than that, I don't want to hear from you. I don't want to hear about you, I don't want to know what you're doing with or to my sister. Silence and obedience, Mr. Hadley." She turned and stalked toward the door, "now clean," she barked, and was gone.

Steve fetched a sponge from the bathroom and got down on his knees to clean up the floor. "What have you told your sister about you and me?" Steve asked Dawn.

"Don't flatter yourself, Steve Hadley, my sister has an imagination all her own, and I haven't added a thing to it." She turned to the old man, "I'm sorry Moses," said Dawn, folding up the soiled trousers, "I stopped and checked on Irene, you know how bad she's getting."

"I hate to be a burden," Moses said, "but I'm slipping too." He pulled on a clean pair of pants and slowly sat back down in his wheelchair, his gaze fixing on the hummingbird that had returned outside the window, darting around the branches of the lilac tree, now in full bloom. "I have a strong feeling that this is my last summer," he said softly, without emotion.

Steve looked at Dawn and she looked back at Steve, neither said a word, but among the three of them in that room, a connection was being formed, something powerful and lasting.

"Nurse Hackett says you're going to have to start going to the cafeteria again for your meals," Dawn said.

"Why do I want to sit around there with all those old people? I'd much rather take my lunch with you and Steve."

"Sorry, just those confined to bed rest can take their meals in their rooms," said Dawn, "now you don't want some doctor prescribing some knock out medication because they think you have some anti-social disorder do you?"

"I'll still stop by everyday on my rounds," said Steve, surprised at how much the old man looked forward to his visit.

"Promise?" said Moses smiling.

"I promise."

Dawn began to see Steve in a new way that morning, maybe she had misjudged him after all, and then there were those blue eyes, a girl could just get lost in those blue eyes. She shook her head slightly, trying to bring herself back to her senses, then checked to see if anyone had noticed her unusual ritual. Could she really be falling for an irresponsible college kid with no more ambition than common sense? She didn't have time to think of something so silly.

"I've got other things to do," said Dawn, "I'll leave you boys to talk about the things that boys talk about." She smiled, and then limped from the room.

"Was that a smile?" Steve asked Moses.

"Looked like it to me," the old man replied, "of course, some days I don't see so well."

"Was it for me?"

"I expect so," said Moses, "I don't know why it wouldn't be."

"What did I suddenly do right?" Steve was still looking at the doorway as if she was still there.

"She's not a bad kid, you know, she's got a heart of gold," Moses said, finally getting Steve's attention, "going through life with that leg has probably put an edge on her she wouldn't have otherwise, but underneath she's a softy."

"You sound like you know her pretty well."

"I count her as one of my closest friends, why?"

"Was she born like that?"

"Like what? With a tongue like a razor?"

"No, with that limp, was she born with that limp?"

"Does it matter?"

"No, I was just curious is all."

"She doesn't talk about it, but if I was to guess, I'd say it was an accident, I mean, it sounds like there was a time in her life when she didn't have that limp," said Moses, watching Steve's eyes. "And to make matters worse, I think it somehow involved her father."

"Her own father?" said Steve trying to make some sense of it, "you're guessing aren't you? Her father?"

"It's hard to believe coming from your world, isn't it, son?"

"Very hard," he said, shaking his head, "that's something you just read about in the papers, it's like it doesn't really happen to real people."

"It really happens."

"And they couldn't fix it?"

"I don't know, couldn't, wouldn't, after all these years, seems like ones the same as the other, it doesn't really mater now, does it?"

Steve plopped down on the edge of Moses bed, and stayed there silently for a long while, a silent rage building and then running through him at the injustice of it all. He wanted to lash out, he wanted to hit somebody, somebody should have to pay for this.

"What happened to her father?" Steve finally asked.

"From what I've been able to piece together, it sounds like he lost his family," said Moses, watching the young man's face, "taking this pretty personally for a girl you barely know, aren't you?"

Steve realized he had been staring off in a daze, and snapped back, "Am I?"

"Seems like," said Moses, "but it happens like that, like a bolt out of the blue when you least expect it."

"What happens like that?"

"Love."

Steve looked into the old man's twinkling eyes, "What are you talking about now, Moses."

"I'm not talking about a thing, I'm just observing."

"Well, I think you're having another bad eye day," Steve quipped, wondering if he really was that transparent.

"We'll see," said Moses, his own gaze drifting off, embracing a memory of a time when life was fresh, and love was new.

As a young man, Moses Bailey wasn't much on celebrating any of the holidays, but Thanksgiving dinner at the Conner's was a chance to be with Sarah, and that was a chance he was not about to pass up. As he rode his motorcycle down Blue Star Highway heading toward Chicago, he examined every curve of her face in his mind. His1922 Harley-Davidson Model W Sport Twin glowed greenish-gold, reflecting the sun. His hands tightly gripping the one-inch tubular steel handlebars, his sandy hair blowing in the wind as the 6 horsepower engine swept him through the gentle curves of the road. He wore a pair of World War I aviator goggles he had picked up at an estate sale on the south side of Lake Leelanau. He had thought it the perfect accessory to go with the flying ace scarf his mother had made him, scared as she was of "those contraptions."

When he reached Chicago he bought a bottle of Chardonnay to take along, unconcerned and unintimidated by the prospect of entering high society with the improper vintage. He parked his motorcycle outside the two-story brick townhouse. The brick was brown marbled with beige, the wood trim, hand carved and ornate, the landscaping fastidious. As he swung open the iron gate and climbed the sandstone stairs, he saw the Conner's Lincoln and two other cars in the drive. Doyle answered the door impeccably dressed in a three-piece pinstriped suit, white starched collar, and a crisp white handkerchief in his breast pocket.

"Welcome, Moses, how was your trip? I don't know why you didn't take the train, isn't that thing dangerous?"

"Hello, Doyle. I didn't know you cared."

"I do care," said Doyle, "I care about my commissions. You can die after, I said after, you become famous."

"God loves an honest man," said Moses.

"Sugar Mo, you made it," Sarah rushed to the foyer and gave him a hug.

"This is for you." He handed her the wine, their eyes met and locked for a moment longer than was appropriate.

"Everybody," Doyle's voice boomed, "I'd like you all to meet, the one, the only, the soon to be famous, Moses Bailey."

Moses was greeted with a mix of jeers, waves, and assorted pleasantries. How he hated these social ordeals, especially the entrances and the exits. It was as if everyone had a script and no one had given him a copy.

"Let me introduce you around," said Sarah, taking him by the arm. Except for Sarah's parents, Marge and Harry, the assemblage seemed to be Doyle's court; all were in one way or another, employed by or dependent upon him or his cordiality. The gallery's publicist and wife, the gallery's accountant and wife, the gallery's receptionist and fiancé, the art critic from the Tribune and guest, and the editor of Chicago Today who treated Doyle as if he walked on water. This deference was quite a mystery to Moses, but he didn't ask.

When they got to the kitchen Sarah's mother was mashing potatoes at the table. This came as a surprise to Moses, by all other appearances he would have assumed that servants were preparing the feast. Sarah tied an apron around her waist, and then kissed him on the cheek and whispered, "I'm so glad you made it." The kiss, and even more so the whisper surprised him, confused him. Then he discounted them as merely the festive spirit of the holiday momentarily overtaking her.

She turned him to the beautiful, mature lady with the potatoes, "Mother, this is Moses, Moses Bailey who I was telling you about."

"I'm glad to meet you, Moses," Marge said. It was more than obvious where Sarah got her looks; Marge was an older version of Sarah, and except for a couple fine lines of wisdom around her eyes, the hands of time had barely touched her. Marge's hair was dark blond with occasional strands of gray highlighting it, as if by design. If it was true, that a woman shows what she thinks of her husband by the kind of wife she gives him, then Marge held Harry in the highest esteem. She turned to Sarah, "Moses is the one who sails, right?" Sarah nodded. "Where do you sail, Moses? Very far?"

"Usually just around Grand Traverse Bay, but once in a while I'll go out to one of the islands, if I'm feeling adventurous."

"Sarah says you live in a barn so you can keep your sailboat in the living room in the winter time."

"Yes, ma'am." He said, reaching for a sliced carrot on the relish tray. She slapped his hand in jest.

"Why do you keep a sailboat in your living room?" she asked.

"It's too big for the bathroom," he said. Sarah and her mother both laughed. "I can work on it the winter that way, and when I really get cabin fever about the end of February, I sit in it, put my hand on the tiller, and take a short sail around the Bay in my mind."

"Mother, Moses keeps his sailboat in the living room, and it's perfect, I'm sure he wouldn't be Moses Bailey if he didn't." She smiled at him openly.

"You and Doyle have really found yourselves a character this time, haven't you?" asked Marge.

"Haven't we though," said Sarah a smile peeking at the corner of her lips as she concentrated on spooning the corn relish into a glass bowl.

Moses hated to force himself away from the sight of her, but he could see they were busy and thought that the polite thing to do would be to amble back to the living room and mingle. Mingling to Moses ranked just under going to the dentist. Why he was leaving Sarah's side to go mingle was something he didn't understand, maybe it was to save himself, to keep him from falling into a hole that would consume him totally and completely.

Pretending to be a socially adept creature of the human persuasion was a trick that was just about impossible for Moses Bailey, nevertheless he tried. In Sarah's house he could do little else. He looked back to Sarah, who was still intently working over the corn relish, and wondered what was going on in her mind. Did she have the slightest inkling of how thoughts of her dominated his mind?

"Come over here Moses," said Doyle, "I've shown Joseph here some of your work, sort of a preview." Joseph Bounderby was the art critic for the Tribune, but everyone was supposed to know that without explanation, and everyone did, except for Moses.

"Your work shows potential," Bounderby said, squinting down his nose, over his glasses.

"Thank you, I think," replied Moses.

Just then Sarah came out of the kitchen and announced, "It's time to eat, gang."

The guests wandered from the living room into the dining room. Moses hung back letting the others find their places, deciding he would take whatever was left, just hoping he would end up with a spot where he could look at Sarah now and then. To his surprise Sarah had made place cards. He watched people find their seats and then saw the one that read 'The Soon-to-be-Famous Sugar Mo Bailey'. He grinned inwardly when he discovered that it marked the seat right next to hers. To his right Sarah had placed one of Doyle's gallery employees, Jenny Seabright, a gorgeous face, buxom figure, bleached blond hair, job unspecified. He did not understand the logic of this arrangement, perhaps this was Doyle's idea, but he did not waste much time trying to make sense of it.

Doyle carved, and Moses sat and watched Sarah move back and forth between the dining room and the kitchen, and for the most part tuned out most of the nonsense that was being talked about. The physical attraction he felt for her was being transformed into something deeper and that was a change he was not prepared for.

"What do you think of Picasso, Moses?" asked Bounderby. "We saw a display of thirty small oil-on-canvas works of his when we were in Paris in February."

"I don't think of him," said Moses. "I just paint."

"And sail," added Sarah.

"It's a strange time to be in the art business in Europe," said Doyle. "In September, the Louvre closed and locked its doors and workman began removing treasures. In London, the National Gallery closed and the stained glass of Cantebury's Cathedral was taken out and buried in the surrounding countryside."

"Let's not let this degenerate into another depressing discussion about the war in Europe," said Sarah's father, momentarily taking charge. "Has anyone read Faulkner's new book, 'The Wild Palms'?"

"Faulkner is inaccessible," murmured Bounderby, serving himself some cranberry sauce.

"Talk about war, how about the civil war?" Jenny spoke up, "have you seen Gable's new movie, the man is a dream."

"Stop dreaming about that one, Jenny," said Marge, "Carole Lombard has him now."

"A girl can dream can't she?" said Jenny.

The feast of American indulgence went on and on, food and wine, and more food and wine. Harry told an amusing story about when Sarah was small, and Moses couldn't help but notice how she went along with it good-naturedly, without the slightest hint of embarrassment.

"So when is the wedding, Cornelia?" Sarah asked, deciding it was someone else's turn on center stage.

Cornelia, mousy-haired, pale and thin-lipped, lowered her eyes, unaccustomed to being the focus of attention. "In February," she said, "it's Robert's favorite month, isn't it Robert?"

Robert nodded, stuffing another bite of turkey into his already full mouth.

"Is she worth it, Robert?" Doyle asked.

"Worth it?" Robert responded, not understanding the question.

"Is she worth giving up all the other women in the world?" explained Doyle. Jenny Seabright looked up from her plate, began to speak, but then thought better of it.

"Do you have all the other women in the world, Robert?" asked Moses.

"Of course he doesn't," retorted Doyle. "You all know very well what I'm talking about."

"Well, if he doesn't have them how can he give them up?" asked Marge.

"I think it's more likely that it's Cornelia who's giving up all the other men in the world, right Cornelia?" asked Sarah

His meal finished, and needing a break from the small talk, Moses rose, took his glass of wine, and excused himself to the front porch for a smoke, a sadness knocking at the door to his conscience. He knew that what he felt welling up inside him probably had nowhere to go. And if it did, it would be a dangerous place, a place where he had no right to go. Some things were better left alone. For a long while, he toyed with the idea of walking back out that iron gate, jumping on his Harley-Davidson and heading back to Sutton's Bay, and the safety and security of his paints and his boat.

"It's a party," came Sarah's voice from behind him, "it's not a day to be so serious."

"Just having a Lucky," he said, "want one?"

"You can smoke in the kitchen, come back inside." She took his hand and he followed her back to the kitchen.

"Let me have those," he said upon entering the kitchen and took a stack of dishes from Marge and walked them over to the sink. He turned on the tap to run dishwater and rolled up his sleeves.

"You don't have to do that," said Sarah, "we didn't invite you to come and do the dishes."

"You have to remember, I live alone," he said, "I'm quite comfortable with dish detail, besides I'm a lot more comfortable with a sink full of dishes than I am out there discussing football. My sport is hockey."

"Hockey?" said Marge, her face brightening, "like the Blackhawks?"

Moses chuckled, "the very same sport."

"Do you still play?"

"Occasionally, I'll go up to the rink and play a pick-up game with the kids, but I'm not involved in any organized way anymore."

"Do you miss it?"

"Not really, I can still go out skating, and fly across the ice and feel the wind on my face, that's usually enough to get me through until spring." He was ready for the subject to change, but continued to politely answer Marge's questions. She was Sarah's mother, enough said.

"We're you any good at hockey, Moses?" Marge asked.

"I set the state record for most goals in a season," he answered, then regretted how boastful it sounded.

"Then you were a star," gushed Sarah, reaching out and squeezing his arm.

He couldn't tell if she was being sarcastic or not, he only knew if she squeezed his arm one more time he would probable melt on the spot. But she didn't, changing the conversation by reciting the dessert menu. He selected the traditional pumpkin pie with whipped cream, and sat across the kitchen table from Sarah dabbing at it. This is why he had come, for the chance to simply look at her on a cold autumn day and wonder, wonder what it would have been like had they met at another time, before she had become another man's wife. But he had to be careful with his looks, because twice Marge had caught him staring at Sarah in a way totally unconnected to the conversation. And mothers have an instinct about the secret thoughts of men, especially when it comes to their daughters.

Moses could only tolerate being in Sarah's presence for a limited length of time, his feelings were too intense, too overpowering, increasing in strength as the afternoon wore on, until he was afraid he would blurt out something and bring the whole thing to an end, tipping off her husband and placing him in exile from Sarah's presence. A fate, he knew might be better, safer at least, but one that at that moment he could not even consider, so about seven o'clock he excused himself with a pretense of being weary from the journey.

Sarah wrapped her arms across her breasts and shivered on the front steps as she said good-bye to him. "Thanks for coming, Sugar Mo, I'm glad my parents got a chance to meet you, they'll see you again at the opening, but they wouldn't have had a chance to get to know you like today."

"Is that important to you? That your parents get to know me."

"Yes," she said. "Yes it is." He didn't ask why.

"I liked them very much, your Mom is a knockout."

"She likes you too, I could tell."

"You better get back inside before you freeze." He couldn't help looking at her long and hard one last time. He wanted to say, "Don't go back inside, don't ever go back. Come away with me; let me undress you button by button, piece by piece. Let my lips delight in dancing upon your nakedness. Run away with me and together we'll make a paradise of our own," but he didn't. He didn't say anything more.

She opened the door and stepped through the threshold, then looked back and set her gray eyes on Moses for what seemed like an hour, her face suddenly serious. A look quite different from any she had ever given him before, as if she were reading his thoughts. She said nothing; she just stood there immovable, just looking at him. Then, she dropped her eyes, her mouth giving way to a coy smile, and closed the door.

The next morning, Moses stood in the lobby of the Drake Hotel where Doyle had reserved a room for him. There couldn't be more of a contrast between the converted barn in which he lived and the decadent comfort in which he now stood. He looked down the flight of steps that led to the front door. He felt the necessity with which the building had been designed, the need to feel above the grit and the grime of the street.

Moses left the hotel, walked a few blocks down Michigan Avenue and turned the corner on Chestnut and down to State. He came to an abrupt halt when he looked down an alley which ran behind a restaurant and saw what appeared to be a couple of boys, ten or twelve years of age, picking their breakfast out of the garbage cans. One was red-haired with freckles, oblivious to an onlooker, but the other, a blond with wide innocent eyes, looked at Moses squarely and at length, before again taking up his task. Moses stood motionless for a moment, resisting the temptation to get involved in their lives and then, resigning himself to the fact that there was little he could do, continued on. He shook his head; Chicago was not the place for him.

When Moses entered the gallery, Doyle was already hard at work with the confidence of a man who had done this job a thousand times. Positioning the lights just so to bring out colors, or contrast, or highlights. Positioning the paintings in a complimentary order so a walk through the show would flow as easy and as natural as a raft ride down a lazy river. Indeed, Doyle was so adept at his craft, Moses wondered why he had insisted on Moses being there. It would have been just as well with Moses, to stay in his hotel room waiting for the opening, thinking of Sarah to pass the time. Or was it waiting to see Sarah, passing the time until the opening?

All the while Doyle was talking, explaining the marketing rationale for this, the promotional aspects of that, and then an aside about how an artist could best benefit from his debut show, along with tips on how to work the crowd, taking particular attention to discern whether he was conversing with a critic, a serious buyer, or a mere passerby. He wanted to interrupt Doyle with, "Don't you know there are children in this city eating out of garbage cans? How can you think about art?" but he didn't, he let Doyle continue on doing what it was Doyle did best, building a world that others could pretend was reality.

Moses kept looking at the door with a hope, more than an expectation, that Sarah might come through it. When two o'clock came, and Sarah hadn't, and Doyle hadn't even mentioned her, Moses was sure he had messed things up, that Sarah and maybe everyone else had been able to see how he felt about her and she decided to nip the proverbial problem in the bud right then and there.

The way Doyle had looked at him first thing that morning when he entered, Moses was sure Sarah had said something to him, and Moses spent all morning waiting for Doyle to hit him with it, to tell him how Sarah was uncomfortable with the way he looked at her, how Doyle was uncomfortable with the way he looked at her, how Moses had made the whole world uncomfortable with the unrestrained passion which consumed him. But it didn't come, Sarah's name was notably absent from Doyle's monolog, he hadn't forbid Moses to see her, he hadn't informed him that she would not be stopping by ever. So what was it, where was she? He was getting tight in the stomach, going through a withdrawal of sorts, from not seeing her. He had been back in her presence one day, one afternoon to be precise, how could he let himself carry on like this? Why couldn't he get himself under control? Why didn't he want to? Why did he relish, in some sadistic way, what she was doing to him? He could not remember any time before when he felt so alive.

Suddenly his heart leapt, she stood in the doorway, looking at him, her hair pulled back. "Hello," she grinned, "Sugar Mo," her expression faded as she turned to her husband, "Doyle."

"Hello," returned Moses.

"Well?" asked Doyle, as if the question were understood.

"We've solved the wine and cheese crisis with the caterer, everything is under control," she said.

"Did you know there are children eating out of garbage cans not four blocks away from here?" He did not know why he said it, it simply came out.

Doyle stopped and looked at him, both perturbed and perplexed, "Why do you bring that up? Did you want to invite them or what?"

"Would you, if I said yes?"

Doyle laughed, "Only if they were buying paintings."

"What if I asked?" said Sarah.

"What is this?" said Doyle exasperated, "how did we get from wine and cheese to hungry children?"

"I've got coffee and éclairs," came an exuberant female voice entering the gallery. It was Jenny Seabright wearing a tight cardigan sweater over tight blue cotton slacks that revealed the shape of her hips all too well. "Oh, Sarah, er, Mrs. Conner, good afternoon," she said in surprise, "Doyle, Mr. Bailey, is anybody ready for a break?" recovering her composure.

"Jenny . . ." Doyle said, as if cutting off his thought before it squeezed its way out of his lips. He looked at Sarah, and then looked back at Jenny, "Moses doesn't need any of that coffee and sugar, he's as nervous as a cat already." He thought for a moment, pretending to examine a four by four waterscape. "Sarah, will you be a dear and get Moses out of here for a while so he can relax, we need him appearing confident and in command at the opening"

What in the world was he talking about, wondered Moses, but he didn't say a word. Doyle was proposing for him to go off alone with Sarah, why would he protest on the basis of mere fact?

Sarah responded without reservation, "Pack up your troubles, Sugar Mo, I'm going to take you places you've never seen."

Hadn't she done that from the very first moment they had met, he thought?

"Confident and in command," Doyle called after them as they slipped out the door, "and not talking about kids eating out of garbage cans, we're not hosting a fundraiser for hungry children you know."

"Maybe we ought to be," said Moses softly, closing the door.

Sarah drove the Zephyr down Michigan Avenue and swung over to Lakeshore Drive and followed the shoreline north. Moses rested his bent arm on the open window and propped up his head with the crook of his elbow. He looked north out across the water, and let the wind rush through his hair as they drove. It was one of those unique, sun-filled autumn days when the bright glow and warmth was reminiscent of summer, but the stillness, the absence of the summer tourists, and the missing clamor of children now in school, provided an intimacy that was only reinforced by the gentle lapping of the waves along the shoreline. The leaves covered the ground in a pallet of burnt orange and crimson in warning of the impending change of season.

He looked across the car at her, "Is it a full time job being that beautiful?" he asked, feeling rather bold.

"No, it's simply heredity, just luck," she smiled softly, but did not look at him, "I really very seldom think about it."

"What do you think about, what do you care about?" he watched her drive, "tell me everything." He wanted all the intimate details of her life. What did she like for breakfast? What was her favorite color? What did she dream about? He wanted every intimate detail of her life, but how could he fit it all into one afternoon? Would he ever have another?

"I love animals, dogs especially. I believe they're God's creatures."

"I didn't notice any pets around your house, did you have them put away when you had guests?"

"Doyle won't have it, pets in the home, pets cause too much disruption in the home he says, besides it might take my attention away from him for two minutes when he didn't have it planned, everything has to fit the master plan with him, all the angles have to be studied and analyzed."

"Is that why you don't have any children?"

"They haven't invented a child that's predictable, prearranged and planned, planned, planned. A child would definitely put Doyle's world in a tizzy."

"Maybe that's what he needs, a child would teach him to relax, maybe even find a sense of humor."

"He wouldn't have it, he'd toss out the child and the child's mother, he's made that perfectly clear."

"You think he'd really follow through with a threat like that?"

"Without a doubt."

"Why do you put up with a one way relationship like that?"

"For better or for worse."

"Your marriage vows?"

She nodded and he saw tears welling up in her eyes. He regretted the turn the conversation had taken, but there was an admiration for her inside him now that was totally and completely unconnected to the awe and wonder he felt about her physical charms.

They parked the car and walked, talking of little things, and then falling into long silences that were curiously not uncomfortable, like an old married couple who have grown together rather than apart and can not only occupy the same space but also the same thought without the necessity of words. How had they so quickly, so magically connected? They both silently wondered the same thought at that same instant.

"What are you doing over the holidays?" she asked, "any big plans?"

He was suddenly and acutely aware that he would not be spending the holidays with the one person in the world he most wanted to be spending them with, yet this was a confession better saved for another time. "No, no plans of any magnitude. Give the sailboat a coat of lacquer, walk up to town and let Sam the barber talk me into getting a haircut before I go up to Northport and spend a couple of days with my mother over Christmas." He smiled in amazement at the change that had occurred within him; this life had always been quite satisfactory before now, before Sarah. Could he tell her that his life would never be the same now that he had met her? Did he have the right to say such a thing? "Other than that, I'll just sit and watch the snow fall, listen to my Robert Johnson record collection, and wait for the kids to come find me for a game or two."

"Hockey?"

"Is there anything else?" He smiled when she laughed; it always made him smile to hear her laugh. "So what about you, what does the king of the Chicago art world and his wife do for the holidays?"

"We'll spend Christmas Eve with my parents, then catch the train for five weeks in Miami."

How could she do this to him? Did she know the type of vision this conjured in his mind? Sweet torture. He thought of Sarah in a bathing suit romping in the sun on Miami Beach. Smoothing suntan lotion on bare shoulders, bare ankles, bare calves, bare thighs, oh my, he was definitely in trouble. "Takes a lot of planning to be gone that long, doesn't it?" His heart suddenly sank as he thought of her blond hair blowing in the wind, and him not there to see it, about her laughing and him not there to hear it, about her dancing the night away under a tropical sky and never thinking of him.

"Yes, it seems like my life is one unending 'to do' list. Bills to pay, interviewing people to look after the house, setting things up at the bank, if Doyle asks me to take care of one more detail for the gallery, so help me I'll scream."

He looked back out at the water, trying to swim out of the emotional undertow into which he had slipped, struggling, gasping for air, suspended for a long moment between the bottom and the surface, and then recovering, forcing a little grin he said, "You think we ought to get back?"

After she dropped him in front of his hotel, he watched her as she drove away, her long hair fluttering out the window. He stepped out into the street so he could watch her just a little longer. She looked back once in the rearview mirror and flung an arm out the window in a final wave, then turned a corner.

SIX

Moses stood at the hotel window and watched the twilight descend upon the city. He lit a cigarette and leaned against the window arms outstretched, hands spread wide apart, and looked down at the street. The constant thought of her would not be quiet. Inside his heart, he was as restless as the November wind.

A need to put his body into some kind of action led him back out onto the street, walking, walking with no other aim than to move, and perhaps in the movement, lose his thoughts. A lifelong connection with the water brought him back to the shoreline. He walked without a purpose, without a direction, without a plan. He listened to the call of the water, but once he arrived at the beach, he was hit with an acute sense of loneliness. He had always been one for whom his own company was completely sufficient, until that moment. He was struck with the realization that Sarah had transformed his life, now his very existence would be forever changed. He cursed himself for longing to be with her, to see her, to embrace her vision with his adoring eyes.

In the quiet of the evening, he admitted his weakness and it pained him. The smell of the breeze off the lake had always been the fragrance of his life, now it was simply a reminder that the air lacked the smell of her perfume.

He turned away from the lake, walked back to the hotel and then past it, retracing his morning route. Was it madness? She would not be at the gallery, he knew that, yet trudged on, as if a man possessed. Did he want to see one of his paintings in the window? He had no idea what was leading him back to the gallery. He passed the alley of the hungry boys, it was empty now, perhaps he would have stopped this time, if they had been there, he didn't know, he didn't know anything except that being where she had been was as close as he was going to get to her that night, and that was what he had to do.

He stopped across the street from the gallery and looked at it, 'Conner Gallery of Fine Art' read the sign, engraved letters of gold in a large cut stone of black onyx. The white painted wood around the massive windows of the front façade was fresh and the glass reflected the streetlights as they came on. The gallery was dark, except for a security light in the back and a light over a service walk that ran down the side leading to the employee's private entrance. He crossed the street. There was no particular haste in his step, the thrill, the excitement, and the anticipation that should have been there was nowhere to be found or felt. Instead, an overwhelming emptiness dragged along with him like a convict's ball and chain. He stood in front of the window and took his pack of Lucky's from his pocket. He lit one, and stood examining his painting displayed on the other side of the glass as the smoke unconsciously rolled out of the corner of his lip.

He began to move toward the big plate glass window on the other side of the door, when he noticed that the front door was ajar. He stepped up to it, twisted the doorknob and it swung open. He stepped inside and closed it behind him. Voices, soft and muffled, echoed through the darkness from the private offices in the back.

Moses' pulse quickened with the prospect of who one of the inhabitants of the back office might be. He stepped past his paintings, walking through the gallery toward the light. As he moved down the corridor he saw the light shone from Doyle's private office, the door was open, and the light from the desk lamp spilled into the hallway. He got two steps from the doorway and then stopped still in his tracks when he saw what was happening inside the office. Doyle stood at the front of his desk, his back to the doorway, his pants and boxers bunched down around his ankles. Jenny Seabright's blue cotton slacks were strewn just inside the door. She lay on the desktop moaning with apparent delight, her cardigan sweater completely unbuttoned, exposing full, voluptuous breasts succumbing to Doyle's ravenous hands, her shapely legs wrapped around him, pulling him close as their bodies moved together.

Moses stopped breathing for a moment, not believing what he was witnessing. Then he turned, and hastily disappeared through the darkened gallery. He closed the door without a sound, and walked briskly down the street and around the corner.

It was dark early that night, as Dawn drove home from the nursing home. The sun had never really shone all day, and now the daylong drizzle had turned into a downpour. A warm shower was about as much as she could concentrate on, even though thoughts of Steve persisted in trying to make their way into her consciousness.

She turned her blue Honda onto the tree-lined street where she lived, only to be greeted by the glare of yellow, blue, and red flashers and intense spotlights illuminating the neighborhood. She pulled to halt at the curb in front of her apartment building and her heart sprang to her throat, and then, just as quickly, fell to her stomach, a sick nausea overtaking her. Firemen in yellow slickers were rolling up hoses and resecuring ladders back onto the fire trucks. Policemen in raingear were directing traffic and securing yellow caution tape around the black smoldering skeleton of the building that only that morning she had thought of as home.

She got out of the car and stood dumbfounded in front of the horrible sight, totally numb to the chaos and the rain. The downpour soaked her uniform and she shivered in reflex, but was unaware of it. She could not move, and stood staring at the blackness and destruction that the fire had left in its wake.

"Got to move along, miss," said police officer Bill Dunn, a portly man with jowly red cheeks sprouting out from under his black-rimmed eyeglasses, now spattered with rain.

She did not answer. She tried to say something, but the words just would not come. She was devastated.

"Miss, please, we don't want anybody getting hurt here, better move along home now." Officer Dunn's voice was getting much more stern; he did not have a lot of his usual patience left; he had been headed off duty when he got the fire call. And with his girlfriend waiting at home with pizza and a video, he had better things planned for that evening. He was wet and irritated, and the last thing he needed now was problems with the uncooperative citizenry.

She did not look at him, but continue to stare at the hulking structure. "I am home," she finally managed.

Compassion swiftly returned to him, "Charlie, bring me that umbrella over here." He held an umbrella over her head; a rain slicker was thrown over her shoulders. "Is there anybody we can call?" he asked softly.

She could think of no one but her sister Nancy, and after nearly force-feeding her coffee for half an hour as she sat in the front seat of a fire truck, Officer Dunn was able to get her to focus enough to give him the name and number and made the call.

Nancy and Barton arrived with daughters Becky and Angela, ages seven and nine respectively, in tow.

"My god!" said Nancy her face grimacing, "Are you all right, Dawn?" she asked, looking at Dawn's condition, she'd seen drown rats that looked better.

"She's taking it quite hard," said Officer Dunn.

"Was she inside?" Nancy asked the officer.

"Just rolled in when we were wrapping it up."

"Is there anything left?" asked Barton, "any of her possessions."

"Nothing anybody's going to be able to get to tonight, if there is anything," he explained, "doesn't appear like there'll be much, the building's a complete loss, and we have to keep the site secure until the fire investigators get through with their investigation and determine a cause. If they suspect arson then they have to remove whatever evidence they find, could take a while depending . . ."

"Why would anybody burn down my home?" came a meek voice from somewhere inside Dawn.

"Didn't mean to alarm you, Miss," said Officer Dunn, "we see 'em all, but this one's probably just accidental, one of the other tenants smoking in bed, or lightning striking in the storm, we'll just have to wait to find out."

"Is Auntie Dawn coming to live with us?" asked Becky.

"Yes dear," said Nancy. Barton shot her a questioning glance, but did not speak his protest. He wasn't sure about having an employee share his roof, even if she was related. He would have to think about this.

"Can she sleep with me?" asked Angela, "like a slumber party?"

"I think we'll give Auntie Dawn Becky's room for tonight and let you girls sleep together until we get things sorted out, OK?"

"Come on, Auntie Dawn." The girls took charge of her and led her toward the Hackett family bus, a maroon Dodge Caravan, parked across the street.

"Go with these good people, have yourself a stiff drink, and put yourself to bed," Officer Dunn called after her. "It'll all look better in the morning, believe you me."

Outside the van, the two sisters embraced. They had, for the most part, lost touch ten years ago when Nancy got married and moved away, until twenty-one months ago when Dawn followed to attend nursing school. Even then, they had mostly stayed out of each other's way in that little town, until finally they came face to face when Dawn came to do the clinical part of her nursing program at the nursing home. Being nine years apart in age, it was as if they were parts of different families, except for the dark history that they both shared. And Barton did his best to insure that whatever family ties remained, were severed after he and Nancy were married.

Barton helped Dawn into the van; she was nearly unaware that his hand was on her shoulder quite a bit longer than it needed to be there. The van pulled away from the curb, splashed through the puddles made by rain clouds and fire hoses and turned the corner. The flashing rainbow of lights bouncing off the rooftops and reflecting in the windows quickly disappeared as Dawn sat forlornly looking out the window, her mind in a muddle.

Barton drove them to a white colonial house on Jefferson Street, freshly painted white clapboard siding, black shutters at the windows, and bulky white wooden columns extending two stories in height. It was evident that Barton was doing quite well as an executive in the health care field. Jefferson Street was quite an elite address in Evergreen. However, most of the neighboring dwellings were presided over by wives who did not work, except for the occasional charity bazaar at the country club.

The entry door was of custom carved maple, distinctively framed by two sidelights with leaded glass. Inside, the Hackett home was elaborately furnished; expensive wallpaper in deep green with gold leaf trim provided a backdrop for deeply polished mahogany furniture, imported light fixtures shone down on parquet floors in the dining room and foyer, and deep plush carpeting throughout the rest of the house.

It was only the third time Dawn had visited in the nearly two years she had been in Evergreen, and she would have again noted the sharp contrast of her sister's home to way they had had to live when they were growing up, but this night she was not capable of noting anything, she was numb. She made a feeble attempt to lift her head as they entered. Barton stepped behind her to help her off with the borrowed rain slicker she still wore. Her abdomen reflexively shot forward, was that Barton's body pressing against her from behind while Nancy wasn't looking? Her foggy thoughts could not contemplate that, or anything else. She turned toward him, but he turned away to take care of the coat, and in turn his own, and those of the girls. Maybe it was accidental, it had to be accidental, and after all, he was family, why would she ever suspect anything else. He turned to face her at a respectable distance and flashed her a dimpled grin that was at once both friendly and fiendish. He rubbed his hands together and said, "Now for that drink, what'll you have?"

"What she needs now is to get out of these soaking wet clothes and into a nice hot shower," interposed Nancy, "girls take Auntie Dawn upstairs." Becky and Angela each grabbed onto a hand and led her toward the stairs where Dawn dropped them and made war with the stairway just like she had with her own on any other day. This struggle somehow restored her focus, and by the time she stood in the shower with a torrent of hot water running over her head an accurate representation of what had transpired that evening began to register.

Soon she was lying in a borrowed bathrobe in a borrowed bed of a little girl, remembering the helplessness of the little girl she had been. Tomorrow there would be a solution, she was sure, but tonight she needed rest.

The next morning she found her uniform cleaned and pressed, draped over the desk chair. Nancy had taken care of this detail after she had fallen asleep, knowing there would be little in her own wardrobe that would be of any value in loaning to her younger sister. She dressed quickly, remembering with a rush where she was and why she was there. Angela and Becky both made appearances seeking assurance that Auntie Dawn had recovered her senses and was now back to normal. "I'm fine," she reassured them, "but I will have to go out shopping for a new wardrobe, any volunteers?" They both nodded and squealed with delight. She had taken them shopping before last Christmas, and had indulged them until their eyes ran brown with hot fudge. That was an afternoon they would not soon forget.

After methodically descending the stairs, she found that Nancy had prepared a breakfast of scrambled eggs and pancakes. She sat down at the dining room table, Barton was already seated, drinking coffee and reading the morning paper. Nancy came in from the kitchen and set a pitcher of orange juice on the table, "Come on girls, get your breakfast," she called.

"I want to thank you for all you did for me last night," began Dawn, "I know what an imposition it must have been, but they asked me who to call and I just didn't know . . ."

"Well of course you'd call your sister," interrupted Nancy, "who else would you call? Now don't think another thing about it, we just were so worried about you, are you OK? I've never seen you take anything so hard." Then she paused, "well not for a very long time."

"I'm fine really," she said, and plunged into her scrambled eggs as if to prove it.

When Barton had finished his breakfast he sat back playing with a toothpick, flashing an unsettling grin toward Dawn whenever Nancy wasn't looking.

"So what are you going to do Dawn, did you have renter's insurance?" Nancy asked.

Dawn wasn't sure if it was Nancy being the big sister or Nancy being the head nurse that accounted for her take-charge tone at that moment. "Yes, I paid insurance even though I didn't know if I had anything worth insuring," she said.

"So now what?" Nancy pursued, "All you have is the clothes on your back, until you get your claim settled."

"I have a little in the bank," said Dawn defensively, "I don't spend every dime I make. I'll pick up a few things after work tonight to get me by for now. I'll take the girls out shopping with me, we'll have a time of it." She smiled.

"Well, if you had a man to take care of . . ." Nancy stopped herself, but it was already said. She looked for something to yell at the girls about to change the subject, but could find no fault.

Dawn rolled her eyes and thought, "yes, just like you dear sister, with your charming husband chasing everything in town with a skirt," but said nothing. Barton had a menacing way about him, sneaking glances and striking suggestive poses only to return to a pretense of the placid when coming under Nancy's gaze. He stroked the edges of his lips with his thumb and forefinger, his eyes issuing an invitation, unsettling and undeniable, and then straightened up just as Nancy glanced his way.

Dawn ignored him and turned her attention to her sister, her poor deceived sister, who couldn't recognize, or better yet, refused to recognize, that she had a husband who thought he had a right to every female he had contact with. In fact, what made it truly scary, was that it seemed as if he thought he not only had a right, but in some perverse way, a duty to them as well. A man deluded into thinking he was God's gift to women in the extreme.

Dawn tried to direct the conversation toward Barton, reasoning he would have to be on his best behavior if he were the focus of attention, "So tell me Barton, do you share your wife's opinion, that what my life really lacks is the attention of a man?" She was not about to confess how close to the truth her sister's nearly unspoken sentiment really was.

"Well Dawny, without sounding harsh," he looked down at his hands and idly played with the empty coffee cup, it is what every woman wants isn't it?"

Yes, damn it, it was, and it was something she would never have, how did she ever let this subject be brought up in the first place. "Not every woman Barton, the convents are full of those who don't?" She looked back to her sister. "Can we leave a bit early and swing by the apartment so I can pick up my car?"

"Are you ready to see that sight?" said her sister, "it shook you up quite badly last night."

"I'm over the shock, thanks to my big sister," she patted Nancy's hand as it laid on the table, "now I've got to put my life back together."

At the door, Barton helped the women on with their coats, first Nancy, who headed out the door, and then Dawn. As he watched Nancy heading out the back sidewalk to the driveway, he touched Dawn at her ribs, just below her breast with a suggestive squeeze.

"Barton, stop it," she said, trying to maintain control of her voice so that she didn't alarm her sister or the girls.

"Excuse me?" he said, his voice dripping with enough innocence to fool a priest.

"If you touch me again, you'll have a fat lip to show for it."

Barton was beginning to realize that this woman was made of sterner stuff than he had ever given her credit for before. "Touch you? Why sister Dawny, what on earth are you talking about?"

"You know exactly what I'm talking about, " she scowled, "and don't call me sister, I'm no sister of yours!"

Barton liked women, and this one in particular had whetted his interest with her sassiness, beautiful dark hair, and her petite frame. No man in his right mind would want the little gimp on a permanent basis, but as a diversion from his boring, overweight wife, she would do just fine. Barton began to anticipate the days ahead.

"OK, is Dawny all right?"

"Dawn will do just fine, if you don't mind," she said sternly, "it's my name. Do you have it clear where your hands are supposed to be?"

"Aren't you the spunky one?" he said, "and brave too, to be talking to your boss in such a fashion."

She sighed in disgust and headed off down the walk behind her sister. "Just keep your hands to home and we'll get along fine, Barton."

He flashed a grin that oozed with charm, charm that would have parted a widow from her pension, and donned his hat to follow her, "I'll let you think on that, a little girl like you might have needs that you don't realize right now."

Dawn returned to work with a heavy heart. Perhaps work would be the best therapy, she reasoned, concentrating on other people's troubles would take her mind off of the fire. But when she entered Moses' room, it was always like visiting her grandfather, and she broke down, her bottom lip beginning to tremble.

He saw the tears welling in her eyes, "Dawn? What is it, dear?"

"I lost my home," a single tear made its way down her cheek.

"Dawn, what happened?" A compassion, one would normally associate only with family, filled his voice.

"The apartment building where I live, where I lived, burned down yesterday."

"Oh, Dawn, I'm so sorry. Were you hurt?"

She silently slumped down on the edge of his bed, as if she didn't hear him. In her mind a vision of the hulking rubble returned. "Dawn?" whispered Moses.

"Oh, sorry," she snapped back, "uh no, I wasn't even home. When I got there the firemen were just cleaning up."

"What firemen?" It was Steve's voice, bouncing and vibrant. Everyday Steve passed Moses' room when making his rounds, picking up half eaten trays of food and engaging in light conversation. He entered the room and saw Dawn's face and his smile vanished.

"Dawn's place burned down," said Moses solemnly.

"Oh, I'm sorry," Steve was wordless beyond that; he didn't know what to say in situations like these. He never knew what to say at funerals either. He had been raised to suffer in silence and never knew what to say at the revelation of another person's grief.

"You lose everything?" asked Moses.

"I really didn't have much, but what I did have can never be replaced."

"Like photographs and such?"

"Yeah, and this little statue of a nurse with angel's wings that my mother gave me, things like that."

"I'm sorry for you, darling," Moses said, wishing he could reach out, take her in his arms, and give her a hug. But things like that were just not done between staff and patients in Nurse Hackett's facility.

"Is there anything I can do?" asked Steve.

"Yes," said Dawn, looking into his blue eyes, yes, he did have blue eyes, "you could change the subject."

"I've got a subject," said Moses, she turned to him, "summer's slipping away, and we should all take a trip to the beach."

Steve looked at Dawn.

"I've asked her before," said Moses.

She nodded in agreement. "Many times."

"I love her to bits," said Moses, "but she has no sense of adventure."

Steve looked from Dawn to Moses, then back to Dawn.

"I can see the wheels turning, Steve, but we could never get permission."

"Whose permission would we need?"

"The nursing home doesn't just let their patients go wherever they want to," she said.

Moses sighed and looked out the window, "I just want to see the sun set over the big water one more time before I die," he said, "I don't know why it's such a big thing."

Steve could see the pain on his face, but had no answer.

SEVEN

It is not my desire to justify the actions of Barton Hackett, which I am duty bound to report later on, but it must be demonstrated that no man is totally evil, and that nothing happens in a vacuum. Even the most contemptuous of us has some trait that has a redeeming quality.

Barton remembered how he used to be envied by every man in the room when he would enter with Nancy on his arm. She had been pretty by anyone's standards. Now he sat with a bitterness in his belly as if she had stolen from him a sacred treasure. But the depth of Barton's disappointment in his marriage had not affected his desire to be a good parent. In fact, it may have had quite the opposite effect, with his two little daughters receiving all the attention that he had to give his small family, to the near exclusion of his wife. He was a good father to his two little daughters, and it was during her stay with Barton and Nancy that Dawn observed the other side of Barton's lecherous nature. It took her by complete surprise to see how completely, totally, and openly her nieces, his little daughters, loved him. How broad and tender was his smile as he bounced them on his knee. How concerned he was at their slightest cough or the hint of a runny nose.

And there was one night in particular that stayed with her for no particular reason other than how common place it seemed.

It was a cool summer evening at Barton and Nancy's house, the stickiness of the past few days had subsided, and Nancy had turned off the air conditioning and thrown open the windows. A gentle breeze rustled the lace curtains now and again. And out in the neighborhood you could hear the sound of a distant lawnmower.

In the family room after dinner, Dawn was perched on the loveseat in a light blue terrycloth jumpsuit, her knees up where she had propped open a book by Kahil Gibran that she had borrowed from the nursing home library. The family dog, floppy eared and golden, was curled at her feet. They had bonded, the girl and the dog, almost from the moment Dawn had entered that home, when the dog came to sleep with her the night Nancy and Barton brought her home in a daze after the fire.

One end wall of the room was completely covered with built-in bookshelves running to the ceiling above a row of six cabinet doors, everything painted in an enamel eggshell. The carpet was a plush, the color of red wine. Small antique tables with intricate carvings held antique lamps of artistic porcelain with frail beige lampshades. Two overstuffed claw-foot chairs and the matching loveseat in a mint green were flanked by the tables and lamps and faced the French doors which led out to a garden that looked for the most part untended.

Angela and Becky lay on the floor at their father's feet, with coloring books and crayons spread out before them. He sat idly perusing the newspaper. The girls were chattering about what color they should make Barbie's dress, and Barton would chime in with his suggestions, all acting as though this were a common occurrence. All natural and at ease with each other. How out of character for Barton, thought Dawn, at least the Barton, she had come to know.

"Let's make her dress forest green," said Angela.

"No, it has to be black," said Becky, "black is the only elegant color."

"Girls," said Barton interjecting in anticipation, before the little girls even knew they were having a problem, "why don't you make two pictures, one with a green dress, and one with a black one. You know Barbie isn't going to wear the same dress every night."

The three of them looked as though they had spent many such evenings just like this. Angela was the image of Nancy as a young girl, the way Dawn remembered her. Thin and graceful, a few freckles decorating her cheeks, her hair more red than blond depending on the light, and her smile warm and captivating. Becky was small and blond with a mischievous grin.

Both wore khaki shorts and cotton tank tops, Becky in a deep purple, Angela in day-glo pink with aqua trim. Barton still wore the white shirt and navy pants he had worn to work, but his collar was open and he had forfeited his tie and jacket since entering his home. His wingtip shoes were parked next to the footstool on which he propped his feet. And there was something about the sight of Barton in his stocking feet that also struck Dawn as unnatural. It was too homey, too casual, for someone she knew as callous and calculating.

The girls giggled and chatted, if there had ever been a competition for their father's attention, it appeared it had long ago been properly and successfully dealt with. Dawn surprised herself with the feeling of admiration that she felt for Barton's skill as a father.

"Auntie Dawn are you sad?" asked Angela, "I would be sad if our house burned down."

"Yeah," she said softly, " I suppose I am, but I sure am glad I have two nieces like you to take care of me."

The girls looked at each other, their eyes wide. "We're good at taking care of things," said Becky, "aren't we, Dad?"

"You're the best, precious," said Barton, picking up his paper once again.

As the evening wore on, the smell of the popcorn Nancy was making in the kitchen filtered into the room, attracting the girls' attention. Nancy brought in a tray of four bowls of popcorn, handed one to Dawn, one to Barton, and set down two for the girls.

"Hey," said Angela, "Becky's got more than I do."

Instantly, Barton snatched away her bowl and was on his feet, "you girls share that bowl, and if you finish it you can have another." He returned the other bowl back to the kitchen, and the girls returned to their coloring book without further comment, occasionally stopping for a handful of popcorn.

When the grandfather clock in the front hallway chimed nine, both girls looked up at their father.

"Whose turn is it to ride up to bed first tonight?" He asked them.

"Mine," said Becky. Angela nodded.

He knelt on the floor in his stocking feet. "OK," he said, "climb on."

She bounced up on his back and threw her arms around his neck and her legs around his waist. "We always get piggy back rides to bed," Becky said looking down at Dawn.

"Lucky girls," smiled Dawn.

"Goodnight, Auntie Dawn," she called as they disappeared through the archway.

"Good night, Becky."

Barton came back moments later for Angela, and she took the same position as her sister and said her good nights.

Nancy came in from the kitchen and sat down in the chair next to Dawn. "He'll be up there a half hour making sure they brush their teeth and reading them their bedtime story."

"He seems to be quite a devoted father."

"A fanatic father," said Nancy, her tone did not sound as if she were trying to be humorous.

"He's not a good father?" asked Dawn.

"He's a great father," said Nancy, "I only wish he was half as good a husband."

Dawn really did not want to pursue the subject any further and was grateful when the conversation dropped into silence.

During the 1930's Doyle Bradley Conner had achieved a reputation for extravagance, and it was well earned. An opening at the Conner Gallery of Fine Art was as close to a Hollywood spectacle as Chicago would have the opportunity to experience. And for the opening for the exhibition of the works of Moses Bailey, Doyle had created an event of newsworthy proportions. Giant spotlights illuminated the front of the gallery, and guests arrived in formal evening attire, women in gowns, which cost more than the highest price Moses had ever asked for one of his paintings, streamed into the gallery escorted by gentlemen in tuxedos. Limousines and the latest model luxury sedans pulled up to the front of the glistening gallery, disembarking passengers. Valet attendants helped the ladies from the vehicles, then jumped in and drove away the shining sedans.

Moses studied the scene as he approached, his collar upturned against the wind, his hands jammed in the pockets of his pants, a cigarette attached to the corner of his mouth. He would, no doubt, feel more at home hanging out with the valets. Even wearing the new tie he had bought to go with his corduroy sport coat was not going to elevate him to this social class, not that he actually wanted to be elevated. Doyle had explained to him that with artists, "it's not attire it's attitude," it was well known that artists were eccentric, no one expected an artist to dress like everyone else.

Moses finished his cigarette as if hoping to somehow draw a little extra courage from it, and made his way across the street dodging the all the confusion occurring at the front door by going down the service walk to the back.

He wasn't in the door more than twenty-five seconds when Doyle angrily confronted him, "You're late. This is your deal you know?"

"Sorry, I suddenly forgot how to tie a tie." His gaze looked past Doyle and scanned the crowd filling the gallery.

Jenny Seabright came up, her ample bosom practically spilling out of a low-cut blue sequined dress, and grabbed his arm, "Well it's about time, Mr. Bailey, time to get to work." She directed him out to the middle of the crowd, stuck a glass of wine in his hand, and the introductions, handshakes, and what passed for intelligent conversation concerning the world of art began in earnest. Jenny stayed within earshot after making an introduction, she would shake her head in disapproval when he would say something like "I just paint," but every time he looked at her he could only think about the scene he had witnessed the night before. Her bare breasts, those shapely legs, and that bleached blond hair hanging off the edge of Doyle's desk, swinging rhythmically with the motion of their bodies.

He listened to comments with one ear, and kept one eye in his present circumstance, with the other he kept scanning the throng for Sarah. Jenny and Doyle kept the parade of patrons and critics coming as if timed with military precision. He thought about asking Doyle where his wife was, but somehow it didn't seem to be a fit piece of conversation to stick in the middle of the flow of oncoming strangers.

When the parade finally began to slow down, he lit a cigarette and leaned back against the wall, propping one foot up on a tall granite ashtray. He exhaled and turned his head, at once locking his vision on to those soft gray eyes for which he had searched. Sarah was gorgeous in her backless black evening gown, the black satin hinting of the aroused nipple beneath it, her dark blond hair piled on top of her head, long diamond earrings dangling at the sides of her face, cherry red lipstick that begged to be kissed, and skin as soft as a daydream on a warm summer afternoon. Moses could hardly contain himself. They held each other's eyes as if not caring who might be watching. Finally, after a long while or an eternity, he couldn't tell which, she lowered her eyes and slowly sauntered toward him. His heart raced, and then began to sink as he thought of what he had discovered the previous night, and the thought of what sharing that knowledge would do to her life.

An art critic from one of the Chicago weeklies assailed him from the rear, as Moses kept his gaze glued upon Sarah. He was a pretentious little man who sported a bow tie and sunglasses even at night.

"What do you think of that Jackson Pollock?" asked the critic.

"I don't," said Moses, without emotion.

"I thought a Pollock was a fish?" asked Jenny.

"He's on the WPA, you know?" the critic continued.

Sarah swept in to rescue him, "Moses Bailey is too busy painting to worry about other artists," And pulled him into motion by his sleeve, "if you two will excuse us . . ."

"Sugar Mo, I think you're a hit," she leaned and kissed his cheek. As she moved, his hand grazed the naked flesh of her back, an electric current charged through him momentarily rendering his power of speech useless.

He looked at her face for a long while, wishing he could reach out and gently caress it. And in that moment he knew, he could never be the one to cause a tear to run down those cheeks. He would die with the secret that he carried rather than be the one to break her heart.

"Cat got your tongue?" she grinned.

"You're beautiful, incredibly beautiful," he finally managed, "with you in the room how is it anybody is even looking at my paintings?"

"Fortunately for you, they don't all share your taste."

She took a deep breath and began to speak again, but paused as a grinning gray-haired gentleman reached between them and shook Moses' hand. "Lovely, just lovely," he said and moved off toward the bar.

She looked as if she were trying to decide whether or not to speak at all, "I probably could a pick a better time to talk about this . . ." She paused again.

He had no idea why his hands were trembling, and stuck them in the front pockets of his pants so he didn't have to think about them. He sensed they were standing at a point in their lives when nothing would be the same afterward, but he could not discern whether it was a threshold or a crossroads.

"Sarah, you've stopped smiling," Moses said tenderly, "I know in the ways of the world we barely know each other, but will you believe me when I say that you can tell me anything?"

"I knew that before you said it, it's just sometimes I have trouble expressing serious things."

"Just take your time, we have nothing but time."

"That's not true, and as I was packing some bags for our trip to Miami Beach, I realized that."

"Realized what?"

"Sugar Mo, I'm going to miss you."

"I'm going to miss you too, Sarah." More than he would ever admit to himself or anyone else.

"What I'm trying to say is that it's more than that, Sugar Mo . . . I'm really, really, going to miss you." She looked up at him and it was as if those gray eyes were looking into his very soul, carving her name upon his heart, "I know more than you think about the way that you feel about certain things . . . about the way that I feel about those things . . . oh Moses, I'm really making a mess of this . . ."

He had finally gotten control of his trembling hands and took them from his pockets, clasping hers between them. "Sarah, go ahead and say what it is you've got to say."

"I know this will sound like I'm assuming something, quite a lot actually, and if I'm wrong you have to promise to stop me and forget I said anything," her gray eyes looked up at him open and vulnerable, "promise?"

"Go ahead."

"You didn't promise."

"OK, I promise."

She looked down at their hands joined together, then looked around and reluctantly withdrew them. She returned her gaze to meet his eyes, "Underneath all the flirtation, witty comebacks, and the laughter we share, there's something else going on, isn't there? Something real."

He stood silent, feeling the memory of her touch on his palms. She had waited all evening for this moment. He felt sure that her absence until now had been no accident, no coincidence. He was not about to interrupt. He wanted her to complete what she had to say, it was time to get it out in the open, wherever it was to lead.

A fat, jolly type with slicked back hair and a blue suit, and a little too much drink under his belt, stumbled backward from one of the paintings for no apparent reason. As he did, he bumped the elbow of a waiter passing him with a tray full of empty glasses, sending the whole cargo crashing to the marble floor. Every head in the gallery turned to look, except for two.

"Well . . . isn't there?" She whispered, but everything else about her indicated she was shouting. "There is something else going on between us, isn't there?" She reached out almost instinctively and grabbed his forearms.

He looked down at her small delicate hands and their immaculately painted nails, then looked back to her face and nodded.

"It's been there from the moment I pulled up your driveway and saw you standing there on your front porch, leaning against that post in that way you have. It's been there since the moment I got out of the car that day, hasn't it? Admit it."

He nodded once more and began to speak as if choosing his words very carefully, " I can remember the very moment when I felt something restless awaken within me. You took off your sunglasses and I looked into your eyes, and it was as if a wind began to blow across my heart, and when I listened to the wind, I could hear it whisper your name." He wanted to tell her more, to tell her everything, but how could he? "It's not a whisper anymore," he paused trying, with every fiber of his being, to stay in control, "and I can't turn off the wind."

She sighed, "Oh Moses, my sweet, sweet, Sugar Mo," her voice was quiet and faltering, sounding almost as if it had a tear in it. She looked away from him, hiding her face. She looked out across the crowd, and then up at the ceiling. He could see her eyelashes flutter as if she had something in her eye. He didn't move. He didn't speak.

"My mother saw it between us, and that was only the fourth time we were ever together."

It amazed him more than a little that she had counted the times they had been together. "She saw how you looked at me, and to be fair about it, the way I looked back at you," she looked back into his eyes, a slight grin made its way to her lips, "or was it the other way around?"

"You tell me, you're doing fine so far."

"She told me to be careful," she continued, "to be very careful."

"Your mother must think I'm a dangerous man."

"I feel like such a little schoolgirl," he could see her eyes welling up and her top lip began to quiver, "I didn't mean to say that. What I mean is . . . isn't there a woman out there for you, someone other than . . ."

He cut her off before she said it, as if preserving some hope, "Are you trying to let me down easy?" He forced a smile.

"I didn't want it to sound like that, it's just that I'm afraid of where this journey might lead if I don't get off the train right now, don't you know?"

"All I know is how I feel about you."

Doyle suddenly appeared at his shoulder, bringing another hand to shake, another white-haired matron to compliment. Sarah turned and faded back into the crowd. He watched the smooth skin of her back move away. She looked back, as if feeling his eyes caress her from a distance, and smiled, but it was a sad smile.

The latest news of the Russian attack on Finland dominated the front page headlines as Doyle sat reading the paper at his favorite table at his favorite breakfast spot, when Moses walked in. The headwaiter raised an eyebrow at Moses' carpenter jeans and denim work shirt as he made his way through the starched white linen tablecloths and royal blue leather chairs to join him. Doyle as usual had the appearance of a man well pleased with himself. An oxford cloth shirt, herringbone tie, and blue cardigan sweater, as usual not a blemish or anything out of place. He did not take his eyes from the paper as Moses approached. Moses sat down, ran a hand through his tousled hair, took his cigarettes from his pocket, and asked the waitress for a cup of coffee.

"I should be furious as hell with you," Doyle said without looking up, "it's your premier showing, and you take off early?"

"I gave it all I could stand," Moses said, and reached for a cigarette.

"All you could stand?" Doyle lowered the paper, "what kind of namby-pamby excuse is that, all I could stand? Don't you realize you could have been throwing money away? Just pissing dollar bills down the sewer?"

"Money's your thing, Doyle, and so are all these people."

As Moses looked across the room toward the back wall of floor-to-ceiling mirrors, Sarah appeared and walked toward them. Was there a time of day when she didn't look incredibly beautiful, he wondered? She wore a loose fitting, white crocheted top over a mint green skirt with matching shoes. The skirt fit snug across the hips and ended just above the knees. "Morning Moses, Doyle." She sat down, and the heads that had turned to watch her cross the room returned to their breakfasts. She avoided making eye contact with Moses and she busied herself sweetening the coffee that had been ordered for her. It was hard enough to keep up the pretense, without having to compound the difficulty by looking at him. How could she be expected to look at those passionate green eyes after what had been said last night? He would just have to think her rude and get over it, that's what he would have to do. Finally, her resolve weakened and she looked across the table at him, and as luck would have it, right into those green eyes of his. She felt herself melting again. What was she going to do about this schoolgirl crush? Perhaps, she would first have to admit it was far more than that. And doing something about it, would take something monumental, if not downright surgical.

"I'm leaving," Moses announced. Her heart sank.

"You don't like the food here?" asked Sarah, knowing full well what he meant, but unwilling to admit it to herself or anyone else.

"I'm leaving Chicago."

Doyle folded the paper and laid it down on the table, looking at him sternly, "What the hell are you talking about?"

"I'm heading back to Sutton's Bay this afternoon." Sarah stared at him, wondering if indeed this were the inevitable conclusion.

"Your show is a success," Doyle was sounding agitated, "don't you know what that means?" He was trying very hard to remain calm. "Now is the time to cash in on your success, not run away from it?" Doyle poured another cup of coffee, but did not drink it. Instead, he pulled an expensive looking cigar from his pocket, snipped the end, and lit it. He blew a smoke ring over the table before continuing. "What is it? You bored? We'll get you a girl? You homesick? We'll get you two girls? You don't like girls, we'll get you a boy, just tell me what the hell it is. What's bothering you? Just tell me and I'll fix it."

"There's nothing to fix, I just don't belong here."

"Not the kids eating out of garbage cans thing again, Moses, you got to grow up. Those kids are going to be going hungry whether you're here or back up there in no man's land."

"It's not the kids, Doyle. And I want to thank you and Sarah for everything you've done for me, but I don't belong here."

"Lord knows I've met my share of idiots in my time, I mean who wouldn't dealing with the 'artist temperament' in this business, but kid, you take the cake. Don't you know you're walking out on a fortune?

Can you imagine what earning power you'll have throughout your career with a start like this?" Doyle was back in control, his voice, the soothing tones of the salesman, "Have you seen the reviews, they're great," he began opening the paper once again, "I've brought them along, wait til you read them, they couldn't be better if I wrote them myself."

"Doyle, none of that matters," Moses was looking at Sarah, "I've got to go." He stood.

Doyle popped out of his seat and stood blocking his path. "Why?" You've got to tell me why, you owe me at least an explanation. If you have no understanding about all the time and money I've invested bringing this off, you must at least tell me why."

Moses looked at the floor, scuffed his shoe against the carpet, then looked at Sarah searching for something, anything, in those gray eyes, then once more he faced Doyle, "Because I'm in love with your wife."

Doyle's mouth dropped open and he sank back into his chair. That was the one answer for which he was totally unprepared.

Sarah began to speak, but all that came out was a gasp of air. She bit her bottom lip, her eyes forlorn and on the edge of tears. Moses took one last long look at her face, trying to engrave it in his memory, and walked out the way he had come.

EIGHT

Moses walked the two short blocks from the restaurant back to the hotel. The angry November wind bit at his eyes. He felt as if he were about to cry, but refused to admit to himself the reason why. It seemed Chicago had gone from summer to winter in two short days. It was definitely time for him to leave.

Doyle Bradley Conner had introduced him to the world, had he done him a favor? Moses did not mean to fall in love with another man's wife; it was opposed to everything that he believed in, but it had happened just the same. And he was completely, desperately, in love.

As an experienced motorcycle traveler, Moses packed light. There wasn't much to it when he went back to the hotel to pack his things together. He looked around the hotel, surmising he would probably never again indulge in that kind of luxury, but in his heart, this knowledge did not bring with it any regret. His only regret had a completely different face. Maybe he should have told her what kind of man she was married to, tried to convince her to come away with him, but just as quickly as it was conceived, the thought was dismissed, he could not be the one to tell her, not now, not ever.

The phone rang. He looked at it as if it were a foreign object. His bag was packed, his mind made up, he was on his way out the door, and his course would not be altered. The phone rang again. Reluctantly he picked it up.

"Moses, I'm down in the bar," Sarah's voice was pleading, "can I talk to you before you go?"

A knot suddenly formed in his stomach. "I'll be right down." Saying good-bye to her a second time would take more courage than he had been prepared for.

He grabbed his bag, threw his jacket over his arm and looked around the room one last time.

When he reached the bar, she called out to him, "Sugar Mo, over here." How could it be, he wondered, that she got better looking every time he saw her? She blushed and waved her hand.

He crossed the room, it was dimly lit, and the large slabs of polished walnut, and the hulking mahogany bar made it even darker. She was sitting in a booth and he slid into the brown leather seat facing her.

She reached out on the table and grabbed his hand, and then suddenly realizing what she was doing, she withdrew and put her hands in her lap under the table. A waitress came over, lit a small candle on the table, and asked for their order. Sarah ordered a wine and Moses asked for a couple fingers of bourbon, it was a whiskey kind of day.

While they waited for their drinks, Sarah made polite conversation, asking about his boat, and when it got brought inside, and if the cherries were any good this year. And Moses wondered why she had come. Although he didn't mind having the chance to look at her one last time, it confused him.

The waitress brought back the drinks and Sarah lifted up her glass, "What shall we drink to, Sugar Mo?"

"A safe journey," he touched his glass to hers, "wherever our roads may lead."

She didn't say anything for a while. He pulled out his pack of cigarettes, lit one, and blew smoke toward the ceiling. Here he was, Moses Bailey of Sutton's Bay, sitting in a hotel bar in downtown Chicago with another man's wife. Why was he here?

She pulled her hands from under the table and placed them in front of her as if experiencing a sudden need to examine her manicure.

"Why are we here, Sarah?" he asked softly.

She didn't answer him right away. She lifted her head so he could look directly into her soft gray eyes. "I didn't come to stop you," she began slowly, there was something in her tone that had with it the finality of a funeral. And the momentary happiness he had felt at seeing her again began to melt.

She paused again and then, "I knew all the words that I wanted to say, but it's much harder to actually say them."

"I already know them, that's why I'm leaving."

"I have to say them, I can't let you go thinking it was all you, that you had a crush on me and that was all, because it's been more than that, and I had to let you know that it's been more than that for me too."

He wondered why it felt as though someone had rolled a giant boulder on to his chest, crushing him.

"But it isn't fair to Doyle, this thing that we've had, I know it and you know it too. I fantasize about you, about us, about how it could be."

"I've had the same kind of thoughts from the very beginning, and if I told them to you, it would make you blush."

She looked down at the table, "and that's exactly why I'm not grabbing you by the arm, and begging you not to go, I know it has to be this way."

"I know."

"Do you? Do you know that I'd really like to take you back upstairs to that hotel room, lock the door, and rip your clothes off, do you know that?"

He tried to force a smile, but it came out as a frown.

"And for that very reason, because I want you more than I've ever wanted a man in my life, I'm going to walk out of here, stand at the curb and wave good-bye as you ride out of my life forever."

"I don't know what to say, Sarah," Moses shook his head. "You already know how I feel about you, I love you. I don't think I've ever been ready to say those words before. But with you the feeling is so powerful and intense they almost seem inadequate. I think I've loved you from the moment you stepped out of that Lincoln and into my cherry orchard, into my world. Do you have any idea of how much I've wanted you, all of you, everything that makes you Sarah? I want you today and every day hereafter, but I don't think it is doing either of us any good for me to repeat it now."

He lit another Lucky and took another sip of his whiskey.

She shook her bowed head and reached inside her purse for a handkerchief. "Don't, Sugar Mo . . . no more." The bartender, apparently aware of what was happening, turned up the radio to cover her sobs. Moses nodded in acknowledgement.

Moses reached across the table and put his hand on Sarah's neck, it was the first time he had ever touched her in that way, and it melted him. Her skin felt like he had imagined it would during all those nights alone, which had been transformed into lonely nights just by knowing her. The sensation traveled through his fingertips and up his arm and came to rest deep inside him somewhere. And the feeling was sad, sad for all the times he would never feel it again, "So you can see why I can't stay in the same town with you."

She lowered her eyes, watching her hands. She slowly folded the handkerchief and returned it to her purse. "I know, there's something about being together that's just too strong for me too." She took his right hand in both of hers and looked back up to his face, "I owe Doyle a lot, and he's been very good to me."

This was taking a path on which he had no desire to go, not with Sarah. She was confusing loyalty with love, and getting tangled up in her own emotions, and he didn't want to listen to it. "You don't have to explain, Sarah." He put a single finger to her lips, silencing her. She kissed it and closed her eyes.

When she opened them he was standing beside the table. "It's time for me to go." She nodded and rose. They left with her hanging on his right arm while he carried his bag in his left. There were tears in her eyes.

They did not speak as he strapped his bag onto the Harley-Davidson, no false promises about writing, or staying in touch, just a long look between them. And then the motorcycle roared to life. He adjusted his goggles, and she rushed to him, pressing herself into him, kissing him full on the mouth. He felt the curve of her breast hard against his chest, their tongues dancing together. And then it was over, tears streaming down her face as she tried to wave, but the muscles wouldn't answer her command to move.

He headed his motorcycle down the Michigan Avenue, wondering how he was going to make it through all the years ahead without her. A car, then a truck, and then another car, fell in behind him, the traffic swallowing him, hiding him from her view, and he was gone.

Finally, Steve had decided to take matters into his own hands, to try and control his own destiny. He stretched out his legs along the brick planter outside the back door of the nursing home, waiting for Dawn to get out off the second shift. The moon was full, hanging low in the southern sky; a cool breeze spoke of rain in the distance.

He stood up, unable to sit still; a nervousness in his stomach moved him to begin pacing around the planter. Why was he nervous? After all, she was only a girl, and he had certainly talked to one or two in his life without feeling this kind of anxiety about it.

Then Dawn appeared at the door and he felt his heart catch in his throat. Was it her long dark hair, her soft brown eyes, or the gentle curve of her cheek? He didn't know, but there was definitely something brewing inside him, something he had never felt before.

"Are you waiting in ambush, Steve?" cracked Dawn, "where are you hiding your mop?"

He smiled, "You're never going to let me live that down are you?"

"Never."

"I'm really here to talk to you about something serious."

"You? Serious? Why does that sound so hard to believe?"

"No, really, what would I have to do to get Moses out of here for a day?" he asked.

"Barton Hackett," said Dawn, "he would have to sign the release, it couldn't be the charge nurse or anything."

"Would he do it?"

"Turn over custody of Moses to you?"

"It'd only be for a day, only an afternoon, well, an afternoon and an evening."

"Turn him over to you?" she was smiling.

"I think you think that's funny."

"It is."

"Why?"

"Why on earth would you think you have even an ounce of credibility with anyone at this nursing home?"

"I'm an upstanding citizen, it's not like I'm a chainsaw killer or anything."

"Like you're here doing community service out of your sense of civic responsibility?"

"I made a mistake, a momentary lack of good judgment."

"You've shown you can't be responsible for your own life, so the nursing home should entrust you with the life of one of their patients, what kind of sense does that make?"

"Well when you put it like that . . ."

"How else can anybody look at it? Facts are facts."

"Facts don't account for what's inside a person."

"No, you can't see what's inside a person," she agreed, "whether it's good or it's bad."

"Well how about you?" his mind was still spinning, "you're Miss Perfect around here, even related to the powers that be, why don't you ask for permission to take him to the beach?"

"I think he's better off here."

"What? How can you say that? He doesn't want to be here anymore than I do."

"No, but it's what's best for him."

"What's best for him, how can you say that? Every day in that cage a little more life slips out of him, I can see it happening."

"And what would it look like if the nursing home let him out for the day and something happened?"

"Like what?"

"Like what? He's eighty-three, anything could happen. He could have a stroke. He could have a heart attack. He could die. What would the nursing home look like then?"

"So they keep him caged up in there, and kill his spirit, then everything is fine, because nobody can blame the nursing home for anything."

"They have to think about their liability. What do you think would happen to the confidence level of all the other families that have trusted this facility with the care of their loved ones? It would take a nose dive, and so would the census, they'd be checking people out of here as fast as those families could find accommodations elsewhere."

"Well excuse me for even thinking you'd be interested, I thought people went into nursing because they cared about the well-being of their patients."

"They do, at least I did."

"You're not even through with the course and you've already left that behind. This place is killing that little old man, what old age isn't doing to him, this place is finishing the job, and you think it's OK, at least the facility doesn't have any liability."

"When you figure out how to make the world perfect, let me know, until then stop pitching a fit because it isn't. You have to grow up, Mr. Steve Hadley, people don't always get what they want, and sometimes they don't even get what they need. It's sad, and I know it's a shock to a pampered rich boy from the suburbs, but that's the real world."

"That's what you think of me? A pampered rich kid?"

"Was there ever anything on your Christmas list that mommy and daddy didn't get you?"

"Of course there was." Where did she get off talking to him like this?

"Like what?"

"Like what? Well . . . I don't know, I can't remember, but I sure as hell haven't always gotten everything I ever wanted, my last name is not Getty or Gates you know?"

"I can tell by the tone of your voice you wish it was."

"I just wanted to know how to get Moses out of here for a little field trip, that's why I waited for you, that's all."

"That's all?" She smiled.

"Now what are you implying by that smirk on your face?"

"What does your girlfriend think about you hanging out waiting for another girl like this?"

"I don't have a girlfriend."

"I'm not surprised."

"What is that supposed to mean?" He felt his cheeks redden.

"I mean, I'm not surprised that you don't have a girlfriend, if you make a practice of knocking them down the first time you meet them."

"That's not my practice, and I apologized for that."

"How did I get so lucky? Am I special?"

He did not respond immediately, then simply, "Definitely."

Neither Steve nor Dawn spoke for what seemed a long time, but neither moved to leave.

"You can be exhausting," he said finally.

"And you can be dangerous," she smiled, "so I guess we're even."

"I don't know about that," he said.

"You don't?"

"No."

"What do think would make us even then?" she asked.

"Well you could give me a kiss, that would be a start."

"Fat chance." Where had that come from? He asked her for a kiss? What man had ever asked her for a kiss? What was wrong with this guy? Was he totally imbalanced? One minute he's arguing with her, the next he's asking her for a kiss. "I think I'd rather leave things uneven if that's the case."

"Well you asked, so I told you."

"I hear kissing is overrated."

"If you think kissing is overrated, you're doing it wrong," he laughed.

She felt the color begin to creep up her neck and was grateful that it was dark.

The security guard leisurely wheeled around the corner on his rounds, saw Dawn's uniform and said, "we can't have people hanging around the grounds after hours, I'll have to ask you two to step back inside or be on your way."

"Will do," Steve replied.

He walked her to her car and opened the door. "I hope I didn't offend you," he said.

"Offend me?"

"About the kiss, you're not the only one who says what they think. I just want to say that if what I was thinking offended you, then I'm sorry."

"I think I was more surprised than offended," she said. She was standing at the car, the door between them. He stood grasping the top of the doorframe, watching the moonlight form a halo about her head. Like a sudden flash, she bent over the door and gave him a peck on the cheek. Before he could turn his head in response she was sitting in the car looking up at him, waiting for him to let loose of the door.

He looked down and smiled. "See, I told you," he said, "you've been doing it wrong." He closed door and gave her a wave. If the truth were known, she thought, she hadn't done it at all, wrong or otherwise. She waved back and sputtered out of the parking lot, her heart racing.

There was no explaining why the hallway did not seem sterile and cold as usual, but it was a chipper, almost optimistic, morning as Steve headed down the corridor toward Barton's office. Steve wore a grin on his face of which he really did not know the origin, and could not explain either. In moments, however, the grin received purpose as he noticed the welcome sight of Dawn coming toward him. For whatever reason, Dawn had taken the time that morning to put on some makeup, a little blush to the cheeks and some lipstick. Steve did a double take, and had to catch himself from running into an open door.

Dawn too was wearing a smile. "Stay away from that mop," she said good-naturedly to him as he approached, pointing to the janitor's closet, "in your hands it is a lethal weapon."

"Good morning to you too," he replied and waved, and turned into Barton's office.

Dawn, if forced to admit it, was absent-mindedly thinking about what a nice specimen of the male form Steve was and had completely missed turning at the side corridor. Or was it that she had subconsciously stayed on a course where she would walk right past Steve, but in either case she realized it, turned around, and just as she neared the door to Barton's office she heard Barton say to Steve, "That Dawn McNally's got quite a mouth on her doesn't she?"

"She's not shy in letting you know what she thinks," said Steve.

Dawn stopped short of the door and listened for more. She was not in the habit of eavesdropping, she had been raised better, but it seemed as if fate, or some other power had brought her to that exact spot at that exact time, so who was she to try to go against such celestial movements? She stood still, at once conscious of the sound of her own breathing, and of the sound that rubber soles make on a waxed tile floor. She did not move.

"She's got plenty of what a young man would like to get his hands on though, doesn't she, Steve?"

Steve chuckled nervously. He did not know quite what to make of this coming from Barton. Was he being treated like a member of the boys club, or was this some kind of weird test that Barton was trying on him? "Well, sir, she got my attention the first time I laid eyes on her."

"She needs more than eyes laid on her," Barton said, "and I let her know that I'd be happy to oblige."

Dawn pressed herself against the wall and almost had to put her hand to her mouth to keep from saying something.

"You let her know?"

"You know," Barton winked slyly, "body language."

"You're quite a devil, Mr. Hackett," Steve tried to keep his tone light, it would be wise, he thought, to not get tossed out of the boys' club before he even knew whether or not he was even in it. Besides, he had to stay in Barton's good graces, he had a bigger mission in mind, "and you a married man."

"I was just having some fun with her."

"What did you do?" Dawn had to strain to hear, Steve was nearly whispering.

"I felt her up." To Dawn, Barton's tone was downright boastful, as if he were announcing that he had won last weekend's bowling tournament.

"What did she do?"

Dawn could hear no answer, but imagined her brother-in-law giving Steve one of his patented "I'm God's gift to women" grins, implying she had somehow appreciated his attention, before Steve finally said, "yes, Mr. Hackett, you're quite the sly wolf." And they both laughed.

Dawn felt the color rise to her face, and the color was unmistakably red. She crept away silent and infuriated.

"The real reason I came to see you this morning is about Moses Bailey," Steve said, "I'd like permission to take Moses on a field trip."

Barton turned suddenly and severely serious, the meeting of the boys' club was adjourned. "In order for any patient to leave the facility, it requires the knowledge, consent, and signature of a family member."

"Well whose signature do I have to get for Moses?"

"There is no one."

"He's mentioned a son."

"His son drowned after falling through the ice while out winter fishing two years ago, and his daughter-in-law, who I gather he was never very close to anyway, remarried and moved to Wisconsin."

"Can't he just sign his own consent form? I mean, there's nothing wrong with his mind. I mean, he's here because other of his parts have stopped working."

"He's here, because someone put him here, because they trusted us to look after him, to do what's best for him. And that does not mean letting him go off with some college prankster to who knows where, for God knows why."

"It's just the beach," said Steve almost pleading, "he just wants to see the sunset over the big lake one last time before he dies. It doesn't really seem like that big of a last request."

"Not without the proper consent and signature on the release form."

"You just told me, there is no one to sign whatever form has to be signed."

"Well then, he can't go, can he?"

NINE

Barton Hackett thought the night had an unmistakable gloom. He had put his daughters to bed with a story, hugs, and kisses all around. Sometimes, he thought, they were the sole source of joy in his life. He poured himself a brandy and sat in the darkness looking at the night outside the window of his den. Tonight, for no conscious reason, he was not distracting himself with work or television, and the undaunting revelation that his life was anything but what he wanted it to be, bore in on him relentlessly.

Some men faced with an unhappy marriage, bury themselves in their work, or find momentary pleasure in some sexual dalliance. Barton had tried both, but on this night the truth stared back at him from the reflection in the window, that of the many choices he had for a life's partner, he had made the wrong one. It did not sit well with him to admit that he was wrong, he took another sip of brandy to try and make the admission go down a bit easier.

"What are you doing sitting here in the dark?" the voice was Nancy's.

Should he say, "Because you look better in the dark?" No, he felt too low to even be cruel. Normally, some little bit of flesh, some small revenge would he extract from the one he blamed for this predicament, but not tonight. Tonight he had admitted that it was his choice, and his fault for being in the clutches of this detestable piece of feminine obesity. "The light hurts my eyes," he said instead.

"You ought to get them checked out, you always procrastinate on everything."

Why didn't she just take her reprieve and go, why did she insist on pushing him? Was there some kind of sickness within her that would not rest until she received the full measure of his cruelty? "First thing tomorrow," he said in a controlled tone.

"Sure, you say that tonight, but tomorrow, you'll find something better or more important to do, that's just like you, say one thing tonight and do something completely different tomorrow. You act like I just met you yesterday, but I know . . ."

"Nancy!" his voice was raised, stern, and commanding.

"Barton? Should I turn on the light?"

"Nancy, go to bed."

She recognized the tone, and made a retreat to her bedroom without another word, once again alone.

He poured himself another brandy, emptied the glass, and poured himself another. He repeated this pattern another time before Dawn came through the front door. She stood in the front entry hanging up her coat, "I like to play with little girls," came the voice from the darkness.

She peered into the darkened den, "Barton?"

"Good evening, little girl." His voice was menacing.

"Why are you sitting in the dark?" Dawn was determined to not let the fear she felt show in her voice.

"So I don't have to look at her, but you can snap the light on, I like to look at you."

"Are you drunk?"

"I'm ready to play." There was nearly a misbegotten laugh in his tone.

"I'd say you're ready for bed."

"I'll take that as an invitation." He chuckled.

"The only thing you should be taking is a path straight up the stairs to your bedroom."

"And just what do you suppose is waiting for me there?"

"That's none of my business, and I don't want it to be."

"Just come over here and play, let me show you how much fun it can be for boys and girls to play together."

"If you don't stop this nonsense, I'm going to have to tell Nancy, as much as it would break my heart to do it."

He seemed unfazed by the threat, "We could be very quiet, so we don't disturb a soul."

She continued toward the stairway, undeterred.

"What are you doing?" he called, his voice a threatening whine.

"What I'm doing is going to bed. Good night, Barton."

She made her way up the steps, knowing he could bound up the stairs and catch her in a matter of seconds. She did not turn around, she determinedly kept going one step at a time, listening for the sound of his foot on the stairs behind her, but the sound did not come. She got to the top of the stairs and looked around, but he was no where to be seen. She let herself into her bedroom, closed the door and sank back against it trembling, her heart racing, and a cold sweat breaking out at her temples.

There was no lock on the door, and she stood there fully dressed for what seemed hours, listening for him to climb the stairs. There was a creak in the floorboards, and he hummed an unfamiliar tune as he made his slow ascent. Step by step, she could hear his heavy footsteps. At the top of the stairway she heard him stop, and then down the hallway she heard him approach. She heard him stop outside her door. She held her breath, her eyes scanning the room for a possible weapon. Her niece's dolls and stuffed animals were everywhere, as a last resort she picked up the lamp from the dresser and held it above her head and waited. Then she heard the door to Nancy's room open.

"Barton, don't you have to get up in the morning?"

"Yes," was all the reply she heard, and then the click of their bedroom door closing behind them and muffled voices from inside. She breathed again and put down the lamp.

The next morning she found herself a new apartment.

"Well, Steve, when are we going to the beach?" Moses asked smiling, as Steve entered his room and flopped down on the bed.

"I don't know," Steve answered, shifting his eyes to the floor. He had been avoiding telling Moses what had transpired in Barton Hackett's office, hoping some miracle or some flash of inspiration would intervene, and Moses would still get his wish.

By this point in late July, Steve had mastered the Pioneer Manor schedule, and found that most afternoons he could quietly slip from George's kitchen and spend up to an hour with Moses. And they both looked forward to the daily visits. Both of Steve's grandfathers had died before he was ever born, and it was during these summer afternoons that Moses became the grandfather that Steve never had. Moses recounting stories of his life, and Steve confessing the fears and frustrations of his own.

"Well my social calendar's open most every day, so you just let me know, all right?"

"Will do, Moses."

Although it had always seemed that on the surface Steve had every advantage, he always felt as though there was something which put him on the outside, that he was never quite as good as those around him, like he was secretly from the wrong side of the tracks, and that everyone would find out his secret any minute. It wasn't until he met Moses that he learned that there was no wrong side of the tracks.

"You can't worry too much about what other people think of you," Moses told him, "where do you think I'd be as an artist if I worried what people were going to think of my work while I was creating it?" He did not wait for an answer. "Frozen, that's where. I would have been as crippled as I am now from the get go."

"It's not really what other people think of me," said Steve, "it's what I think of myself, I think of myself as inferior. I feel like a second class college student, in fact, it feels more like I'm still in high school, living with my parents and commuting to the university on the edge of town." And if Steve really had to confess the truth, it wasn't just college. He looked at other guys and just knew they were better looking, he played ball with them and knew they were more athletic, he told jokes with them and knew they were funnier, and when he watched them with girls, he knew they were more accomplished with women.

"That's because you're comparing yourself to them on their terms. In your mind, you're giving them the home ice advantage. You're comparing yourself to them in areas that they are good at instead of areas where you excel."

"Like what? Eating chocolate chip cookies?"

"A bright kid like you will find it, I'm sure. And when you do, you won't feel the need to compare anymore. It will all work out believe me."

"It doesn't work out for everybody, otherwise there wouldn't be homeless bums drinking themselves to sleep on the curb every night."

"People do get broken, that's true," said Moses, looking at his arthritic hands, "are you afraid of that happening to you?"

"Yes, no . . . I don't know."

"Some people try and fail, and some get broken in the attempt, but far more people fail to try. Instead of listening to their heart, they choose something safe, and then spend their lives moaning about how unhappy they are." Moses put his hand on Steve's shoulder, "do yourself a favor, don't be one of those. In a strange way, the bum on the curb who has lost everything trying to fly, is happier than the one in the suburbs who has locked up his wings in the closet, never to see the light of day."

"Poverty of the spirit versus the kind of poverty we usually think about, is that it?"

"Pretty close." Moses grinned, "I think I'm getting too philosophical, I don't want to bore you with the musings of an old man. So why did you choose to go to that school, if going there makes you feel inferior?"

"That was the only way I was going to afford a college education."

"So you're not the spoiled rich kid that Dawn thinks you are?"

"She said that to you?"

"Not in so many words, but I definitely got that impression."

"Well, that's not the only thing she's got wrong about me."

"You kind of like that little girl, don't you?"

"Why does it show?"

"Only to anybody who's looking."

"I don't know if it matters much," said Steve, "I think she's been avoiding me."

"I think you may be right," Moses said, his eyes twinkling in a way that showed he knew more than he was telling, "I'd say she's a bit miffed at you."

"What did I do now?" Confusion seeped into Steve's voice, "I haven't knocked her down, I only asked her for a kiss."

"I think that's something you're going to have to discuss with her."

"Why what did she say?"

"I thought I was the one with the hearing problem," said Moses, grinning, "That's something you are going to have to discuss with her, but maybe it's all in my imagination, maybe she's just preoccupied with her new apartment."

"She's got a new apartment?"

"Yes, she's moving in tomorrow, from what I hear."

"It appears you hear far more than you're willing to tell."

"Maybe that's why I hear things worth telling."

Dawn's furniture was a mish-mashed collection of odds and ends, rummage sale specials, bargain basement gems, and a prize or two from the Salvation Army. They were short on aesthetics, but functional when it came to holding the people or possessions they were designed to hold. Dawn had stretched her meager savings to put together a household. There was a fight with the insurance company looming in the future, but she couldn't wait for that to be settled, she had to put some distance between her and her brother-in-law.

"Don't worry about the rain," she told the deliverymen, "just bring it on in here."

"Maybe you should spend another night or so with us until you get settled," said Nancy.

"This will do me just fine," Dawn replied, directing the location of the davenport.

Dawn had rented the bottom half of a two-story house on Euclid Street. What paint was left on the building was white, or had been, the covered porch which protected her entryway was droopy, and the shrubbery which surrounded the place was overgrown.

"Why you want to live in a neighborhood like this is beyond me," said her sister.

"It's what I can afford right now," Dawn was getting annoyed, "besides I don't live on the outside, and the inside has been freshly painted and has brand new carpeting. It's not like I'm buying the place, I'm only renting."

"But terrible things can happen in a neighborhood like this."

"Terrible things can happen in your neighborhood, too," Dawn shot a look at Barton as he stepped onto the porch. For her sister's sake, she didn't want to get any more specific than that.

"You've found yourself another piano," said Barton.

"That's why I couldn't afford to spend much on the rest of the furniture."

"That's what I was going to point out," he said, "if you'd come to me ahead of time I could have spared you such foolishness."

"Are you calling my piano foolishness?" Why was she even bothering to converse with him, this moron who made her the butt of lewd jokes behind her back, who boasted about 'feeling her up' all the while married to her unsuspecting sister. Why was she even trying to be civil?

"Didn't I make myself clear enough?" He asked.

"You're clearly an arrogant ass," she muttered. If her mother hadn't raised her to be a lady, she would have spoke it right out and spit it in his face. "If you're just going to parade around with your hands in your pockets, you might as well just parade yourself right home, I don't need any spectators."

"Barton, why don't you at least try to look useful," Nancy chimed in.

"Why don't you try to look like something other than a cow," he said to himself as he walked around the corner of the house. He would just have to have a cigar and consider what was to be done with this kind of insult. These women had to learn, or be reminded, that he was not a man to be trifled with. Maybe he ought to get Nancy two blinking yellow lights and a 'wide load' sign to wear on her ass, maybe then she would remember her place, and what she was making him endure.

The deliverymen unloaded the bed and mattress, the last pieces on the truck, and presented a delivery receipt for Dawn to sign. They said polite good-byes to the ladies and they were gone.

"How did you get all that used furniture delivered? I mean, you bought a piece from here, and another piece from there, how did you arrange to have it all delivered on the same truck?"

"I called up the trucking company and told them where all the furniture was, where it had to go, when I wanted it, and which insurance company to bill for it and they took it from there."

"Do you think the insurance company is going to pay for it?"

"Well, what I know they won't do is, they won't come and 'undeliver' my furniture. Did you see the time those guys had with my piano? Can you imagine some insurance claims adjuster trying to come over here and take it back to the secondhand store so they didn't have to pay the delivery charge?"

They both chuckled at the vision.

Nancy looked out the kitchen window from where she was putting dishes away in the cupboard, and watched Barton pacing, and smoking, and stewing in the rain. "I better go," she sighed, "you know how he gets."

"No, I don't," said Dawn, enjoying the thought of Barton worrying if the rain was going to ruin his expensive suit, "but I'm sure you do. Thanks for the help, Nancy, but by all means go if staying is going to lead to problems."

"Whenever I talk like I have a mind of my own it hurts his ego, and there's hell to pay for a week afterward," Nancy said, buttoning up her coat.

"Well then you better go, or else just shoot him right now and put him out of his misery." The sisters both laughed and Nancy kissed Dawn on the cheek before turning and heading out the door.

She watched them from the kitchen window, Nancy waddling to the car, Barton flapping his jaw, Nancy waving off his hot air with a flick of her hand. If husbands were like that, thought Dawn, maybe she was better off without one after all.

She wandered into the living room and sat down at the piano. For some inexplicable reason she was suddenly and completely happy. Perhaps it was the thought of not having a husband like Nancy's or anyone else to answer to, perhaps it was the realization that she once again had a home of her own, but the joy soon found its way to her fingertips and out through the piano it came, raucous, rollicking, and playful. She smiled, closed her eyes, and let her fingers dance upon the keyboard.

Steve leaned against the doorjamb relaxing, his hands tucked up under his armpits. He watched, listened, and wondered what kind of girl would sit and pound on her piano with the front door wide open to the rain, ignoring the hundred odd moving-in chores to be done.

With a flourish that would do any Carnegie Hall impresario proud, Dawn ended the song, threw her arms in the air, twirled on her seat, and found herself staring into the blue eyes of Steve Hadley.

"You could have knocked," she said in instant irritation. She turned back to the piano, closed the cover, and rose to her feet.

"I didn't want to interrupt, you seemed to be enjoying yourself so much that I . . ."

"Like you in Barton's office yesterday?" she interrupted.

"What?"

"You were having a good old time yucking it up about the gimp girl, weren't you?"

"I don't know what to say, I went to Barton about Moses, and you know I was going to go, he just started talking about you."

"And you just sprang to my defense, didn't you?" Her eyes shot daggers at him.

"I didn't know what to make of what he was saying to me, he caught me completely off guard, but I don't remember saying anything bad about you."

"What do you want, Steve?" what little patience she might have had for this rich kid was completely gone.

He straightened up off the doorframe and entered the living room, "I thought you could probably use a hand."

"No thank you, Mr. Steve Hadley," she said his name as if it were a toxic substance, "I can mange just fine." She picked up a box of cooking utensils her sister had brought over to donate to the cause, and began to turn toward the kitchen. He stepped to her side and easily plucked it out of her hands. She gave him a scowl, "haven't you got somewhere to go? Maybe some little old lady to lie in wait for, so you can mow her down at the crosswalk, or something?"

"Sure I do," he smiled, "about this time on Saturday afternoon I'm usually poisoning the neighbor's cat, but I thought I'd take this week off, give the cat a break, and come over here and bother you instead."

Why did he have to smile, she wondered, he was so hard to hate when he smiled.

"Where do you want this?" He asked.

"In the kitchen." He carried it through the archway into the kitchen and she followed along. She couldn't help but notice the taught flex of his arm, exposed by the short sleeves of his white tee shirt as he set the box on the floor next to the cupboard. Not that she wanted to, mind you, she just couldn't help but notice, it was just that simple, she just couldn't help it. How many times would she have to repeat it before she believed it?

She caught herself before her daydream even got a good foothold, "Look, Steve, I heard you whispering with my ass of a brother-in-law yesterday, and I got a pretty good idea what it was all about, what you really think of me. But you see, I'm just not the man-hungry gimp he makes me out to be, and you're not going to get lucky, or whatever it is you expect to get hanging around here, so why don't you just say your good-bye and leave me to my chores."

He straightened up and jammed his hands into the front pockets of his jeans, "Dawn, I think you got me all wrong."

"No, Steve, I think you've got me all wrong. I'm not stupid, I know men, at least well enough to know what they want, and what they talk about. At least give me credit that I know what you and Barton were whispering about."

Steve looked at her silently for a long while, he had never known a girl like this before. And, in fact, he didn't really know why he was still hanging around there, he had never let anyone give him a tongue lashing like that without his volcanic temper exploding, but composure and compassion reigned, and upon reflection, he decided he had to try to set things right.

"I'm sorry, Dawn, you're right, it was no way to be talking about a lady. Please accept my apology."

"No." She opened the box on the kitchen floor and began to remove the pots and pans.

Steve didn't know whether to laugh or reach down and pick his jaw up off the floor. He had never had an apology, that is, of the few he had ever given, thrown back in his face. He saw that she was not joking, "You won't?"

"No, I think you're just a little boy in a man's body, and I really don't want this relationship, or whatever it is you want to call it, to progress any further. We have to see each other at work, and I'll have to tolerate that, but you'll finish your sentence, your community service, and that will be that."

He stood silent; this wasn't how he had intended for this visit to go at all.

"I'll be damned," he finally said.

"Good," she exclaimed, "that would suit me just fine." She turned and disappeared into a back room he supposed was the bedroom, leaving him to stare blankly and scratch his head. He was torn between holding onto the last of his pride or following the instruction of his heart, between retreating out the door or following after her. He swallowed hard, sometimes pride sticks when going down, and went after her.

From the doorway he watched her starting to put the bed frame together. This is why he had come, to do these things for her. She blew a straggling piece of hair from her face with a blast of air out the side of her lips, mopped the perspiration from her forehead with the back of her hand, and picked up the hammer to beat he frame into submission. He just watched and did not again tender any offers to help.

"I'll be heading home then," he said.

"Please do, you probably still have time to catch the neighbor's cat."

"I'll see you at work then."

"Yes," she said, "and when you do I'd appreciate it if you didn't stare at my backside like you're doing right now. I hope I've made it perfectly clear, Mr. Steve Hadley, that I'm simply not interested."

He let out a deep sigh, "Abundantly."

She took her hair down and redid her ponytail; she turned to find him still standing there. "Why are you still here?" she asked.

He let out another sigh, "Heck if I know," he muttered, and turned his back to her and stomped through the house. She heard what sounded like a hesitation for nearly a minute, and then heard him stomp across the porch, and out into the rain.

She threw down the hammer in frustration, stood up and put her hands on her hips. She had told him exactly what she thought of him, so why didn't she feel good about it? She went back to the kitchen to fetch her cup of tea. This day had started out so joyous, now look at it, she thought. She went into the living room and flopped down on the couch.

On the coffee table was a box that she did not recognize. It was not a moving box for it was wrapped in silver paper with a large red ribbon and bow. She set down her tea and picked it up. On a small card attached to the ribbon was written, 'Welcome home – Steve'. She sighed and sank back into her chair a little deeper, looking at the present. Her feeling was not the excitement and anticipation that normally accompanied receiving a gift. The feeling was, in fact, quite the opposite.

She slipped off the ribbon and slowly loosened the paper. Inside was a white box, and she gently lifted off the cover. She pushed back a layer of tissue paper and there inside it was her small statue of a nurse with angel wings, with the edge of the wings charred from the fire. Steve must have combed through the rubble piece by piece to find it. She held it to her chest with both hands and tears streamed down her cheeks.

It was a rainy morning in Evergreen, and Steve felt somehow as if it were raining somewhere deep inside him as well. Dawn's face was the first thing he saw when he entered the door for work, and his first instinct was to turn immediately and avoid her path. Then he noticed that the anger, that had flashed fire in her eyes last night, had been replaced with something that was completely different.

"Thank you, and I'm sorry," she said, coming to him.

"Is that code?" he asked. She loved how his blue eyes twinkled.

Dawn looked behind her; it was one of those rare moments when they seemed to be all alone in the nursing home corridor. "I'm sorry I had the wrong idea about you and what was going on in Barton's office," she lowered her eyes to the floor, "at least on your part."

"You don't have to apologize for that, I let him talk about you with disrespect, and I'm sorry I did." He gently cupped her chin between his thumb and forefinger and lifted her face to look into her eyes.

She grabbed him by the arm with both her hands, he looked down into her eyes and saw what looked like tears welling up, "and thank you for my angel nurse," she lifted up her lips to his, closed her eyes and kissed him on the mouth. "You must have spent hours digging through the debris and ashes to find it," she went on, "I think that is probably the nicest thing anyone has ever done for me."

"You deserve it."

"How can you say that after the way I've treated you?"

"You know what I think?"

"What?"

"I think that little nurse angel is you."

She smiled and looked away. When she looked back, he was frowning. "What is it? What's wrong?"

"How happy I am about you right now, makes me think about how sad Moses is going to be when I tell him that they aren't going to let him out of here to go see his sunset. I've been putting it off, but I'm no good at keeping secrets, especially from people I care about."

"That's good to know," she smiled kindly and touched his hand, "he'll be disappointed."

"I think it was the only thing in his life that he had left to look forward to, his last shred of hope, and I have to be the one to squash it."

"It's not your fault," her voice was soft. She reached up, stroked his cheek, then laid her hand on the side of his neck, gently pulling his head down to her waiting, open lips, but her timing could not have been worse. At that very instant, Nurse Hackett came trudging around the corner, catching them, indignation instantly firing in her eyes.

"Do you think this is what you're being paid for, nurse?" said Nancy, she was all Nurse Hackett at that moment, without the slightest hint of sister. "And you Mr. Hadley . . ."

"I know, I know," interrupted Steve, "the kitchen's waiting for me." And he was off down the hall before she could continue her reprimand. Nancy turned back to her sister and she was gone down the hall the other way.

That afternoon, Dawn found Moses alone and contemplative at the window of his room.

"What does it feel like to be in love?" Dawn asked him.

Moses turned from the window, saw it was Dawn, and his face brightened. "Is this just research, or have you finally fallen for me?" He smiled.

"No, really, how do you know if you're in love?"

"I'd say if you have to ask, then you're not." He studied her face for some clue. "Is this about you or just conversation?"

"Could be."

He chuckled, "which?"

"I was just wondering if it had symptoms," she said, "after all I am a medical person you know."

"Hmm, yes I know." He waited for an instant until he caught her eye, "and just exactly what are your symptoms?"

"I, I . . ." She stammered and turned red.

"Do you think our friend Steve might be infected with the same disease?" he asked.

"Why would you say that?"

"My eyesight might be going, but I'm not blind, yet."

"Do you think," she was anxious, serious, and excited all at the same time, "do you think he cares for me?"

"I wouldn't be surprised."

"But how would I know?"

"Start by giving me another reason why somebody would spend three days sifting through ashes and soot?"

"Three days?"

Moses nodded, "it sounds like love to me."

Just then, Steve entered the room with all the fanfare of the circus coming to town, and Dawn wondered if he could ever do anything quietly. Where did that thought come from, she wondered, and what exactly did she have in mind?

"Are you two talking about me?" Steve asked good-naturedly.

"We're talking about love, Steve," said Moses, "if you have some expertise or insight on the subject we'd be happy if you'd share it with us."

Dawn silently turned red when Steve's eyes locked upon hers.

"All I know is, if it's as bad as the songs make it out to be, maybe somebody in the medical field should be researching a vaccine for it."

They all laughed, then Moses asked Steve, "What is it you truly love, Steve?"

Steve looked at him with a mischievous expression on his face.

"I mean besides your mother, fast cars, loud music, and the occasional practical joke," then Moses shifted his gaze to Dawn, "and whatever young lady happens to be quickening your pulse at the present."

"I don't know," answered Steve, "I've never really thought about."

"How can you not think about it?" asked Moses, irritation and excitement both creeping into his voice, "that's what life is all about, love, Steven, love."

"My father says life is about work, a man's work speaks for who he is."

"I would agree with that, if we're talking about a man who's doing what he loves."

"I think that's easy for an artist to say," said Steve.

"Or a nurse," said Dawn, "I do what I love."

"And I think it speaks volumes about who you are," said Moses, a wry smile slipping to his lips.

"But what about those that just do a job to get paid?" said Steve, "there's millions of those people."

"Why imitate their errors?" asked Moses, "Do what you love."

Steve's mouth curled at the corners, "Do you think I can find someone to pay me for sitting around looking at Dawn?" he asked.

She blushed as she finished taking Moses' blood pressure, and left the room without looking back at either one of them.

Steve watched her go, and Moses saw the fondness on Steve's face turn somber as his eyes turned from the doorway back to Moses. Steve had put it off as long as he could. The last thing he wanted that afternoon was to see the hope vanish from Moses' eyes, and he was sure that it would.

"I've got something to tell you, Moses," said Steve, his voice soft, hesitant and solemn.

"Should I sit down?" Moses grinned, looking up from his wheelchair.

"I wish I could joke about this, and I wish there was another way to break it to you, but they're not going to let me take you to the beach." Steve looked out the window rather than look Moses in the eye. "They say you have to have a relative sign you out, so you're stuck."

"Well, isn't that the biggest pile of crap you've ever heard?" cursed Moses, "they act like I've lost my god damned mind. Do they even have a clue why I'm here? It's my body that's failing me, not my mind. My mind is the only thing I've got left. My mind and my memories."

"I'm sorry," said Steve, "I wish there was something I could do."

"It's not your fault, boy, I appreciate you taking a shot for me, and I don't think it was wide of the net, I think the game is rigged." Moses fumed silently for a long while, looking out the window. "I ought to sue the bastards, but they've probably got all the angles covered six ways to Tuesday. But now they got me riled, there's a principle here, how and when and where did I lose the power to make decisions in my own behalf, you know? I hire this outfit to do a job, to look after to me, and all of a sudden in the process I lose my freedom and my power of choice, this just isn't right."

"Did you want me to get in touch with an attorney?" Steve asked.

"No, probably something was signed in all the piles of papers that had to be done to check into this establishment, they probably got something that says they have the power to do what they're doing, but it's not right, it's not fair, and it's not just, and I'm just not going to sit here and take it like some dumb animal they can put in a cage and wait to die. I'm not." He was angry, and growing angrier the more he thought about it.

Dawn came back into room to retrieve the chart she had left behind during her hasty exit, the glow on her face quickly changed to concern when she saws Moses' seething expression. "Is Steve getting you all worked up, Moses?"

"My boy, Steve? Hell no. It's that bastard, brother-in-law of yours, that runs this place has my dander up."

"Well if it was up to me, I'd cut him off the family tree entirely, but what did he do?"

"He's imprisoned me." Moses said flatly, "Mr. Barton Hackett and I are going to have to have a heart to heart talk."

"That's going to be a little difficult," said Steve, "I don't think he has one." Dawn threw him a glance that said he was speaking her thoughts.

"Is he here? Do you know if he's here?" asked Moses, rolling toward the door.

"He just left," said Dawn, "I saw him go just before I came down here."

"Ducking out on a fight," Moses said, "the coward."

As they left Moses' room together, Steve looked at Dawn, his expression turning suddenly serious. He tried to fight the nervous butterflies that had taken flight in his stomach to no avail.

She could tell there was something making him uncomfortable. "OK, so spill it."

"What?" Had she guessed, he wondered, was it that obvious that she had turned him into a nervous little school boy, all over trying to ask her for a date?

She was ready for the 'I'm getting too close to the gimp' speech. No matter how they sugar coated it, it always came, she had never met a boy or man yet who could get passed her limp. "You've got something on your mind," she said, "I can tell."

"When I'm not being the class clown," he confessed, "I'm actually quite nervous around beautiful women."

"Are we changing the subject?" she asked, "what does that have to do with what's on your mind."

"What I'm trying to say is," he touched her lightly on the arm, "you make me nervous."

She felt the redness creep up her neck and looked down at the floor. She had never heard the infamous speech begin in quite this way.

"I think your beautiful," he continued, finding the courage from where he did not know, he blustered on with his confession, "and I'm afraid you'll turn me down when I ask you to go out with me."

A date? Was she to believe her ears? Was he actually about to ask her for a date? Now it was her turn to be nervous. "Why would you be afraid of that?"

"You're so beautiful, and I'm so . . . so Joe Average, I know you could do a lot better than me." He looked at her and she was grinning. "Did I say something funny?"

She suppressed a chuckle, "I just never would have thought of you as modest or humble either one, but you've almost got me believing you really believe what you just said, that you think you're plain, or Joe Average, as you put it."

"I do feel that way."

"Well, I won't tell you what a woman sees when she looks at you because it would just go to your head, but what she doesn't see is Joe Average."

"Maybe that's just you."

"Maybe."

He turned and began to walk away, then he suddenly stopped and turned around, "So that means we've got a date right?" he asked.

"You haven't asked me yet." She smiled at his awkwardness.

"Would you like me to get down on one knee or what?" he cracked.

"An engraved invitation would be all right," she said. He caught the mischievous flutter in her brown eyes, "engraved in blood."

He took her hand and enclosed it with the two of his, and her heart melted. "Let me take you out driving Saturday, I'll pick you up in the morning and we'll make a day of it."

A date, she had actually been asked out on a date, it had finally happened, just when she had given up on it ever happening. She opened her mouth, but her voice caught in her throat. Finally, she collected her composure, at least some of it, and said, "You haven't told me where you're taking me."

"I'd like you just to trust me, there's places I'd like to share with you."

"Trust the most dangerous man in Pioneer Manor?" She smiled.

"Yes," he said confidently, but his eyes were pleading.

"OK, but I don't know if I'm being courageous or foolish." She did not laugh, but felt like literally exploding with joy.

When Barton Hackett returned from his luncheon meeting, his mind was still filled with the vision of the waitress who had attended his table, and the way her salmon-colored uniform clung to her tight, young buttocks as she swayed past his seat, nearly screaming for him to reach out and touch it. He could spend the afternoon in a daydream such as this, enjoying the replay of that vision, and the fantasy that accompanied it.

Moses Bailey sat in his wheelchair, waiting for him at the door to his office.

"Mr. Bailey, and how are we today?"

"How are we?" asked Moses, incredulous, "I'll bet you're just fine, you can come and go as you please, choose what you want for dinner and where you want to eat it. As for me, I'm pissed off."

"The oatmeal lumpy this morning? Or did we just get out of the wrong side of bed?"

"How many times have you been throttled by an eighty-three year-old man in a wheelchair?"

"Mr. Bailey, there's no sense in getting yourself over-wrought, whatever it is, we can get it fixed. Batteries for your remote control? Extra lemon custard? Light bulb burned out in the bathroom? Just tell me what it is and I'll have it fixed, don't let it worry you in the least; I'll take care of it. Looking out for you is what I'm here for."

"I'd call you a liar, except you'd probably take it as a compliment. If I didn't come down here, you would never give the name of Moses Bailey a thought."

"But you did, Mr. Bailey, you did come down, so what ever it is, you must think it is important enough for me to interrupt my busy schedule to take care of it, to put all the concerns and care of the other two hundred and seventy-nine patients on hold just so I can take care of what it is that's bothering Moses Bailey. So what is it?"

"I want out."

"Mr. Bailey, I don't have time for this nonsense. Now if there isn't any real issue to discuss, I'll have to get back to my work."

"You're not listening, you condescending prick, I said I want out," Moses was raising his voice, "prepare my release or whatever form you need me to sign and call me a cab, I'm checking out of this little dude ranch for the almost dead."

"Mr. Bailey, if you don't lower your voice, I'll have to have the orderlies return you to your room and have you sedated."

Moses looked at him dumbfounded, and didn't say anything while he recovered his composure. "Are you deaf?" he asked, finally. "Or simply thick headed?"

"Mr. Bailey, your son admitted you to this facility, he signed all the papers as your guardian, only your son can make any changes to your care arrangements"

"That's crap."

"Did you give your son power of attorney?"

"The arthritis in my hands, I just could not sign checks or anything anymore."

"Don't avoid the question, did you or did you not, give your son power of attorney, the power to admit you to this facility."

"Yes."

"Then only your son can change it."

"My son is dead."

"I can't help that," Barton turned his back on him, "good day, Mr. Bailey."

The Christmas season of 1939 had arrived for Sarah complete with all the trimmings, complete except the joy. She sat in the silent gallery looking around her at the emptiness, the snow swirling outside against the plate glass window. Everything, but one Moses Bailey painting, had been sold or put away in anticipation of their trip to Miami Beach. She rose and walked over to it, she had to wrap it for a customer who was coming by in less than an hour to pick it up, but she had put off the task until last. She studied it and gently ran a finger down the frame. Something tightened within her that she did not want to name.

The opening of the front door took her attention momentarily from the painting.

"Didn't mean to startle you ma'am," it was a neatly dressed young man in a khaki delivery uniform. "I just have this one package to deliver, before I can go out and finish up my Christmas shopping. Do you mind signing for it? It was supposed to be delivered here yesterday, but you know how it gets at Christmas." He shrugged and handed her the clipboard and pencil.

She signed her name and examined the small package as he left. 'Anderson & Co., Jewelers' was emblazoned on the box. She suddenly felt like a little girl snooping in her mother's closet. It was supposed to be delivered yesterday he had said, yesterday when Doyle was working alone in the office. She knew she should just walk into his office and put it on his desk, but it was awful tempting to just have a look. What would one look hurt, after all, she could still look surprised on

Christmas when he gave it to her couldn't she? It wouldn't be that hard to look thrilled, especially if it was something magnificent, like she was sure that it was.

She entered Doyle's office and sat down at the desk, putting the tempting little box in front of her. She supported her head in her hands and stared at it, as if waiting for the box to somehow give her permission to look inside. Then, she decided the only fair thing to do was to give it a test. The hardest decisions were always made easier by a test. If she pulled on the slender white ribbon and it came untied, then she reasoned, it would be all right for her to look inside. That test was straightforward enough, better than flipping pennies two out of three times, or trying to fly a paper airplane so it landed in the wastebasket.

She tugged at the ribbon, but it did not move. Her hand slipped, that was it, the test can't count if your hand slips. She picked up the ribbon once more, this time wrapping it around her finger and bracing the package with her other hand before giving the ribbon a hearty yank. The ribbon came loose and unfurled. It must be destiny, it was simply meant to be that she open this present early, why else would it have come open in her hand?

She lifted the cover and gave out a squeal, then quickly looked around to see who might have heard her. Inside the box was a necklace of beautiful, large shining emeralds surrounded by clusters of small, sparkling diamonds. Reassured that she was still alone, she slowly, delicately, lifted it out of the box and held it up in the light in front of her. Since meeting Doyle, she had traveled in a social circle that included some of the wealthiest and best dressed people in the city, in the country, for that matter, but this necklace had to be the most expensive piece of jewelry she had ever seen. How the jewels shined. Glistening green rays of light bounced off her grinning face.

Somewhere inside her, below her ribs and above her stomach, an indescribable warmth glowed as she put the necklace back into the box and rewrapped it. She smiled. After all the turmoil of Thanksgiving, and the way Moses Bailey had turned her life upside down, was this the reassurance of love from Doyle that she needed to go on? She had to admit it, since meeting Moses she had had her doubts, and wondered more than once, no, who was she kidding, more than a dozen times, more than a dozen dozen times, whether marrying Doyle had been a mistake. Doubting not only her feelings, but those of Doyle as well.

When Christmas Day came, Sarah thought, for some reason, that it would be a day she would always remember. Christmas Eve with her parents had been fun, perhaps a little too much wine, and at times perhaps a little too quiet, and her mother had looked at her quite odd when the subject of Moses had come up, but it was not something she was going to ask her about. She was not going to talk about it, in fact, she was not even going to think about it. Except for times when she couldn't help it, like right now, or an hour ago when she looked out at the snow and wondered what winter was like in Sutton's Bay, or when she drove by Grant Park and looked at the water and the thought jumped in her mind, with no help from her whatsoever, that it was the same lake, the same water, that ran all the way up to Grand Traverse Bay.

But no time to think of those things now, it was Christmas morning, a time for her and Doyle to share the holiday alone, before hopping the train for a luxurious vacation in Miami Beach. How could life be better? After all, wasn't she about to get the most expensive piece of jewelry in the entire world? She knew that thought was an exaggeration, but not much of one she was sure.

She was dressed in a pink velvet robe, the edge of a white lace nightgown peeking out at the fold. Her hair was pulled back, but uncombed, and there next to the sparkle and the splendor of the Christmas tree, Sarah Conner looked every bit the little girl. The tree was decorated with strung popcorn, as was her family tradition, and a collection of ornaments that her mother had kept for her, a new and special one added every year as she grew up. She looked at the little plaster bird ornament that had been added to the collection when she was seven, the year she had to spend Christmas on the davenport with the chicken pox.

She sniffed Doyle's cigar as he read the paper and sipped his coffee. His blue corduroy housecoat with satin lapels was immaculately pressed, his hair brushed, his attitude distracted. He sat in an overstuffed burgundy armchair, his feet propped up on a matching ottoman.

"C'mon Doyle, it's Christmas, there's no news that's so urgent, that it can't wait for you to catch up to it on vacation. Just think about those long leisurely afternoons on the beach when all you have to do is smoke your cigars, read the newspaper, and drink a pina colada.

"And worry about how much you spent shopping the morning before."

She frowned. "Is there a problem you haven't told me about?"

"Haven't told you? He was your discovery, your wonder boy, why would I have to tell you?"

"You sold out the show, didn't you?"

"Ha," he put down the cigar in an ashtray formed in the head of a dragon, and looked out the window, "at half the price we could have got if the artist had been there."

"I'm sorry, I thought we did all right."

"We? What the hell did you do except scare him off? You ruined the whole thing. What the hell did you do to that country bumpkin, anyway? Nibble on his zipper and roll his eyes back in his head for him? Or did you go all the way and lift your skirt for him?" She looked at him in silent rage. "Was that it? Did you give him your scrawny ass?"

"You know I didn't do any such thing." She cried, and ran from the room with tears in her eyes.

He didn't apologize for the things that he said, he never did. But what tore at her most was the guilt, for she had wanted to, and even if she could never admit that to Doyle, there was no denying it to herself. She had wanted to nibble on his zipper, lift her skirt, and more, more than Doyle could ever imagine. But she didn't, why wasn't she given credit for that? She didn't, and it was for Doyle's sake that she hadn't.

Something had gone wrong in her marriage, if it had ever been right in the beginning. It had been there for a long while, now this acrimony had brought it into sharp focus, it would be hard to sweep it under the emotional carpet this time. Sometimes, she thought, people stay together simply because they don't know what else to do, and not much else. "We're riding a tired horse," her thoughts escaping her lips. Startled by the sound of her own voice, she looked around to see that she was still alone in the room.

After an hour of sulking, and waiting for an apology she knew would never come, she rejoined him in the living room. He hung up the phone as she entered, but did not speak to her.

It was a cold Christmas. They handed each other gifts in a perfunctory way, without comment, and whenever possible without eye contact. Had it turned into a business transaction, trading gift for gift? Or something even worse that she refused to name? She longed to be back at her parent's house, smelling Christmas dinner cooking in the kitchen and listening to her father hum Christmas carols while starting a fire in the fireplace with the discarded present wrappings.

It is said that love too can go through its own season of winter, and this was theirs, no tenderness, no warmth, no joy, and curiously as she looked at the stack of opened presents under the tree, no emerald necklace. Her anger faded and gave way to sadness, discouraged, not knowing if the winter of their love would survive to see spring.

The driver from the limousine service rang for them at four o'clock to take them to the train station. He loaded the bags in the trunk and ushered Doyle and Sarah into the comfort of the gray velvet interior. The ride to the train station was silent, except for Doyle's spits of conversation with the driver about road conditions from the snow, and a bit about the war in Europe, that Sarah knew he used to keep from interacting with her. He would probably be silent all the way to Miami Beach, if she didn't do something to smooth it over. But she wasn't up for anything like that right now. Her face was expressionless, almost lifeless, as she looked out the window watching the buildings pass.

At the station, Doyle and the driver saw to the bags. Sarah stood at the curb, wrapped the mink coat tightly around her, and absent-mindedly watched the people come and go. Why was no one smiling today, she wondered, it was Christmas. Was there no joy in Christmas for anyone?

An attendant in a blue uniform with brass buttons held open the door and they walked inside. Underneath the high arched ceilings suspended up in the sky by massive stone columns, some people hurried as if their very lives depended on it, while others lounged and fidgeted as though they couldn't get the time to go fast enough.

Through the crowd bobbed the bleached blond hair of Jenny Seabright, "Doyle, yoo-hoo, Doyle," she called.

Doyle turned his head and saw her, then stopped. He took a sideways glance at Sarah as Jenny caught up with them. Jenny was dressed in a long black wool coat that ended just above matching high heels. Her face looked freshly painted, and around her neck . . . Sarah's mouth fell open. Around her neck was the emerald necklace.

"I just had to wish you two a safe trip," Jenny gushed, smiling up at Doyle.

"That's quite a necklace," said Sarah, trying to regain her composure.

"It was a present," said Jenny still looking intently at Doyle.

"From whom? Rockefeller?" quipped Sarah.

"From my . . ." Jenny paused, searching for the right word, "from my boyfriend."

"Jenny's boyfriend is quite generous, wouldn't you say, Doyle?"

Doyle cleared his throat. "Uh, yes, yes he is."

"If you two will excuse me," said Sarah, her face reddening, "there's something I have to do before the train leaves." She crossed the marble floor away from them, her strides long and full of purpose. Neither Doyle nor Jenny spoke or turned to look after her.

She caught up to the attendant with the brass buttons, who was carrying their luggage and tapped him on the shoulder. His head snapped around with a start. "Follow me," she commanded. She marched off as if on parade with the attendant and luggage in tow.

"Wait here," she said as they approached the ticket counter. When she got to the ticket window she asked, "When is the next train leaving north?"

"Wisconsin or Michigan?" asked the agent.

"Michigan," she answered without hesitation.

"The one right behind you out those doors," he motioned with his finger, "is leaving for Grand Rapids and points beyond in about ten minutes."

She opened her purse, "One ticket, one way."

The ticket agent made change and stamped her boarding pass, "Safe trip," he said without looking up.

"Those bags on that train, please," she pointed, directing the attendant. His face was more than a little confused, but he followed his instructions without question. She stepped onto the train, paused on the steps and looked back through the glass doors into the lobby at Doyle and Jenny. They appeared to be totally engrossed in their own conversation. She felt no guilt and no regret and turned up and into the train. She found her seat and sank into it with a great sigh. She leaned back, tilted her face toward the ceiling and closed her eyes. Her favorite song, Cole Porter's "Easy to Love," began playing in her head as the train started to move.

TEN

The train rumbled along, passing through the gray concrete and brick, past the rusted iron skeletons and the hulking smokestacks, and out into the snow-white countryside. Pine trees and farmers fields passed one after another. For the first hour and a half, Sarah found it to be quite easy to keep her mind a blank just by staring out the window. She wanted to feel nothing; she did not want to waste her energy or tears on anger or sadness. She pushed down the humiliation she felt, swallowed hard, pushing back the tears, and stared out into the solitary whiteness of the snow.

After a while longer, another rustling rose from deep within her and she decided to call it hunger, and made her way to the dining car. She sat down and smoothed the starched white tablecloth without a thought.

"Are you traveling alone?" A handsome young man was standing beside her, his dark eyes focused intently upon her.

"Yes," she said without emotion.

"May I join you?" He smiled, flashing a set of perfect teeth.

"I'd rather be alone," she said flatly.

"As you wish," he said, and he disappeared down the aisle. Normally, she would have been flattered, normally, she would have at least engaged the young man in some friendly conversation before sending him away, but nothing about this was normal. She didn't feel friendly, she didn't feel flattered, she didn't feel anything.

When the train finally came to rest momentarily in Benton Harbor, she climbed down from the train to stretch her legs. In the station, three sailors in uniform, slouching with their duffle bags, watched her every move in silent appreciation. She spied a drug store across the street, and her high heels made a clicking, clattering sound as she scurried across the brick pavers. A small bell gave out a single ring as she entered.

"Help you, miss?" The man behind the counter was thin, his dark hair slicked back away from his wire rimmed spectacles.

"Do you sell cigarettes?"

"Of course, miss, we pride ourselves in being a full service drug store."

"A pack of Lucky Strikes, please."

When she was back on the train, and it was again rolling north, she sat back in her seat and idly played with the package of cigarettes with her fingers, thinking.

In Grand Rapids, she left the train and checked into the Pantlind Hotel for the night, a single bottle of wine delivered by room service, her only supper. She spent a restless night in a big, half-empty bed, it seemed so strange to be sleeping alone. And the empty hours dragged, she woke, one o'clock, she woke again, two fifteen, the night dragged on.

The emptiness crushed in upon her, but she could not quite figure out what made her feel that way. The anger at betrayal was understandable enough, but the emptiness, where had that come from? She tossed and turned, and tossed some more, first pulling the covers up around her chin and then tossing them off. What was it she missed? Was she going to miss being an ornament in a rich man's world? Was she going to miss soothing his ego in whatever way he demanded? Was she going to miss the isolation of living a life without animals and children? Of seeing her family only on the holidays? Was she going to miss seeing Doyle's distracted, irritable face across the breakfast table each morning? No, she would miss none of that. So where had the emptiness come from?

Then suddenly, she bolted upright in the bed, as if the heavens had opened up and hit her in the head with a divine revelation. It was not Doyle for whom she yearned, it was Moses. She flopped back onto the bed, a big grin exploding across her face, her eyes closed, embracing a vision of him.

In the morning, a trail of questions brought her face to face with the large, kind eyes of Norman, who ran the Pantlind Hotel parking garage. He was bald, thin, and spoke in a friendly manner as if he'd known you all your life.

"I made a call this morning," he said, "there's a filling station down around the corner that has a black Desoto for sale."

"I don't know what questions to ask," said Sarah. She looked fresh and eager for adventure in a red angora sweater and tight slacks. "Does it run well? How much?"

"I asked the same thing," said Norman, "and Bud down there is an honest man so he told me that the Desoto runs out fine but has a noticeable tick in the engine and a crack across the windshield."

"As long as it won't strand me in the middle of nowhere, how much does he want for it?"

"Bud said you could have it for two hundred, he went a little overboard for Christmas and could really use money more than an extra car."

Sarah smiled, "Norman, I could kiss you."

"I'd rather you didn't," he said, "I wouldn't know how to explain it to my wife."

She laughed. "Do you always go out of your way for strangers? Or am I just a lucky damsel in distress?"

"I was raised on the story of the Good Samaritan," there was a smile hidden behind his eyes, "and I've just tried to live my life that way. Do a good deed and pass it on, now it's your turn."

"I'll remember," she said.

Bud brought the car around and Norman helped her stuff her luggage into the trunk. She climbed in, adjusted her mirrors, and the two men watched as she checked her hair, and then her make-up. She mouthed, "Thank you," and gave Norman a wave as she pulled out onto Pearl Street and then swung north on Division Avenue.

The road from Traverse City to Sutton's Bay wound along the shore of Grand Traverse Bay, and although Sarah had made the journey to Sutton's Bay a few times during summer weather, it appeared totally changed in the winter. Drifting snow had narrowed the road to little more than one lane, snow covered ice had stilled the usually rollicking water by the shore, and icicles hung from the bare fruit trees.

It was mid afternoon when she arrived in Sutton's Bay, 317 miles from Chicago. She drove out to the cherry orchard, and down the path to Moses' house, but hers were the only tracks in the newly fallen snow, there was no other sign of life. She waited the rest of the afternoon and into the evening, but still he did not come. She fell asleep waiting, and woke to moonlight flooding the orchard, but still there was no sign of Moses. Forlorn, she retraced her route back south to Traverse City, and took a room at the Park Place Hotel.

There was something freeing about not having Doyle to answer to, she thought, but when she was addressed as "Mrs. Conner" by the hotel staff, it now suddenly seemed uncomfortable. She dined alone without incident, but felt as if everyone in the restaurant were staring at her. Was it so unusual for a woman to be eating alone? What was it they were all staring at?

In the morning, she went to see Mr. McKinney at Traverse Treasures where she had first discovered the beautiful and uniquely original paintings of Moses Bailey. The man, like his work, was an original, she thought.

Traverse Treasures stood across State Street from the Park Place Hotel. It squatted low in comparison, and inside, it was long and narrow leading to a small bay window in the back from which you could see the water. The walls were covered in burlap and mounted with shelves from floor to ceiling. Every manner of knickknack, carving, and pottery was on display, most produced by local craftsman. In the center of the store were three walls of weathered wood forming a self-supporting triangle. On these hung the paintings of Moses Bailey. Traverse Treasures was owned and operated through its twenty-nine years of existence by Mr. Gerard McKinney. A man, who from first meeting, made it more than evident that he loved what he did, and the niche he had made for himself in the world.

Mr. McKinney wore his seventy-two years very well. He moved like a man much younger, and looked Sarah up and down with the appraising glance of a man whose flame still burned bright within him, as she entered his shop. A continuous gray eyebrow crossed his lined face above round horn-rimmed bifocals. The mention of the name of Moses Bailey brought a smile to his lips and a twinkle to his eye.

"Hi! Mr. McKinney isn't it?" asked Sarah.

"It is," he said.

"Mr. McKinney, you may not remember me, but . . ."

"I remember you," he interrupted, "if you don't mind an old man saying it, you don't have the kind of face a man can easily forget."

"Thank you," she blushed, " but I . . ."

"You bought the Moses Bailey painting this past summer, and you liked it so much you pestered me until I told you where he lived."

"I didn't mean it to be pestering."

"I'm sure I'm exaggerating a bit," she noticed a hint of an accent in his voice, "with pretty girls it doesn't take much for me to give them whatever they want. Lucky for me, my trade is with the old fat ones with blue hair, or else I'd go broke."

They both chuckled.

"Do you know where I might find Moses," Sarah continued, "I went out to his house, but there doesn't seem to be any sign of life."

"No," said Mr. McKinney, "I'm afraid I can't help you there, darling. I haven't seen Moses in quite a while. In fact, I thought it was kind of curious, his motorcycle is parked out back and tarped."

"Is that unusual?"

"It is for him to not stop in and mention it. I mean he'll do it from time to time, if he's going to spend a few days here in town, or like the year before last when took the bus to Detroit to talk to the Red Wings, but he would always tell me about his comings and goings. I've been expecting him to pop his head in the door any day now and fill me in on his latest adventure."

"You two are pretty close then?"

"Well, I don't know if you know, but sailing's a pretty big part of Moses' life."

"So I've gathered," she smiled, "I don't think I've ever met anyone who lived with a boat."

He chuckled. "Well when it's in the water, it's moored in a slip at my place down the way. And since his father died, seems like we kind of fell into this habit where he'd come in after a day's sail, and we'd talk, and have a lemonade," he grinned, "or a toddy or two. "

"What would you talk about?"

"Just anything he'd want to talk about, things I imagined a father and son, or maybe a grandfather and son would talk about, just things, whatever was rolling through that imagination of his at the time."

"So I guess if you don't know where he is, probably no one does, is that about right?"

"Well I can't say that, there's always Ida, I don't think the boy ever kept a thing from her."

"Ida?" Sarah felt the color rush to her cheeks and her heart fall. There was another woman? She had never even guessed, never even given it a thought that . . .

"Ida Bailey, his mom, the spitfire of Northport, that's what I call her. If anyone knows where he's gone off to, it would be her."

Sarah felt herself breathing again. Of course, his mother, she knew that. "So Ida lives in Northport? Or has she transplanted herself like Moses?"

"There's no transplanting that woman, though there's many that have tried. If I were twenty years younger I'd be trying it myself. Fine woman, but she won't mince words with you. If she's thinking it, you're knowing it, that's just the way she is."

"Would mind very much giving me directions, Mr. McKinney?"

"You know how to get to Northport?"

She shook her head.

"But you've been to Sutton's Bay though, right?"

She nodded.

"Well just stay on the same road and keep going, and as long as you don't slide off into the bay you'll get to Northport. When you get into town the main road will make a turn to the right," he looked at her in the eye to make sure she was getting it, "after it turns take that street down until it hits a cross street that runs along the docks and such, and turn right one block, and turn right again and it's the second house on the right. It's a big gray one, with the front door painted green last time I was there."

"To Northport right, and right again, second house on the right." She was looking at the ceiling, tucking away the information in her head.

"Do you got it?"

She nodded. "I got it, Mr. McKinney, thank you."

"You want me to draw you a map." He wasn't too sure about the exchange.

"No, really, I got it, I can see it in my head, it's not all that much harder than finding my way around Chicago. Thanks, Mr. McKinney, you're a life saver." She turned toward the door.

"So can I ask," he said, and she turned back to him, "is it because you're sweet on him?"

She broadly grinned at him. "He doesn't tell you everything does he?"

"I'll take the expression on your face as a yes."

"You may, Mr. McKinney, you may."

"So if you catch up with him, could you tell him that Mr. McKinney said he could use another couple of paintings?"

"I shall."

"Good luck to you, darlin'."

She was headed for Northport and rolled back into Sutton's Bay once more. Even in the snow, Sutton's Bay had the feeling of home. Why was that? She had been there but four times in her entire life, and then just for a few hours at a time. Sarah did not understand the feeling, but embraced it just the same. The little village hugged the gentle curve of Grand Traverse Bay, with hills dotted with orchards gently rising around it.

Along the water's edge, now lined with banks of snow along the ice, she could see the abandoned wooden piers and docks where in the summer time the masts of pleasure craft of all sizes would share moorings with the remnants of Sutton's Bay's fishing fleet. St. Joseph Avenue gently curved through the business district of town like an unfurled ribbon, low wooden structures, painted and polished, embroidering the edges on each side.

The air was cold and crisp, and carried with it the unmistakable smell of the great expanse of freshwater that lay wild and unforgiving outside the bay's safe embrace. The iron streetlamps were still decorated with holiday tinsel, and the hitching post outside the general store remained painted and waiting for a patron that might never return to use it.

This feeling of homecoming that blossomed within her, beckoned her to do something to mark it, and it was at Sutton's Bay that she decided to stop at the Bayside Grill for a Reuben Sandwich and a hot cup of tea. The bartender was a friendly sort with coal-black hair, eyes that squinted as if he needed spectacles, and a missing front tooth.

He approached the booth where Sarah sat. The window at her side faced out overlooking an alley and then out across the bay. "I'm Bill, and this is my place." He wiped his hands on a bar towel and then threw it over his shoulder.

"I'm glad to meet you, Bill." She smiled at his small-town friendliness, as if he had all day just to look after her needs.

"My waitress ran off and got married yesterday, just up and eloped, so you'll have to put up with me waitin' on you, ma'am."

"I'll try to trouble you as little as possible."

"Visitors are never a problem," he grinned, "they're what keep the lights on." He saw a couple of the local gents sitting at the bar staring at the beautiful stranger, "What are you two looking at?" He barked at them, and they turn back to their drinks and their own business.

While she ate they carried on an intermittent conversation about the local weather and Bill's plans for redecorating before spring. He made a "waitress wanted" sign for his front window as they talked.

"Do you know Moses Bailey?" she asked during a lull in the conversation.

"Who doesn't? The Blackhawks sure missed a bet there." He eyed her again as if reconfirming that she didn't have the look of a bill collector, "you a friend of his?"

"Yes, we got to know each other last summer, he's quite an artist."

"I don't know about that, I guess the tourists down in TC go for his stuff, but I do know he was quite a hockey player, could skate rings around any man on the ice. Still can, most likely."

"You happen to know where he is?"

He raised a suspicious eyebrow, "I thought you said you were a friend of his?"

"I know where he lives," she said defensively, "I've been to his house, but there's no sign of him, so I was just wondering. I'm headed up to his mother's house this afternoon."

Bill relaxed. "Moses stopped in here just before Thanksgiving, he was gonna be heading to Chicago day or two later, and I haven't seen him since, could still be there as far as I know."

Sarah decided against sharing the information she knew to the contrary and returned to her sandwich.

Mr. McKinney's directions had been precise, and Sarah followed them accurately. The afternoon sun shone over her shoulder as she stood on Ida Bailey's front porch and knocked on the door. She was more than a little nervous, what would she say to him? What would she say to his mother if he weren't there?

The green door pulled back revealing the face of Ida Bailey, thin lips, furrowed forehead, thin hair pulled back tightly against her head, and intense green eyes, eyes Sarah recognized instantly.

"Mrs. Bailey?"

"You can call me Ida, Sarah, come in out of the cold."

It took more than a moment for Sarah to recover from the shock. "You know me? But how?"

"Pictures."

"Pictures?" She didn't remember giving Moses any . . .

"My son's an artist, he paints pictures," said Ida, stating the obvious, "but you know that, why am I telling you?"

"He painted me?"

"He paints whatever he loves." Ida's voice was polite and in the tone of merely stating fact.

"But I didn't think he would even want to think . . ."

"My boy broke his heart over you," said Ida. "I think he did some paintings trying to work it out of him," she shook her head, "but it didn't work."

"Is he here?" Sarah asked looking past her into the house.

"No, and I don't expect him anytime soon either," said Ida, "you better come in and sit a spell." Sarah followed her to the kitchen. This was the house where Moses was raised, she thought. The house was simple, but clean and meticulous, the built-in cupboards, benches, and window seats testified that it had been the home of a carpenter.

"So it's a bit out of season to be just visiting Northport," Ida said, coming to the point, "is there a reason you came to call?"

"Mrs. Bailey," said Sarah bowing her head, "I'm in love with your son."

"Now the way Moses tells it, you've already got a husband." It was more of a statement than a question.

"Not for long."

Ida looked sternly at her, "you leaving him for Moses."

"No, I let Moses go, even though it almost killed me, because I was married," Sarah tried to explain, "only to find out my husband was cheating on me."

Ida shook her head, "Every time I hear about the goings on in the big city it reassures me that I'm not missing a thing."

"There are wonderful things in the city," said Sarah, "plays, and music, and art and great restaurants."

"And cheating husbands."

"I'll bet you can find those just about anywhere," said Sarah.

"I expect that's true," Ida said setting a cup of coffee down in front of Sarah, "sugar's in the bowl," she pointed.

Sarah wanted to know everything, from Moses' first words, to his first date, but did not know where to begin, and did not know how her questions would be received.

"Why Moses?" Sarah regretted saying it as soon as it had escaped her mouth; it was an awkward way to start. "I mean you don't seem to be Jewish . . ." this started badly and was going downhill. "Why did you name him Moses?"

"Jesus would have been a sacrilege," Ida replied unfazed, "Moses was a heroic figure."

Sarah prepared her coffee and Ida looked her over critically, she could understand how Moses had lost his heart to a cute little girl like this, but Lord knows she didn't do much cooking or housework with nails painted and polished like those.

"So you came all the way up here from Chicago looking for Moses?"

"Yes ma'am."

"And what did you expect to find once you got here?"

"Expect to find?" repeated Sarah, not really understanding the question, "I guess I expected to find Moses."

"And then?" asked Ida.

"And then I'd throw myself at his feet and beg him to let me be a part of his life."

"Like hell."

Sarah's face held an expression of pure surprise, "I would, I will," she protested, "you just don't know how much Moses means to me . . ."

"A woman must never beg," Ida said, "never."

"But I have to give this a chance . . ."

"A man will never respect you if you beg."

"All I know, Mrs. Bailey, is that I feel my husband did me a favor by giving me a reason to leave. I've never met anyone like Moses in my whole life."

"There isn't anyone like Moses."

"I can tell you're not really big on the idea of your son taking up with a soon to be divorced woman," said Sarah staring into her coffee cup, "and I can't say that I blame you."

"It's not easy to see somebody you love go through the kind of hurt that Moses is going through," said Ida. "But you can't hold yourself to blame, he knew you were a married woman and he lost control of his heart anyway. But that's Moses," she shook her head, "I guess it's that emotional openness, or whatever you want to call it, that makes him an artist, I don't know."

"You've got to believe, Ida, I never meant to hurt him."

"He hurt himself, I told you that before." Her coffee had gone cold and she dumped it in the sink, poured herself a new cup, and refilled Sarah's.

"I'm telling you straight out, Mrs. Bailey . . ."

"Straight out's how I like it," Ida interrupted.

"I'm in love with your son," Sarah said looking her straight in the eye, "and I'm out to make a life with him if he'll have me."

"Well, if you mean it, you've got quite a test before you."

"A test?" wondered Sarah, Ida had confused her again.

"Yes, you have a hill to climb, so to speak, to get to where you want to go."

"I thought you liked it straight out, Ida."

Ida Bailey smiled at her, she could get to like this girl, she had gumption. "That boy of mine has gone off and joined the merchant marine, he shipped out on an iron ore freighter two weeks ago."

"How long will he be gone?"

"Don't know, could be months before he hits a port that's close enough to visit home," she was looking for something more than the disappointment in Sarah's eyes. "And that's if he wants to, he probably won't be going anywhere that reminds him of you when he does get close."

"And you think his house reminds him of me?"

"I expect so."

"Is his boat there?" asked Sarah, "In the living room?"

"Where else but?"

"Then he'll be there sooner or later."

Ida smiled. "You got to know my son pretty well in just a short time." She was in no little way impressed with this young lady. "You're gonna have to wait, maybe a long time, do you think this life you're dreaming of is worth it?"

"Mrs. Bailey, I've been waiting for Moses my whole life, I just didn't know it, I'm on the home stretch now."

"So what's your plan?"

"Well, I'll either move to Sutton's Bay, or camp out in your front yard, but one way or another, if waiting is what I have to do, then waiting is what I'll do." Sarah ran her finger around the rim of her coffee cup, "You know in a way it's like my penance, and I'm prepared to pay it."

"Are you sure about this," asked Ida, suddenly dead serious, "you're prepared to stake your whole life, your future, on that boy, not knowing what his answer will be when and if he returns?"

"I couldn't live with myself if I didn't."

"Well, you're going to need a place to stay," Ida said fumbling in a catchall drawer beside the sink, and finally pulling out a key, she laid it on the counter, "so you might as well move into his house."

Sarah was astonished, "You think it would be all right."

"I saw the boy before he left, and I think I know what his answer will be." There is something magical about mothers, at least some mothers, and it was as if Mother Bailey instinctively knew that this was the woman for her son.

Sarah had a smile on her face that lasted all the way back to Sutton's Bay. She parked the car on St. Joseph's Street in front of the Bayside Grill. She strode in with a friendly confidence, yanked Bill's newly posted "Waitress Wanted" sign from the window and handed it to him as he stood behind the bar watching her. "You found your waitress," she told him.

"Aprons are hanging just inside the kitchen door on the left, better put one on it's about time for the dinner trade."

"OK, boss," she moved toward the kitchen sliding off her mink coat as she went.

While Sally Rand made $6,000 a week doing her fan dance in Chicago, the girl, who in the mind of Moses Bailey, was the most beautiful woman in the world, settled into a waitressing job at the Bayside Grill in Sutton's Bay for $35 a month plus tips.

Steve finished gassing up his Mustang and hung the nozzle back on the pump. He ran a hand across his stomach as he waited for change at the gas station counter. What was the deal with this nervous stomach every time something with Dawn came up? So he finally had a date with her, why was that any reason to have a nervous stomach?

Dawn did not remember ever having a real date. There were times in high school when groups of them would go to the movies or to the mall, and there would be boys in the group, but no male had ever gotten past her limp before, not to take her out one on one. And she had begun to doubt if it was ever going to happen, and now she was nervous that it was about to.

She checked her hair in the mirror on the back of her bathroom door for about the thirty-eighth time, and finally succumbed to putting on lipstick. He saw her every day without it, wasn't this going to seem as if she was trying too hard? Wasn't she?

It was a day trip, dress casually, that's what he had said. That meant jeans, right? Where was all this doubt coming from? If all this turmoil was what dating was all about, maybe she was glad she had missed it.

The blue and white striped blouse accented her figure, she checked the mirror again. In the right light you could see the outline of her bra at the white stripes, what would he think about that? Would he mistake that for some kind of sign that she was . . . that she was something she wasn't? Should she change, maybe something more conservative? A knock came to the door, too late, answer it.

She opened the door to Steve's smile. "I love to see you out of uniform," he blushed, "that didn't come out exactly right, did it?"

She nervously laughed, "I think I know what you meant."

"Well the skies are sunny and the highway awaits," he announced.

"Are you going to tell me where we're going now?" she asked.

"Exploring."

So their first date, and Dawn's first date ever, began. At the car, he closed her door and patted her hand. He wanted to let her know that he remembered what had transpired between them without making her feel threatened, or obligated to kiss him again, though he knew already that it could easily become a habit.

Steve guided the Mustang onto the two-lane highway and north out of town. He pushed the accelerator and the convertible roared in response. Dawn tilted her face up to the sun, closed her eyes, and let the wind play with her hair. "This is wonderful," she sighed.

He smiled at the beautiful girl beside him, and thought that this would be simply a great moment for time to stand still.

"How much exploring have you done since you moved here from Indiana?" he asked.

"I've looked around Evergreen, that's about it."

"Well that must have taken all of a half hour." He grinned.

"So does this babe magnet have any music in it or what?" she leaned to the dashboard and started playing with the knobs on the stereo.

"Sure, what kind of music do you like?" There were so many things to learn about her, Steve thought, it could take a lifetime.

"All kinds, let's hear something fun."

He pushed a few buttons until he found a station that was blasting some suitable driving music, and he slid on his sunglasses. This day was going to have fun engraved upon it in big, bold letters. They roared down the tree-lined highway, green limbs hanging over the road making it appear a tunnel, the stereo pumping, the both of them smiling.

An hour and a half later they stopped for lunch at a roadside restaurant that Steve had stumbled upon in his wanderings. Now he wanted to share it with Dawn. He was out to make a memory of this quaint little roadside café and entwine it with this vision of Dawn. He swung open her car door, "you make me want to invest in a camera," he said.

She did not know what to say and simply smiled.

The small cafe looked out across a small inland lake, it was calm with nary a ripple except those caused by the occasional fisherman trolling in front of the restaurant. Inside, the eatery was finished with dark walnut, navy blue carpet, and blue and white curtains pulled back to display the view.

She ordered a chef salad, and he watched her pick at it as they talked. Did she always eat like a bird, he wondered? So many things to learn about her, came the refrain once more from somewhere inside him.

An hour after they finished lunch, they coasted into Grand Rapids, rolling down Monroe. She cranked her head up to look at the Amway Grand reaching up into the blue sky. "I feel like such a child," she said, "I've never been anywhere or done anything."

"I like that about you," he said.

She looked at him, he was more of a mystery than she had thought, "Why?"

"So I can be the one who gives you the world." His blue eyes flashed excitement, "I can be there for all your firsts."

"That's pretty presumptuous for a first date, don't you think?" she asked, but wished she could have the words back. Here he was dreaming of times together, of a future together, and she was raining on the parade.

"I'm sorry," he said, the smile falling from his face, "I just thought you were having as good a time as I was."

"Oh, I am," she grabbed his arm, "I don't know why I said that, I'm sorry, I really didn't mean to be a party pooper. Can you forget I even said that?"

"Said what?" His smile returned. He tooled around a corner, "Hey look," he pointed, "the Grand Rapids Art Museum, you want take a look inside?"

"I've got a lifetime of firsts to look forward to, and you're my guide, lead the way."

He parked the car, swung open the door, and took her hand as she rose up out of the convertible. He turned to look at the gray granite building, and she kissed him on the cheek.

"I'm not complaining or anything," he said, "but what was that for?"

"For today." She smiled, and he hoped he could always remember that smile.

She hooked her arm through his and drew herself close to him. As they climbed the steps toward the front door, he felt her breast through her shirt graze against his bicep, setting him aglow inside.

It was soon evident, that although they now counted a former painter as one of their closest friends, Steve and Dawn knew very little about art. Neither one could tell a Monet from a Picasso, they simply knew what they liked, and what they liked most of all was sharing it all with each other. They strolled through the marble corridors, admiring the old building with the tall columns and high ceilings as much as the paintings that hung upon the walls.

"I'd like to hang this one in my living right above my new couch," said Dawn.

"I think you'll have to wait for another starving artist sale, I think this stuff is all out of our budget," he said. Did she hear him right? Did he just say "our"? What was she to make of that?

Steve's nervousness had vanished with the Evergreen city limits sign, and had taken a remarkable swing in the opposite direction. He felt as comfortable with Dawn as he had ever felt with anyone in his whole life. Was that an exaggeration? He thought on it for quite a while, gazing blankly at an impressionist exhibition.

"What are you thinking?" she asked.

"I was thinking about how at ease I feel with you." He regained his focus and looked at her, "I think I could tell you absolutely anything."

How she loved those blue eyes, she thought. "Me too," she said.

"Do you really mean it?" he asked, not quite believing her.

"Sure I do." Didn't she? Was there something that she wouldn't tell him? Then she pleaded silently for him not to ask her how she felt about him. That was something she had yet to admit to herself.

"Then tell me about it." He said softly, "tell me about your limp, is it something you can talk about?"

She had been unprepared for that, no one had ever just asked her so outright about it, it had always been some indirect inquiry, or some behind the scenes investigation for the few who had ever been interested. "Only if you buy me an ice cream when we get done here," she was trying to keep the day light and fun, but the subject he had brought up was anything but.

"Deal," said Steve attentively.

"I fell down the stairs when I was young."

"I sense you're giving me the Reader's Digest version of the story."

"It's an old story, I don't want to bore you with ancient history."

"Does it hurt you to talk about it?" He was showing more insight and compassion than she could have possibly given him credit for. "If it does, you don't have to talk about it, I just want to know everything about you." That melted her like little else he could have said.

"It happened very fast, so there's not really much to tell." He watched her face become sad as she thought back to that fateful night. "I was seven years old, and had just fallen asleep for the night, I shared a bedroom at the top of the stairs with Nancy. She was not home yet, she would have been about sixteen then, and was gone about every evening with her friends."

"What sixteen year-old doesn't," said Steve, "go on."

"My father though, he did come home, drunk as usual. He yelled at Momma so loud that it woke me. I lay in bed and tried to cover my ears, but there wasn't anyway I could block out the sound. They were fighting right outside the door to my room at the top of the stairs." Dawn's eyes began to fill with tears. "Then I heard him hit her, and I heard her cry for him to stop. 'Stop John, please stop,' she cried. But he hit her again, and again."

Steve moved to her and put his arm around her shoulder, they were alone in the cavernous gallery. He pulled a handkerchief from the back pocket of his jeans and handed it to her.

"I couldn't just let him go on hitting her, I had to do something, it was my momma. I got out of my bed and went to the door. When I got there I saw him raise his hand to strike her again. I jumped up on his back, threw my arms around his neck and screamed, 'no, Daddy, no.' But he just shrugged, and tossed back one of his big forearms and threw me off, sending me bouncing down the stairs."

"Oh my God, Dawn, your own father?" Steve's heart ached for her.

"Well, I did stop the fighting." She took a deep breath and wiped her tears, "but it was quite a price to pay for it. My mother took me, and left him on the spot. I heard his liver gave out about three years later and he died, but I never saw him again." Just at the instant that she had thought she had succeeded in steeling herself against the horrid memory of the past, just when she was about to put it all back into the locked box in her mind where she kept it, all the years of suppressed feelings came crashing down upon her, and the floodgates let loose her tears. She turned to Steve and buried her face in his chest as she wept.

He cradled her in his arms, and gently kissed the top of her head. "I'm so sorry," he whispered.

When the cry, that had been long overdue, had finally run its course, she looked up at him with red eyes and a shining nose. "I'm a mess aren't I?" she asked.

"Not from where I'm standing," he kissed her on the nose, then seriously, "I didn't mean to ruin your day."

"No day is ruined that has ice cream in it," she said, and gave her eyes a final wipe with his hanky. "Look!" she pointed with amazement.

He wheeled around, his gaze following her finger. On the wall behind him hung a painting, Dawn walked over to it with Steve trailing right behind. The gold plaque with black letters on the lower right said, "Sarah By The Shore by Moses Bailey."

"Awesome," marveled Steve.

"Well, I'll be . . ." said Dawn.

"Quite a piece, isn't it?" came a voice from beside them. They turned to see a middle-aged man in a blue blazer and gray pants that had the appearance of a uniform.

"Yes," said Steve, "the colors of the water are incredible."

"Moses Bailey is known for that," said the man.

"Is he famous?" asked Dawn.

"He's one of Michigan's best kept secrets, not a lot of his work has been found. This one is supposedly of his wife. The story is that after she died, he painted dozens and dozens of pictures of her. Then one night in drunken agony he burned them all, or so the story goes. Torched em' in a giant bonfire in the middle of a cherry orchard somewhere up north." The man in the blue blazer gently shook his head, intently admiring the picture, "this is the only one that survived."

"She's beautiful," said Dawn.

"Yes, she is," said Steve, but he was not looking at the picture.

She blushed, "Why are you looking at me like that?" she asked

"Because I want to remember you in exactly this way."

"Do you think we should ask him about it?" Dawn asked Steve, trying to recover her composure.

"Moses?"

She nodded.

"It sounds like it was quite a painful time in his life, I think he'd probably tell us if it was something that he wanted to share."

"I think we should ask him."

Later, as they approached Evergreen, Dawn sat licking the last of her mint chocolate chip ice cream cone. "I don't want today to end," she said

"Can we make one more stop before I take you home?" he asked.

He could take her anywhere he wanted, she thought, without even having to ask. "Sure," she said.

He pulled his Mustang into his parents' driveway and turned off the engine.

"Where are we?" she asked.

"I want you to meet my mom."

"Steve, no," she shrieked, "look at me, I'm a wreck, my hair's been windblown all day long."

"You're beautiful," he said, "I don't think it would be possible for you not to be, you were beautiful scrubbing the floor of your new apartment, I'll bet you're beautiful when you roll out of bed in the morning."

"Yeah, right."

"So it's a bet then?"

"What?"

"I'd have to be there when you rolled out of bed in the morning to settle that bet, which of course would mean that I would have to stay the night."

"Have you ever had a girl really fall for that line?"

"I've never tried it before," he smiled. "How am I doing with it?"

"OK," she twisted his rearview mirror to assess the damage the wind had done, ran her brush through her hair, and pinched her cheeks, "let's meet your mother."

Audra Hadley was on her knees pruning her roses in the backyard when her son and the beautiful girl with the limp ambled up the paving stone path and stood before her.

"Mom, this is Dawn. Dawn, this is my mom," said Steve.

Steve's mother rose, smiled, removing her gardening glove, and extended her hand, "Call me Audra."

This wasn't the spoiled rich kid's home that Dawn had conjured up in her imagination. This woman seemed real, and the house, although nice, was ordinary.

"Steve, why don't you go get us all something to drink, there's a pitcher of lemonade in the fridge," suggested Audra.

"Back in a flash," he said, and disappeared through the back door.

"We'll take our refreshment on the patio," Audra motioned across the lawn with her open hand.

"You have a lovely garden," said Dawn.

"Thanks, I don't really have a green thumb, but I try hard," she said, looking over her domain. They walked toward the patio, Audra slowing to keep pace with Dawn. "You know he's quite taken with you," she said, looking straight ahead rather than at Dawn.

"How do you know that?" asked Dawn, "this is our first date."

"Oh, he's talked to me about you."

Dawn gave her a confused look and eased down on to the overstuffed cushion of the rainbow striped patio furniture.

"I can coax a little information out of him now and then," Audra continued.

Dawn tried to read her, but only came up with the old assumptions. She didn't want her son dating a gimp, right? "Do you meet most of the girls Steve dates?" she asked.

"He doesn't date much," her look was unflinching, "that's why I bring it up. Most boys Steve's age are trying to see how many girls they can sleep with, as if they were in some kind of contest to prove their manhood, but Steve's not that way."

"He's not?"

"No, I'm afraid my son is looking for love, not sex."

"You sound like you think that's bad?"

"I'm only afraid of him getting hurt," she said, "that's why I bring it up. If you're going to break his heart, do it now, you'll only hurt him more by waiting."

Dawn sat in stunned silence, just then Steve came through the French doors that joined the patio with the dining room, "are my ladies getting to know each other?" he asked.

"Your young lady is simply charming, Steven," said Audra.

Dawn sat back in her chair and Steve handed her a lemonade. She had had many dreams and fantasies of a first date, and even a passing fear or two of meeting a young man's mother along the way, but she had never envisioned something such as this. Being cast as the femme fatale, the heartbreaker, was totally beyond anything that she could have imagined.

The moon hung big and yellow in the eastern sky as Steve drove her home. Dawn was still silent. Nothing could describe the happiness he felt at having her by his side, but he could see that something was troubling her.

"Dawn, where has that smile gone?" he asked.

"I was just thinking about how different you are, how different your life is, from what I imagined."

"You say that like I've disappointed you somehow." He pulled to a stop in front of Dawn's apartment.

She leaned over the car's console, ignoring the jab in the ribs from the gearshift, and gave him a kiss, full on the mouth and unreserved, "Nothing could be further from the truth."

"So how about next week we go dancing?" he asked.

"I can't dance," she said.

"Have you ever tried?"

"Why would you want to humiliate me in public like that?"

"In public? No," he smiled. "Nobody else is invited, I want you all to myself."

As Steve drove home, he was filled with her, his heart so swelled that he feared that it would burst.

ELEVEN

It was a new morning, and somehow a new Dawn. She studied herself in the full length mirror on her closet door, and she had to admit it, it was not the shape of her legs that were deformed, it was their movement, in fact, when she stood there posing, she thought her legs were actually quite shapely. What had happened to her, she wondered, she had never even been able to look at herself for an extended period of time before, now she was actually admiring herself, what had caused such a marvelous transformation?

Dawn all of a sudden had an intense interest in her appearance, make-up and hair, picking out her clothes in the morning, even toying with the idea of shortening her uniforms because she knew a certain blond fellow liked to look at her legs. This transformation did not go unnoticed by her sister, and she had commented on it in no uncertain terms. Jealousy was not the least of Nancy's emotions, for having a form a man liked to look at was nothing but a distant memory for her.

"He's the best thing that's ever happened to me," said Dawn, her voice dripping with elation.

"He's the only thing to ever happen to you," said a jealous Nancy.

Dawn was unfazed by her sister's comment; she only knew that she could barely wait until the next time she could see him.

Dawn and Steve stood in Moses room, waiting for him to return from his daily meditation in the chapel. He was late. Not that they minded, Steve was more than a little preoccupied with how kissable Dawn's lips looked that afternoon. They had by this time fallen into the habit of meeting in Moses room to listen to stories of Moses' life, and through his stories, setting their own daydreams and fantasies free. Having Dawn alone to himself though, was an opportunity that Steve could not pass up. He crossed the room to where she stood looking out the window and put his arms around her from the back, nuzzling her ear.

"Oh my God," she cried.

"What?" said Steve freezing, and then he suddenly caught sight of the same thing she saw out the window. It was Moses in his wheelchair, rolling down the hill of the drive, out toward the road. Without an instant's hesitation, Steve was off on a dead run, out the room, down the corridor, and bursting out he front entrance of the nursing home.

Moses had reached the road by the time Steve came into Dawn's view running at full speed down the driveway.

The momentum from rolling down the hill had Moses' wheelchair going at a pretty good clip, and he smiled as he felt the wind rush through his hair, he was sailing, and it felt good. He felt the breeze blow across his face and closed his eyes. He did not see the truck coming around the turn from town, increasing speed as the driver pulled away from the city limits sign.

The driver was Len Crawford taking a load of empty propane tanks from Evergreen back to Gobles. He came around the turn, tromping on the accelerator, hurrying to get back in time to take his son Tommy to little league practice. He had taken this road a hundred times, maybe a thousand times, he knew every inch of it, but this was the first time he had ever come face to face with a little old man in a wheelchair. And that kid running there along behind, what was he doing in the middle of the road? What was either of them doing in the middle of the road? He blew his horn, and blew it again. He would always remember the old man's startled look as he opened his eyes to see the oncoming truck. "Ah shit," said Len, just as the kid caught up to the little old man in the wheelchair. He cranked the wheel and put the rig onto the shoulder of the road, the gravel flying, and the rear end fishtailing.

Steve leapt to grab the wheelchair and gave it a giant push off the road away from the careening truck. He landed face down in the road with the effort. Moses wheelchair hit the weeds at the top of the roadside ditch and came to an abrupt halt, catapulting Moses head first down into the drainage ditch.

Len brought his truck to a halt in a cloud of dust and dirt, and breathed again. "Mary, mother of God," he muttered and put his bald head down against the steering wheel.

When Dawn arrived on the scene, the first thing she saw was Steve lying face down in the middle of the road, the truck pulled to the side of the road and dust and dirt flying everywhere. "Steve, no!" she screamed, and ran as best she could to where he lay. She bent down and knelt over him, reluctantly, touching his temple.

"Are you always going to say 'no' to me?" said Steve, turning over with a smile.

She took a deep breath, closed her eyes, and lifted her face to the sky, as if silently giving thanks. Then she belted him with a fist to his shoulder, "Don't scare me like that."

When they reached Moses, they found him drenched, sitting waste deep in water. "What in the hell'd you do that for?" he yelled.

"Today's not your day to die," said Steve.

"Why not?" asked Moses, "not that I was trying to."

"Cause you haven't seen your sunset, yet."

Moses gave Steve a sideways glance. "What do you think I was doing?"

"Going to see the sunset?" asked Steve shaking his head.

"Bet your ass I was."

"Moses, the beach is thirty miles away."

"I could have made it by tomorrow's sunset, if some young know-it-all punk hadn't fucked up my ride." Moses was mad and didn't care who knew it.

"Think what you like, Moses," Steve's nostrils flared, and the back of his neck turned red with anger. Steve walked away as two orderlies and Nurse Hackett arrived to haul Moses up out of the ditch. Steve assessed the scrapes on his left forearm and the underside of his left elbow, shaking his head as he walked.

"Mr. Bailey, I thought you had more sense," said Nancy, getting as close to him as she could without getting her feet wet.

"And just what do you think that truck would have done to your ride, if Steve hadn't risked his life to save you?" Dawn asked Moses in a stern voice.

Len watched the assemblage retreat back into the nursing home, "Hey," he called to Nancy, "everyone all right?"

She nodded and raised a hand as if dismissing him. He eased his truck back onto the road and headed once more to little league practice.

Dawn walked silently beside Moses as they wheeled him back into the nursing home. She knew he owed Steve an apology, but decided the only thing to do was to wait for him to come to it on his own.

Moses wiped the water from his face and breathed a heavy sigh. Why do they think it would have been such a bad thing to take on that truck, he wondered? Just because they weren't ready to go, didn't mean he wasn't. He had been ready for a long time, a very, very long time. Back in his room, he sat alone with his thoughts and watched once more through the bars at his window as the daylight faded on the other side of the distant hills.

Three days later, Barton Hackett stood at the front of the nursing home cafeteria in his navy blue suit, dominating the attention of most of the staff. The rest were preoccupied with the coffee and donuts or busy wondering if they were going to get paid for this meeting.

Dawn had taken the time that day to wear makeup and had left her dark hair down, riding on her shoulders. She had worn a skirt that day, an event so unusual, that it could only be called rare. She had never done anything that would call attention to her legs and her perceived deformity. She did not know exactly why she had worn the skirt, was it some kind of final test for Steve before admitting him completely into her heart? A lowering of the Phantom's mask? She did not know, but the wearing of it was somehow connected to Steve in some mysterious way.

As they sat listening to Barton's lecture, Dawn would see Steve's eyes roaming to her and appraising her legs every now and again, as if drawn by a magnet. He seemed completely absorbed in the task, almost as if he were daydreaming. Daydreaming of what, she wondered? He was unaware he was being watched, and the expression on his face was not one of mock or disgust, she could see it was genuine appreciation. She did not understand it, but she enjoyed it immensely. She could not remember any time since the accident when a boy, and then later men, had looked upon her as something of beauty. But Steve did, she could see it in his eyes. It was as if her defect to him was invisible.

The lights were a little too bright for Steve and he tried to shade his eyes while still pretending to pay attention. What really occupied his mind was Dawn sitting across the aisle. She had worn a skirt that day, the first time he had seen her in a skirt, and he kept looking at her legs. They were delicate, yet toned, with the shape of a dancer, attractive, in fact perfect, he thought. It surprised him, and pleased him more than a little bit, but he did not know exactly why.

Barton was lecturing on bomb threat protocol, evacuation routes and "systematic procedures to provide for the patients' care and well-being in the event of such an occurrence. First and foremost, it is the duty of the staff to effectively evacuate the facility . . ."

Suddenly it struck Steve, and he was at once listening intently to the lecture, this was the way, he thought, the way to make Moses' dream come true. He looked up at Barton, and the mind of the prankster was already racing, a grin spreading to his lips. He looked over at Dawn; she was already looking at him with a sly smile on her face as if reading his mind.

When the lecture ended, Steve grabbed the last of the donuts off the table at the back of the room, turned, as if a wide receiver running a hook pattern, then hurdled too rows of chairs and caught up to Dawn at the doorway. "You look gorgeous today," he whispered from behind her.

She did not turn around, or even acknowledge him immediately; she did not want him to see that she was blushing. She recovered her composure in a matter of seconds, but when she turned to face him, she saw only his backside walking briskly down the hall away from her, carrying his donut. She sighed, nice backside, too.

"I'm sorry, boy," Moses said as Steve entered the room, "I'm sorry I showed no gratitude to you for saving my life, it's just sometimes, I don't think I have much worth saving. I apologize, I was rude and ungrateful to one of the few people in this world who cares if I live or die."

"Well, I'll expect better of you in the future, young man," said Steve, affecting a comic tone.

A hint of a smile pushed at the corners of Moses' mouth.

"Does it bother you for me to talk about the future?" Steve asked, setting down the donut on Moses bedside table.

"Why?" grinned Moses, "don't you think I have a future?"

"Truthfully?"

"Is there any other way?"

"Well, I don't think you have much of one, I mean, you've already exceeded the average life expectancy."

"Steve, my boy, this life as we know it is just a blink of an eye in the whole scheme of things. But life goes on. And on and on, for eternity. And you'll be happy to know, so does love."

"Speaking of love," said Steve, "we're going to need the help of my love, if we're going to break you out of this joint."

Moses face widened into a broad grin. "We're breaking out?"

"We've got a date with a sunset," said Steve, standing at the window his hands jammed under his armpits.

"And Dawn's going along with this?"

"She doesn't know it yet."

Dawn entered the room and looked at Steve, "you were sure in a hurry to get out of that lecture."

"Had something I wanted to talk about with Moses."

"Can I ask what?"

Steve shot Moses a knowing look. "You can ask," he said, "but I don't think you'll get an answer until later."

"Sounds mysterious."

"That's my aim," said Steve, "to remain a mystery. Women love mysterious men don't they, Dawn?"

"Seriously?" she asked.

"When have you ever known me to be serious?" he replied.

"Well seriously, women like a man who does have an aim in life, someone who has some ambition to do something with his life."

"What's your purpose, Steve?" asked Moses. "What's the purpose of your life?"

Steve's face took on a quizzical expression, "to answer the age old question, 'can man survive on peanut butter alone?' Could I be dedicated to any greater cause?"

Dawn threw a pillow at him.

Nurse Hackett stuck her head in the room, "I hate to break this up, Mr. Bailey, but Steve here is not the social director of this facility despite what he might think to the contrary." She glared at her sister, "and Dawn, I expected better from you."

"That's OK, Nancy," said Moses, "I was about to lay down and take a stroll down memory lane anyway, and these two have lives to live."

"You here that, Mr. Hadley," she barked, staring at Steve alone, "so get back to living your life, preferably back in the kitchen where you belong," and then under her breath, "and say a prayer of thanks that it's not a jail cell."

"That donut is for you, Moses," Steve pointed. "Dawn, you're sweet enough already."

Dawn grinned despite the searing glance from Nancy.

Steve laughed and scampered from the room. "And Nancy, no matter how hard you try, you'll never steal my love from your sister," he called back as he sauntered down the corridor.

You could buy breakfast for a dime, eggs, potatoes and coffee, and Father Francis Cavanaugh spent his dime five days a week at the Bayside Grill. He was a middle-aged man of fair complexion, dark hair with a round, untroubled face. And it wasn't long before his friendly way uncovered that Bill's new waitress had been raised in the church, and Sarah soon found she had a new friend with whom she could confide anything.

Sarah Conner poured him another cup of coffee, he wrapped his fingers around the mug, feeling the warmth. And there was a warmth in his eyes as he listened to her.

"I'm beginning to doubt if he'll ever come back," Sarah confessed.

"I'm sure if he knew you were here waiting for him," he gently patted her arm, "he'd be here as quick as he could."

"What if he doesn't want me anymore?" Her fear was distressing, "what if he's found someone else while he's been away?"

"Those doubts are just your mind working overtime," his voice was kind and soothing, "what does your heart say?"

"It aches, Father. I don't think I've ever loved anyone or anything this much in my entire life."

"Listen to your heart."

She had settled into her new life, made new friends, and seldom thought of Chicago and the world she had left behind. But there were times when the loneliness was overwhelming, crashing in upon her suddenly and without notice. She fixed her eyes on the door each time it opened, looking for that one particular face in the doorway which could fill her emptiness.

Long weeks at sea did not help Moses forget Sarah, if anything it had made it worse. And he missed painting, and when winter turned to spring, he missed sailing. The big freighter plodded along with a constant drone of the engine. It just wasn't life on the water as he had come to know it, as he had come to love it. Below decks he could have been in a factory somewhere, totally removed from the sound and the movement of the water.

He had done a small painting of her, a picture that captured how she looked that day when they walked along the beach in Chicago. It now hung beside his bunk below decks in the cramped quarters of the freighter. He sat back on his bed, his head propped up with a pillow, looking at it.

"You have one beautiful lass there, my boy," said Scotty, an ancient shipmate, his voice thick with accent, and his face wrinkled and leathery.

"And that's just the surface," said Moses wistfully, "just the tip of the iceberg."

Occasionally, he would find himself getting angry. Irrational and totally unfounded, he found himself far too often as near to rage as his mild-manner was capable. How could she have done this? How could providence or destiny or God be so cruel? He did not know whom to blame, but the injustice of meeting the woman of his dreams after she was married to someone else continued to eat at him. And the knowledge that her husband had no appreciation of what a treasure he truly had, somehow made it all the worse.

He played idly with an unlit cigarette in his fingers and wondered how long, how many nights would he have to try to sleep with this aching inside him? From the painting, she looked out at him, the waves crashing on the beach in the background, the sun setting her face aglow, her hair pulled back and up, but creeping down toward her shoulders, loosened by the gentle breeze. He sat there for hours staring at it, remembering and aching from the want. He remembered every curve of her face, and then the flood of visions cascaded down upon him, the turn of her ankle, the delicate slenderness of her fingers, and onward the visions flowed, her bare back in her evening gown, her long legs in her shorts. He did not know how he could go on living a life without Sarah beside him. He tried to tell himself he never wanted to see her again, but lying to himself was fruitless. He had been away seven months, and it hadn't changed. He tried to defend his heart from the nightly assault, but with little success. He turned away and buried his face in his pillow drowned by the memories.

July was hot and sticky, and when they had seen the most of it, two days of rain came to polish it off. It was a dark moonless night as Dawn emerged from the back door of the nursing home, and walked across the staff parking lot to her car. She always felt so weary after doubling back to work the three to eleven shift. The rain had stopped, at least for the moment, but the pavement was still wet and she had to avoid puddles in her path. She heard water drip from the trees surrounding the parked cars. It always seemed spooky when she was the last to leave at night, and the wet and the dark made it even more so.

She set her purse in the passenger seat, shoved the key into the ignition and gave it a quick twist. Her blue Honda cranked and cranked, but would not kick. She let go of the key, pounded the top of the steering wheel with her palm, and threw herself back against the seat. Why now? She thought. She tried again, but received even less of a response. And trying three more successive times, only succeeded in draining her battery completely. "Damn car!"

A navy blue Cadillac started on the other side of the lot, its headlights switching on, putting a wet glare on the entire landscape. It slowly rolled toward her, then came to a stop beside her. The driver's window powered down revealing Barton inside. "Do I see a damsel in distress?" he smirked.

"The stupid thing won't start, I guess I'll have to go in and call the garage."

"You won't get anybody to come out tonight," he said, "why don't I just take you home and you can deal with it in the morning."

"I don't want to put you to any trouble," she said, "I could just call a cab."

"What trouble, I'm going right past your place anyway."

The idea of just going home and getting into bed sounded too good to resist. Out of instinct, she scanned the parking lot for another alternative as she climbed warily into the seat beside him. He smelled of whiskey, although his tie and collar were still fastened and in place as if he were just starting his day. Barton insisted on everything being in its place, from his attire, to his home, to his office and the facility that he ran. Neat on the outside, a moral mess on the inside, thought Dawn, studying him as they turned out into the darkness.

"I'm family, how could I possibly leave you stranded?" He was not looking at her and almost sounded as if he were speaking rhetorically.

"Working awfully late aren't you?" she asked.

"Just goes with the responsibility, all those patients, all those staff members, it really is quite a burden. No one really understands what a weight it really is."

Was he looking to her for sympathy? She wondered. "Yes, Barton, and it's a responsibility you handle so well." At least she could be nice.

"You haven't been over to the house since you got your new place," he looked over at her, "we've missed you."

"I've been busy, had a lot to do setting up a new household, dealing with the insurance company, you know."

"You left in such a hurry, I couldn't help but think there was some unfinished business between us."

Dawn searched her mind for something to say, to put him off in a new direction, but she only fidgeted in her seat silently.

"You're a little jumpy, Dawny," he said pulling out a cigar from the inside pocket of his coat. He bit off the end, hit the power button for his window, and spit it out. "Light this for me will you, darling? The lighter's in front of you on the dash."

She handed him the lighter, but he did not take it from her.

"No, why don't you light it for me." His face held an evil grin.

"I really can't stand cigars," she said, and threw the lighter back up onto the dashboard.

"Wait a minute," he said, grabbing her left wrist with his right hand, "don't I get any thanks for helping out a lady in distress?"

"Thank you, Barton," she wrenched her arm away from his grip, "now could we just go home without all this talk?"

"That's not much of a thank you," his voice was almost a snarl, "I was thinking of something a little more symbolic of your appreciation."

In the darkness ahead the headlights landed upon a sign, 'Brady Park', and Barton turned in response, steering up the hill and over, out of view of the road.

"What are you doing, Barton?"

He threw the car in park, and turned off the engine. "You didn't want talk, so it's time for a little action," he said, his smile was devilish. He turned to her and this time grabbed both of her wrists, pulling her hard against him, his whiskey mouth breathing inches from her nose.

"Let me go, Barton," she screamed. She began to pry at his fingers, and he released her left hand. He yanked on the door handle and she fell flat on the seat under his pressure, as the door gave way behind her.

"And just why would I let you go?" His voice was sinister, yet calm. "I've noticed you've taken to wearing skirts, and I can't help but wonder what may be found under there? I'm sure there are some things that simply don't run in the family, shall we find out?"

She was able to force her free arm between them, "Barton, stop, let me out."

"You've been avoiding me ever since you moved here from Indiana, but not anymore, not tonight." He pushed his face to hers trying to capture her mouth, but she turned her head aside.

"Barton, please . . . stop!" Terror was rising in her voice.

"Let's see what your hiding under that skirt."

"Barton, don't!" She yelled, but her panic seemed to spur him on.

"Show me, little Dawny." He tried again to kiss her as she struggled beneath him.

"Control yourself, you drunk bastard."

"Now Dawn, don't be such a miser, share that little treasure of yours." He reached down between her legs, grabbing the fabric of her skirt. She wriggled under his touch, the struggle intensifying along with her fear.

"Stop, Barton, stop." She forced her wedged arm down and then seized his hand, but he continued groping her.

"Don't tell me you don't like this, Dawny." She tried to knee him but they were too close, and he was too crafty. "A gimp like you should be grateful for the attention."

"Let me go, you bastard."

He brought his hand up from between her legs, and she was powerless to stop it. He violently grabbed her hair, twisting her head so her face opened to his, and kissed her, forcing his tongue against her gritted teeth. The pressure from her pulled hair felt as though it was about to split her skull. The smell of whiskey filled her nose. She fought against his burly chest as he continued to bruise her lips with his mouth.

She lashed out with her free hand, landing a fist to the side of his face. He instinctively recoiled and she was able to bring up her knee in the small gap between them. Her bad hip roared with pain as she thrust her leg into his chest knocking him back against the steering wheel. He gasped for breath at the impact and she turned over on her belly and slid out the door and onto the ground.

She began to climb to her feet, but he once again snared a fistful of hair and yanked her back against the car. She screamed into the night. Her head struck the doorframe, momentarily stunning her. She slid down the wet side of the car and landed half back on the seat and half on the ground.

He scrambled out the open door, never letting loose of her hair. "Where you going, little girl? The party's not over." There was no more laughter, sinister or otherwise, in his voice. Her head throbbed with pain.

"Barton, you're hurting me!" She flailed at his chest as he straddled her thighs, his hand in her hair keeping her in a position where she could not hit his face. With one stroke of his meaty right hand he tore open the buttons on her blouse.

He lowered his face toward her breasts, bringing it in range, and she nailed him with a fist to his cheek. "Damn it," he yelled, rolling off balance to one knee. She rolled from under him and pulled herself to her feet. She made only one small step toward the back of the car before he grabbed her by the skirt, tugging her back down to the ground. She landed, sprawled on her back only inches from where she had started.

He reclaimed his grip on her hair, then straddled her chest with his knees, pinning her arms to her sides. "I'm tired of your little game, girl." He reached inside the car and grabbed his cigar and lighter with his left hand. He let go of her hair with his right, letting her head hit the ground. He lit his cigar and watched the embers of the tip begin to glow in the darkness. He exhaled smoke into her face and she coughed. "You're going to give me a little," his voice was almost a whisper, "and your going to do it now." She kicked away at the ground with her heels.

With his right hand he reached down and grabbed her neck, with his left he waved the hot orange coal of his cigar in front of her eyes. She screamed and kicked away again at the ground, still unable to move. He tightened his grip on her throat, his teeth set firmly, his face twisted and vile, his cheek beginning to swell by his eye.

"You're going to stop fighting, even if I can't get you to admit you want this as much as I do. You are going to stop struggling, aren't you?"

She looked up at him in terror. She heard the chirp of crickets in the darkness, but saw only the glowing fire of his cigar.

"Until now you've always been the gimp with the pretty face, I don't want to change that, Dawn. But if you make me, I will. Then it won't be your limp that they run from, it'll be your deformed face, and it will all be your own fault."

"Can't breathe," was all she managed.

He sensed his power over her and shook her by the neck banging her head against the ground. "You think you're too good for me or what?"

Her eyes began to get glossy, her head throbbing against the cool ground, "Can't breathe," she repeated.

He loosened his grip just enough for her to take a breath, and moved the cigar from under her nose. "I got women all over town just waiting to lift their skirts for me, what's so special about you?"

She searched her mind for something that would change his violent, angry course, something that would appeal to his humanity, something, anything that might matter to him. "I'm a virgin, Barton," tears began to stream down her face.

"Well, I'm just the man to give you your first lesson."

He slid himself down off her chest, below her hips, and took a position straddling her thighs. He grabbed one of her loosened hands and brought it to his lap, "Go ahead," he commanded, "unzip me."

"You'll have to kill me before I do," she cried.

"No, I don't think so." He brought his cigar back up to her face and positioned it under her chin, "have you ever smelled the smell of burning flesh?"

Her eyes looked up at him terrified and pleading.

"Don't make me burn you, just to teach you to do what a man tells you, now undo me."

She tried to roll her face from the heat of the cigar, but it followed her movement. "Barton, please . . ." Her tears blurred her vision of him.

"Do it now," he ordered, and touched her with the cigar.

She screamed. And then closing her eyes, unzipped his pants.

"Now you," he said. Her eyes remained closed in horror and shame. She heard the clink of his belt buckle. As he crushed her stomach with a knee, she gasped, and then began to openly weep. Although she did not move to help him any further, the rest for him was easy. He pushed her skirt up around her waist and ripped away the silk fabric beneath. He clenched his cigar between his teeth and exposed himself, forcing apart her thighs with his knees.

She bucked as he came down with his weight upon her, and tried to throw him off, again flailing at him, trying to scratch his face. "Hmmph," he grunted and pinned her wrists above her head on the wet ground.

She tasted the salt of her tears, and felt an excruciating pain in her loins as he penetrated her, stealing her virginity. "It's not supposed to be like this," she tried to say, but the words caught in her throat. She had learned at a young age to endure pain, and she set her teeth, determined to endure this as well. She let go of her body, rising above the beast which pumped away at it, the whiskey breath, the puffing cigar, and sweat on the beast's skin. She closed out his grunts and listened to the crickets, and through her tears focused on the stars in the sky above.

Finally, his frantic pumping ceased, and he shuddered and then groaned, and it was over. Barton withdrew and sat back on his haunches, letting loose of her wrists. She folded her arms across her face muffling her sobs. "Lesson's over, little girl," he said, but she did not move.

He placed a hand on her pelvis and pushed himself up to stand over her, forcing a last scream of agony out of her. He pulled up his pants and tucked in his shirt. "It's not everyday I give a gimp the benefit of my experience," his voice took on its familiar boastfulness.

With an arm still hiding her face, she reached down and pulled at her skirt in an attempt to cover herself, then remained motionless, waiting for him to leave.

He grabbed her arm, "You can get up now, Dawny."

She snapped it away from his grip, "don't touch me, don't ever touch me."

"This is your own doing, kid, I tried to be nice, I've tried to be nice for weeks, but you kept resisting."

She did not move her arm to look at him, "Now you're trying to justify the crime you've just committed?" She was sick, but she would not allow herself to suffer the degradation of vomiting in front of him. "Get your fat, sweaty body out of here before I find a rock and kill you with it."

He did not speak to her again. He slammed the passenger side door of his car, walked around and climbed in. She heard the car start and then begin to move.

He gave her a last look as he pulled away. She laid frozen in the grass where he had raped her, her arms still covering her face.

As she heard his car disappear in the distance, more tears came and a terrible trembling shook her body. She rolled to her side and curled up into the fetal position, trying to reclaim control. She wept quietly as the full impact of what had happened crashed in upon her. An argument ensued within her, 'get up' said one voice, 'your knees will buckle from under you,' countered the other. She remained curled on the ground, waiting for the shaking to subside.

TWELVE

Steve stood naked from the waist up in the glow of the open refrigerator, a chocolate chip cookie in the hand which propped open the door. He reached in for the jug of milk, but pulled back without it when he heard the doorbell ring.

From the kitchen, he heard the screen door rattle as the front door was pulled open and then his mother's voice, "Oh my, oh my dear, what's happened to you?"

He could not hear the reply, but recognized the voice as Dawn's. He hurried through the dining room, flipping on lights as he went, and into the living room where he saw her. First her bruised face, then the grass stains and a smattering of blood on her white skirt. His mother had Dawn by the arm and Steve ran to her side.

"Dawn, what's happened, what's wrong?"

"I was in the park, I didn't know where else to go . . ." her knees gave way, but he caught her before she hit the floor, scooping her up in his arms.

Battered and bruised, she had made her way to Steve's home, and to ask her, she would have not known how. Dazed and confused, she did not know where else to go. Was it survival that had brought her to his door, or was it something more?

He felt a shiver run though her body as he carried her over to the couch.

"What happened, dear?" said Audra, kneeling beside her.

Dawn look into Steve's mother's eyes, "I didn't mean to be a bother, I know it's late," her voice was soft and remote, her eyes bewildered.

"Nonsense," said Audra, "you're no bother."

"Dawn, what's happened to you?" Steve spoke softly, and pushed her matted hair out of her face.

She stared at him a long time without speaking, as if trying to make sense of where she was, or trying to form the words to describe where she had been. Then she turned away from him, and faced the back of the couch, as the tears once again made their way down her cheeks. She choked on the words as she spit them out, "He raped me."

Audra gasped.

"Who?" asked Steve, "who did this to you?" Unable to say the word, momentarily unable to comprehend such villainy.

"Barton," she sobbed.

"Oh my God," Steve shook his head, "that arrogant bastard." A vile vision filled his mind, and anger began to rise within him. "Barton raped you?"

She nodded, the tears streaming down her cheeks.

"Oh, my poor, poor girl," said Audra, kneeling down beside Dawn's head, all motherly reservations about this girl instantly vanishing.

"I fought him the best I could, but he was just too big." Dawn sobbed, "my first time just wasn't supposed to be that way."

"No time is supposed to be that way," said Audra, stroking Dawn's arm.

"Where were you when he did this?" Steve asked.

"Over there in the park," she pointed, "I just got out of work, my car wouldn't start and he offered to take me home. He was drunk and he pulled into the park and then he . . ." The memory of it flooded her mind, and she covered her face with her hands, trying to force herself to stop crying.

Steve looked at where the buttons had been ripped off her blouse, the grass stains, the bruises on her wrists and her face, and the blood on her skirt, cataloging the evidence.

"We need to put something on this," he said, putting his finger beside the burn under her chin, "did he do this too?"

"I told him I'd rather die, and when I wouldn't stop fighting him, he burned me with his cigar."

"Oh God," said Steve, his heart was breaking for this beautiful, innocent girl. He longed to pull her to him, and with his embrace drive out all the evil that had invaded her, but he hesitated, thinking that probably the last thing she wanted or needed at that point was the touch of a man.

"You know how they always say that girls who get raped were asking for it?" she said from behind her hands, "I didn't do anything, you got to believe me. He's my sister's husband."

"Nobody asks to be raped," said Audra, "let me get something for that burn."

"I screamed, I hit him, I scratched him, but nothing made him stop."

"Nobody doubts you, Dawn," said Steve. "I've got to call the police, this bastard's going to jail." He reached for the phone on the end table next to the couch, but she caught his hand.

"Don't, I can't do that." She looked up at him, her eyes pleading. "Please."

"But why?" Steve was confused, " he deserves to be locked away for a very long time."

"I know, I know," she said, "but if I go to the police, my little nieces will lose their father, then I will have something to feel guilty about, and I just couldn't live with that."

"Are you sure, Dawn?"

She nodded, "I know what it's like to lose your father, it hurts more than anyone can describe, and mine was a no good one." Steve returned the phone back to its cradle.

His mother returned with some ointment to doctor the wound, and as Steve watched her treat the inflamed pink blister, the fire of rage stoked within him. His heart raced, thinking of how the scene must have been as Barton inflicted the wound, and then one grotesque vision after another piled on, flaming his fire higher and hotter, until he was totally consumed by burning, blind vengeance.

He took her hand in his and squeezed it. "Take care of her, Mom," he said, "I'll be right back." He rose from beside the couch, his hand sliding from her grasp.

"Where are you going, Steven?" his mother called after him. "Steven?" she raised her voice, but received no answer.

They heard the back door slam, then the Mustang roar in the driveway, and the squealing of tires as he left.

"I'm sorry," sobbed Dawn, "so very sorry," and despite all her resistance, she was again crying freely.

"Everything's going to be all right, don't worry," said Audra, stroking Dawn's temple, but unable to hide the mother's concern on her own face. "I couldn't help but overhear your conversation with Steve, are you sure about the police?"

Dawn nodded, then tears welling up in her eyes once more, she asked, "What if I'm pregnant?" She hadn't let herself think of the possibility before, but now the frightening thought got the best of her.

"Well, as my mother used to say," said Audra, "no sense borrowing trouble, but I suppose there is a precaution we could take."

Dawn sighed, and Audra wiped away the tears. "She was right I suppose," whispered Dawn, "a precaution?"

"How about a bath?" asked Audra.

"Oh, yes, yes, could I?"

"Here let me help you." Audra helped Dawn hoist herself off the couch and steered her toward the bathroom. "Let me find you a robe, and then you can give me those grimy clothes and I'll fetch something of mine for you to wear." She smiled openly at her, "of course they'll be about a mile and a half too big, but we'll manage." To Audra, Dawn had been transformed from the dangerous threat to her son's fragile heart to an injured child, and all barriers had been torn away.

"Thank you so much," said Dawn, "Steve's so lucky to have a mother like you." How she needed a mother right then to wipe away the tears, but the memory of her own mother provided no comfort. It wasn't as if she disliked her own mother, but somewhere, way back in the subconscious fog, she had never forgiven her for failing to protect her from her father.

"Are you sure you can do this on your own?" Audra asked, returning with douche and a pink terrycloth bathrobe.

"I'll manage," said Dawn, "thank you very much." She took the bathrobe and the box from Audra, laid it on the counter, and faced the mirror hanging on the wall above the lavatory. The first glimpse of her appearance was quite a shock, she stepped back, and then brought a hand to her face, examining her swollen bruises with her finger. "I know it doesn't look like it, but I'm really quite strong."

"A lot stronger than I would be," said Audra, grabbing the doorknob and pulling it toward her as she shuffled out to give Dawn some privacy. "Just call out if you need anything, I'll be right in the living room."

"Thank you. I will."

Alone in his car, in the glow of the dashboard lights, Steve's rage erupted, volcanic in it's intensity. The tires spit gravel, and Steve scowled as his tight grip of the steering wheel maneuvered his car around the corner onto Jefferson Street. His pulse quickening with each passing block, with each passing house, until the molten lava of pure vengeance ran through his veins.

The Hackett's house was dark except for a singular light burning in Barton's den. In fact, the whole neighborhood appeared asleep, except for that solitary light.

Steve pounded on the carved maple door with his fist. "Barton Hackett, get your ass out here, I want to talk to you."

Steve's pounding was met with silence, so again he railed against the door and cursed its owner in a scream. An upstairs bedroom light flipped on in response.

He banged again, and called, "Barton, come out here or I'll knock this damn door down and drag your carcass out here."

More lights came on inside the house, and the porch light from across the street.

"Barton, you know exactly what this is about," he yelled, "and you can come out here and settle it, or I can come in there and settle it in front of your family, you decide!"

Nancy Hackett looked down from the upstairs bedroom window which overlooked the front porch, her daughters, only half stirred from their sleep and still groggy-eyed, were at her side.

"What is it, Momma? Is it time to get up?" asked Angela.

"It's still dark out!" observed Becky.

Nancy went to the top of the stairs and yelled down, "Barton, is that Steve Hadley on the front porch?"

Barton emerged from the den with a whiskey bottle in his hand, and looked up at his wife and daughters from the bottom of the stairs. "Put the girls back to bed, I'll take care of it."

Finally, the porch light came on and Barton opened the front door a few inches and peered out, "Hadley, are you crazy? It's the middle of the night. Get the hell out of here before I call the cops."

"Go ahead and call them, you cowardly rapist, or get your yellow ass out here, before I kick that door open and drag it out here. Either way, being a spineless bastard is just making it worse for yourself."

Barton looked down at the pajama bottoms he was wearing, and suddenly couldn't think, the alcohol forming a cloud in his mind. He looked at the whiskey bottle in his hand and couldn't decide what to do with it, or where to set it. He finally lifted his head once again and addressed Steve. "Is this about, Dawn?"

"Is there somebody else you've raped tonight, Hackett?" Steve was screaming.

Barton shot a worried glance toward the stairs, but Nancy and the girls were not within earshot. Steve was seething and forced open the door, stepping inside.

Barton puffed out his chest indignantly, put his hands on his hips and commanded, "You get out of here this minute, or I'll press charges."

Steve grabbed the lapels of his bathrobe, twisted in the doorway, and threw Barton across the porch and out onto the front lawn. The whiskey bottle broke as Barton landed on it with his rump. He did not squeal or scream, but looked up at Steve in horrified surprise.

Steve was across the porch in two short strides, reclaimed his grip on Barton's lapels, and yanked him to his feet. He struck him the first four times with his right fist, while maintaining his grip with his left. The blows landed to Barton's cheek, jaw, and nose in rapid succession, bright red blood quickly appearing at Barton's left nostril in response.

"Why are you doing this?" Barton whimpered.

"Atonement, you once told me it was up to you to administer my lesson of atonement." Steve spoke gravely, "Tonight, Mr. Hackett, it is you who must learn the lesson of atonement." Steve wound up and landed an uppercut to Barton's unprotected, jiggling belly, then released him with a knee to his genitals, delivered with all the fury of his rage. Barton bounced back against the concrete of his front steps, a rib cracking as he landed and Barton screamed.

When she heard Barton's howl, Nancy rushed back to the upper bedroom window. "Oh my God," she gasped. She thought about phoning the police, but did not move. What was this about? She wondered.

She watched as Steve continued to pummel Barton without resistance, hauling him to his feet time after time, and then knocking him down with an assortment of furious blows. Until finally, Barton could no longer stand, his legs turning to wet noodles, and collapsing beneath him.

"Enough, enough," Barton tried to say, but the wind had been completely knocked from him.

"Don't go anywhere," Steve commanded and disappeared inside the maple door. He emerged less than two minutes later with one of Barton's finest cigars clenched between his teeth, the end glowing big and red. "This is for Dawn," he said, descending on the sprawling Barton, supporting himself with a knee on Barton's chest, "but let's not hide it, this is probably the only justice that she'll get." He pushed the lit end of the smoldering cigar squarely into the middle of Barton's forehead and Barton let out such a tremendous yowl that lights sprang on all over the neighborhood.

"You fucking asshole, you fucking asshole, you've burned me, you motherfucking asshole," Barton writhed in pain, shaking his head back and forth across the ground.

Steve looked down and saw what his anger had done. He fought back the feeling of regret that tried to rise within him, and tossed the cigar across the lawn. He increased the pressure of his knee into Barton's chest and stuck his finger in front of his face. "You so much as look at her cross-eyed, or say an unkind word to her and I'll be back."

He rose to a standing position and looked down at him. Barton remained motionless on the ground. Steve cast his eyes up to Nancy who was still standing in the bedroom window shaking. His face took on an expression she could only label as sympathetic when he saw her. He looked back down and then turned and walked back to his car. He drove away slowly, his rage and fury spent, and as the house disappeared from his rearview mirror, he began to tremble.

"What was that all about?" Nancy asked coming out the front door and bending over him.

"Just help me inside," Barton said, "you ask too many questions."

"We got to take you in to emergency and do something about that forehead, they could probably do something about that split lip too."

"I'm not going anywhere," he said harshly, as she helped him to his feet with a hand supporting his right armpit, " what's the use in being married to a nurse if she can't take care of me? You know how to treat a simple burn don't you?"

She sighed, "Let's get you to the couch and I'll look for something in the bathroom."

"If we don't have anything here, I'm sure you can go to work and find something."

"I'm sure I can." Business as usual, she thought.

Dawn stayed in the bathtub until the water turned cold, then added fresh hot water and stayed soaking until the water turned cold once again, before finally prying herself out. She stood naked before the mirror which covered the entire wall above the bathroom vanity, toweling herself dry like she had done thousands of times before, but this time she wondered if she would ever feel clean again.

Audra knocked, "Are you all right in there?"

"Just taking my time," answered Dawn, "sorry to worry you."

"Take all the time you need."

When Steve entered the house Audra was sitting at the kitchen table. She looked up at him, observed his bruised knuckles, but did not ask where he had been. In her heart she already knew the answer, and said a prayer of thanks that he had not been arrested.

"You ought to convince that girl to stay the night," she said, "she really shouldn't be left alone tonight."

"Have you talked to her about it?" He asked, "has she refused?"

"I haven't said anything, I'm not the boyfriend."

"And you think I am?"

"By the looks of things, you're a long way out on that limb for someone who's not."

"I'll talk to her."

She rose from the table. "Well, I'm going to check on her one more time, and then I'm going to bed, just come in and ask if she needs anything else."

"Good night, Mom," he said, and kissed her on the cheek, "and thank you."

Steve ran cold water over his knuckles in the kitchen sink, and watched the fog settle over the landscape out the window. He thought again of the cruelty he had inflicted, and wondered if, in the clear light of morning, he would think that he'd gone too far.

Dawn limped into the room, her movements exaggerated more by exhaustion than injury. She wore a matronly jogging suit Audra had found for her, purple with a green plaid caterpillar embroidered across the chest, her hair wrapped up in a towel atop her head.

"I've never seen you limp that bad, even that morning after you fell on my wet floor, is that from what he did to you?" he asked softly, turning off the water and drying his hands on a dish towel.

"I limp more when I get too tired, that's all," she sat down in the chair at the table vacated by Audra, "I just need some rest."

"Mom says you're welcome to stay."

"I know, she mentioned it when she stopped in the bathroom to say good night," she looked down at the gleam of the chandelier in the shine of the table top, "but I'd really rest better in my own bed, I think." Then she looked back up to him and into his blue eyes, "would you mind taking me home?"

"Whatever you want, Dawn."

The hum of the engine was the only sound as they rode along without conversation. Dawn stared out the side window into the darkness, trying to blank everything from her mind. Steve sat beside her and worried if agreeing to her plea to not involve the police had been the right thing to do.

Dawn's house was dark as Steve parked the car. He opened the car door for her and she pulled herself up using his forearm. He put a hand under her elbow as they walked toward the front door, but as they reached the front porch her leg gave way and she began to fall. He caught her on the way down, threw an arm under her knees, picking her up and carrying her the rest of the way.

She unlocked the front door still cradled in his arms. He carried her across the threshold and straight to the bedroom where he softly laid her down on the bed.

"You need anything?" he asked standing over her.

She shook her head, "No, I'm so tired I'm not even going to change, I'm just going to sleep."

He caressed the side of her face, and then kissed her on the forehead. "If you need anything, I'll be on the couch."

She nodded and he turned to leave. "Steve," she said softly, and he turned back to face her, "thank you."

He found a spare pillow without much investigation and the summer heat required no blanket. He laid out on the couch, stuck his hands behind his head, and looked up at the ceiling. From the bedroom he heard the sound of her soft, muffled weeping. He closed his eyes and his heart began to ache.

When Dawn woke to the sunlight streaming through the bedroom window, it seemed as though the night before had been nothing more than a bad dream, but only for an instant. She touched the burn beneath her chin and winced, and the reality of it all came crashing back upon her.

She knew she could stay away from work and no one would blame her. She knew that anyone who understood the story of what had happened to her would justify her taking the day off, indeed, they would probably justify her never returning to that place. But she was not about to give Barton that, he would have to face her, today and everyday, knowing what he had done to her, until she decided when it was time to move on.

She walked into the living room and saw Steve curled and asleep on the couch, his mouth hanging open, looking like a little boy. She bent over him and kissed him on the nose. His eyes snapped open and he smiled upon seeing her.

"Are you taking me to work?" she asked.

"We could make a habit of it if you'd like," he answered.

"What do you eat for breakfast?"

He smiled, his face reddened in embarrassment, and he looked at the floor, "my mom makes me oatmeal in the morning."

"Will you settle for toast until a can lay in a supply?"

He looked back up to her smile. "Anything will be fine."

Dawn watched Barton Hackett slither into the nursing home lobby, he kept his face lowered as if trying to pass through without notice. She saw the damage that had been inflicted upon him, and a small sense of justice or retribution began to gnaw against the mountain of anger inside her. Barton looked liked he had had the hell beat out of him, there was no hiding the truth. His bottom lip was swollen and split, the blood crusted. A welt decorated his cheekbone, his left eye blackened. A souvenir from Dawn's fingernails showed just above his shirt collar.

If it had been enough to heal her she would have smiled, for there was a certain pleasure in seeing him like that. She took particular pleasure in noting that he was limping. How unfortunate, she thought, that it would probably only last a day or two, what he had done to her would last her whole life. She felt like she wanted to step out in front of him as he crossed before her, just so he had to look her in the eye, but she could not make herself move.

The receptionists, the nurses, and his secretary all noticed, but none of them ventured a question. It was a combination of fear and genuine disinterest, seldom had there been a boss who was so universally loathed. The only one who worked for him who would have dared to venture a question was Nancy, but she already knew the answer to all the questions but one, the one answer she had not been able to get out of Barton was to the question "why?"

"Are you going to tell me why your boyfriend beat the hell out of my husband?" asked Nancy, walking up behind Dawn, joining the spectators to Barton's entrance.

"Is he my boyfriend?" returned Dawn coldly, without looking at her.

"Isn't he?"

"You'd have to ask him." Dawn watched Barton disappear into his office and close the door. She started to move down the hall to get back to work, but Nancy reached out and grabbed her arm.

"Dawn, don't play word games with me like we are kids or something, tell me, please," Nancy pleaded.

"You're going to have to ask Barton," said Dawn.

"I have asked him," she looked at he closed door to his office, "do you think I can get him to tell me anything if he doesn't really want to?"

"I can't help you, Nancy."

"You can't or won't?" She cast a critical eye.

"You act as if I was there."

"I know you weren't there, I could see the whole thing happening perfectly well out on the front lawn, but I couldn't hear a thing. Hadley showed up at the house yelling for Barton to come out, calling him all sorts of names. I told Barton to just call the police, but of course he didn't listen to me. He just walked around the house like a strutting peacock, told me to take care of the girls with his 'mind your own business' tone, then went to the front door and had the shit beat out of him."

Dawn's heart suddenly swelled at the vision the description provided.

"Not that I haven't wanted to do the same thing myself on occasion," Nancy continued. "I just couldn't help but think that somehow the whole thing was about you."

Dawn could not look her in the eye, and she could not lie to her, so she just stared at the floor in silence.

"I'm sure if I could be a fly on the wall when Barton tells Hadley that he's going to the judge to have his community service probation revoked and that Steve is going to have to serve out his sentence in jail, I'm sure then I'd learn everything."

Dawn lifted her face to her. "When he what?" she asked.

"When he has his probation revoked, you know good behavior clauses and all that," said Nancy matter-of-factly. "I know Barton, and I know he won't miss the chance to deliver the news in person. He gets some sick sense of pleasure from watching the pain his power can inflict on other people. I know it's true, and I hate it, but it's not like there's a damn thing I can do to change it." Nancy was looking at Dawn directly, searching for some kind of answer in her face. "What is that under your chin, little sister? Is that a burn, it looks like a burn?"

Dawn ignored Nancy's question about her face. "Barton gets beat up, so he gets Steve sent to jail without even having to file charges against him?"

"Yes, Barton's clever that way, he always sees the angle, the shortest distance to get to where he wants to be, or the result he wants to achieve. It's what makes him a great medical facility administrator."

"And a perfectly useless human being."

"You sound as if you're taking Steve's side in this," Nancy said, "to do that you must know what was behind the whole thing."

"Listen," said Dawn, "I didn't say I didn't know, I said you'd have to get it from Barton."

"But we're sisters."

"You'll have to get it from Barton, he's your husband."

Dawn could see the hurt in Nancy's eyes, but knew how much worse the truth would injure her.

"How can you do this to me?" said Nancy, yelling in every way but volume, "first, I lose my father because of you, now this."

Dawn was stunned by the reference to the past, how could her sister blame her for that?

"Don't ask your big sister for anything," Nancy continued, "in fact, you can just forget that you have one, and the next time your house burns down, call somebody else." She stomped away in anger, and Dawn had no words to change it.

Dawn turned her attention from watching Nancy waddle away to Barton's closed door. She approached it, then stood outside it, waiting, trying to decide whether or not to knock. Finally, she just twisted the knob and pushed it open.

Barton looked up with a startled expression on his face which fell quickly to something of a cross between anger and irritation. He had taken off his coat and hung it on the back of his chair. In his hand he held a small make-up mirror with which he had been examining his wounds.

Barton pulled open his top desk drawer, put the mirror into it, and banged it shut. "What do you mean barging in here without so much as a knock."

Dawn was speechless for a moment as she recognized, with a small measure of pleasure, that the wound in the middle of his forehead was a burn.

"Don't get that tone with me, Barton Hackett," Dawn said, righteous anger rising within her, "just be glad it isn't the police."

"The police? Why would they be here?"

Dawn was incredulous. "Don't play games with me, remember I'm the one you raped, you can play innocent with anyone else you please, but not with me."

"Rape? When two adults pleasure each other it isn't rape."

"Pleasure each other?" Dawn was doing all she could to keep from yelling. "And just what pleasure do you think I got from you raping me?"

"I wish you'd stop using that word."

"I'll keep using it, because that's exactly what it was, rape." She leaned toward him, placing two hands firm on the desk, "the main reason you're not in jail this morning is because of your two daughters."

"How's that?"

"I know what it's like to grow up without a father around, and I have no desire to see that happen to my nieces."

"Is that why you came in here this morning, to tell me you were forgiving me?"

"Who said anything about forgiveness?" said Dawn, "just because I'm not having you arrested doesn't mean that I've forgiven you. Besides that, I have yet to hear you ask for forgiveness."

"You said that my daughters were the main reason you weren't involving the police in our affair, is Nancy the other reason?"

"One of the other reasons," said Dawn, "but don't characterize your crime as an affair, when a woman says 'no' to you and you ignore her, and violently take advantage of her, it's rape. Why is that concept so hard for you to understand? I know you're not an ignorant man, why are you pretending to be so stupid about this?"

"Is that all? Or do you think this somehow grants you the privilege of talking to me any way you like?"

"No, that's not all, and yes, I think I can talk to a rapist without showing any trace of respect, especially since I have none."

"Well say what it is you have to say, and let's get on with it," Barton's impatience was showing.

"The other reason I'm not sending you to jail, is that I think Steve Hadley has extracted a small measure of justice from you on my behalf."

"Is that what you call it? 'Extracting justice?' I can't see where it has a thing to do with justice. He's a thug, and he's going to regret it."

"Nancy said you were talking about making trouble for Steve with the judge."

"That's exactly right, Hadley will have a nice stay behind bars to think about what he did to me last night." Barton began to smile, but then winced from the pain of his split lip.

"If you do," Dawn spoke sternly and businesslike, "you might as well reserve the cell right next to him for yourself, because I'll see that you get put there."

"What about your devotion to my daughters, Aunt Dawny?"

"Don't push it, Barton. If you go after Steve, then all deals are off."

"Is it love that I'm hearing?"

"What it is between Steve and I is of no concern to you?"

"What does he think about getting seconds? I won't say sloppy seconds, but seconds never-the-less."

She slowly walked around the desk. He swiveled in his chair to face her. She hauled her arm back and swung at him with all her might. The blow landed with such an impact that she wondered for a split second if it was heard outside of his closed office.

"Ow, Jesus, Dawn, can't you stand a little kidding?" The slap had reopened the split in his lower lip and he fished in his pants pocket for his handkerchief.

"You're a perverted criminal, there's nothing to joke about."

"You never had much of a sense of humor anyway, as I remember it."

"I'm not joking, if you mess with Steve, I'm messing with you."

"You could never prove a thing, it's your word against mine."

"You sound as if you have experience at this kind of thing. I don't, but what I do know is that if I file a complaint against you, they'll arrest you, and we'll have a trial, and your lawyer can try to denigrate me all he wants to, and you can say to the jury that it's my word against yours, but what do you think your board of directors is going to be doing and thinking while we have this little trial to see who is believed?"

Barton did not answer right away, as he sat mulling over his options. "All right," was all he managed.

"You'll have to do better than that," admonished Dawn.

"All right, I won't do anything to Hadley, let's just put this all behind us." He shook his head and looked down at his desk.

"I don't think I'm ready to put this behind me, I think I'll be carrying the memory of last night with me forever. You've given me a nightmare from which I'll never wake, don't you understand that?"

"We can make better memories to replace last night, you just have to show a little cooperation."

Dawn's rage flamed anew.

"Listen, you arrogant bastard, get this straight once and for all. I love my sister, and my two little nieces, so I'm not inclined to send their daddy to prison, but if you so much as breathe on me again, I'll cut your balls off while you sleep and feed them to the dog."

Dawn walked to the door of his office and put her hand on the knob, and then turned back to him. "You know I am inexperienced about sex, I told you I was a virgin, do you remember?"

"Yes." He did not think he was admitting too much by agreeing to that, but wondered where this was leading.

"So, being so inexperienced, I'm curious," she hesitated for effect, as he raised his eyes to meet hers, "are all penises that small?" She did not wait for his answer, but held onto the vision of his shocked expression as she made her way back to work.

It was well past two in the afternoon before Steve and Dawn's paths crossed in Moses' room. Dawn and Moses were engrossed in conversation as Steve entered with a concerned look in his eyes.

"You know we didn't bring it up the other day," said Dawn, "but we found out about you on our trip to Grand Rapids."

Moses noticed some type of swollen sore under Dawn's chin, but did not ask about it. He thought the rest of her face was quite fresh and alive. He thought also that her recently adopted practice of wearing makeup made her even more attractive, this he also noted without comment.

"And just what did you find out about me that you didn't already know?" Moses asked.

"We found out you were famous," said Steve.

"You have a painting hanging in the art museum," said Dawn.

Moses laughed as he watched the two of them. "My real claim to fame," he said, "is that I was once married to the most beautiful girl in the world. I could sit for hours on end and just look at her and wonder how I ever got so lucky that she chose me to be the one she was spending her life with. After I lost her, I was bitter for a long, long time. How could the world, or God, or fate be so cruel as to take something so precious from me? I had what I wanted, what other men only dreamed of, and then my life with her was gone, as if that's all it was, just a dream. But gradually the bitterness seeped out of me, and what replaced it was gratitude. I was grateful for just having the privilege of having shared time with Sarah, no matter how short the time was. I learned that it's like going on vacation to some perfect little piece of paradise, when it's over you have to go home, and you can either be angry about it or cherish the memories. Now I cherish the memories of my life with her, and my only regret is that I didn't realize at the time that all you have is the moment, if you live your life like there's always tomorrow, to do what you want to do, to spend time with the people you love, to say the things you long to say, then you're only fooling yourself."

Steve watched the twinkle in his eyes in silence. "When you find that one who means the world to you," Moses continued, "cherish every moment of every day you get to spend with her, and when that day is done, and it's time to close your eyes for a night of rest, pray to God that he gives you another day to spend with her. And in the morning when you find that he has said 'yes' to your prayer, give a prayer of thanks, because the day will come, and you will not know whether it is sooner or later, but whenever it comes it will be sooner than you'd have wanted, the day will come when the answer is 'no'."

"I can see how that would go for your painting as well," said Steve.

"Certainly," replied Moses, "anything that means anything. What if I would have waited until I was eighty-three to start painting, then where would I be?"

"Then there wouldn't be a painting with your signature on it hanging in the art museum," said Steve.

"And I would have missed a whole lifetime of doing the thing that I love."

When Dawn walked out the back door of Pioneer Manor after working another double shift, Steve was waiting for her.

"Are you my protector now or what?" she asked.

"If the job's not already taken," he said quietly.

She did not answer, she only looked into his blue eyes.

"You didn't tell him," said Steve.

"Moses?" she asked. He nodded. "About Barton?"

He nodded again. "He's like your Grandfather, and now you're keeping secrets from him?"

"He loves me," she said softly, "I know that, what do you think it would do to him if he knew? You and I can go home at night, Moses has to live with those people, why make it any harder for him than it already is?"

"I'm going to break him out," he said, "it's the right thing to do, but I could really use your help."

The night was cold, the stars bright. He was filled with the smell of her perfume as he wrapped his jacket around her shivering shoulders.

He waited for her protest, but "How?" was all she asked.

"Barton gave us the way in his lecture."

"A bomb threat?"

"Exactly."

The plan was simple enough, simple enough in theory. On paper everything looks easy. Steve would call in a bomb threat to the nursing home from a nearby public phone and drive an anonymous vehicle to the staff parking lot where he would pick up Moses and Dawn after they had evacuated the building. Dawn and Steve would load Moses up in the midst of the confusion and drive away.

It's in the details where things began to get sticky.

"We have to plan alibis for ourselves," said Dawn, "if Moses came up missing while in my care, I'll be held responsible."

"Good point," said Steve, "I'm already glad that you're my partner in crime."

"And if you're at the beach with Moses when you are supposed to be at work, you could be held in contempt of court."

"You're right." All that had to be worked out, the right day in the schedule and the right time of the right day.

The evacuation order would have to come right after Dawn punched out at three o'clock, but before she left the building, and both of them should be scheduled off the day following. When Steve realized that Dawn still had a key to Nancy and Barton's house, he wanted to give the plan one final, perfect twist. The bomb threat should be called in from Barton's house.

They discussed, and debated the plan like they were an old married couple planning next month's budget. She especially liked Steve's last final twist. "You're quite a clever fellow, when you put your mind to it," she said. "Just think what you could do, if you put your mind to something serious."

His smile faded from his lips, "This is serious."

"I mean . . . oh, you know what I mean."

"Something serious like being in love with a dark-haired woman?"

She sighed, "no, that's not what I was talking about."

"Oh, so I should go looking for a blond?"

She hit him softly on the shoulder, "I'll poke out your eyes if you do."

He wrapped her in his arms and kissed her. "How can I go looking for somebody else when I can't take my eyes off of you?"

THIRTEEN

Light frost lay on the grass of early autumn when Moses Bailey finally rode his Harley-Davidson back into Sutton's Bay. As he came into town on St. Joseph Avenue he noticed someone walking toward him, someone familiar, yet out of place in this time and in this place. He looked, and looked again in disbelief, it was Sarah. She wore an old pair of denims and hiking boots, her hair pulled back in a ponytail under a blue stocking cap. The city girl had been left far behind. "Hello, Sugar Mo," she said with practiced calm. She had been rehearsing this scene every morning for the last nine months.

"Hello, Sugar Mo?" he exclaimed, "That's what you say? You walk out of my dreams and into my hometown and you say simply 'hello'?"

"Welcome home," she added.

He showed a grin inside five days of whiskers. "OK, what are you doing here?" he insisted.

"I'm on my way to work, we're expecting a big breakfast crowd this morning."

"Work?" He shut off his motorcycle and parked it. "What? Where?"

"I work for Bill at the Bayside Grill, I'm the head waitress."

"Bill only has one waitress."

"Oh, so you don't have amnesia after all?"

"Amnesia? What?"

"I was just telling your mother yesterday that I thought you had forgotten where you live."

"My mother? You know my mother?"

"Why yes, in fact I count her as one of my closest friends." She smiled.

"You're enjoying this far too much," he said, grabbing her by the arms, "tell me what's going on, where's that husband of yours and what the hell are you doing here."

"First of all, I don't have a husband," she looked him in the eye, "and second of all don't hold me like this unless you're going to kiss me."

"What?" he was dumbfounded.

"Did they speak a foreign language on that boat?"

"Ship, it was a ship."

"Well did they?"

He pulled her to him and placed his mouth on hers and tasted her like a thirsty man in the desert, all the loneliness and aching pouring out of him.

She threw her arms around him and buried her face in his chest, it was not a day for tears, she did not want him to see her cry, at least not today.

They stayed that way for a long, silent moment, the wind was but a gentle breeze off the bay, and the color had just begun to show itself in the trees. There are moments of perfection that we would like to frame and mount on the wall so we could go back and visit them when ever we wanted, this was one for Sarah and Moses, when they both wondered, in that instant, if life could get any better.

"Come on in and let me serve you one of Bill's breakfasts," she said finally, looking up into his face, both of her arms wrapped around one of his.

"I'd rather have you to myself," he said wishfully.

"Let me help Bill get through breakfast, he'll understand that I'm taking the rest of the day off after that."

"How about the rest of the week?"

She smiled, and they entered the restaurant with her on his arm. When he saw them, Bill broke into a big grin, revealing his missing tooth. "All shall come to him who waits," said Bill, "or her as the case may be."

Moses slid into the booth by the back window where he had always sat so he could look out at the water, but it was not the water on which he fixed his gaze that morning. How he loved to watch that girl move, to see the delicate curve of her cheek, and caress her soft skin with his eyes.

"You really don't have to do this," Bill said as Sarah tied up her apron in the kitchen doorway.

"How would I ever show my face again in Sutton's Bay if I skipped out on Bill Malone?" she said with a joyous lilt.

"No, really," he got a more serious tone, "if I'd been waiting for nine months for something I didn't even know would ever really happen and then it finally happened, well I think I'd . . ."

"So I take it that it would be OK if I took off after the breakfast rush?"

He chuckled, "Whatever you want, darling. It's just good to see you happy."

Moses finished his breakfast and sat drinking coffee as he watched Sarah expertly handle all the tables in the small little restaurant, getting all the customers their food as soon as it was hot and ready, while maintaining the conversations at each booth without missing a beat. He marveled at her. All that talent in that trim little package, he thought, she could probably do just about anything she put her mind to.

Outside, Moses stomped on his motorcycle and it roared its response, "You want a ride, lady?" he asked.

"Well, I am very used to walking, but I guess I won't get a wide bottom from riding just this once." Somehow he could not see her getting a wide bottom ever. She climbed onto the seat behind him and wrapped her arms around him. She had never been on a motorcycle before, but it seemed like the most natural thing in the world for her to move her body with his, leaning into the curves, totally trusting his every turn. The Harley-Davidson moved smoothly through the streets of Suttons Bay and out into the countryside. Moses could feel her body pressed tight to the small of his back, her arms coiled about him. He inhaled the freshness of the day.

She laid her cheek against his back, closing her eyes. She slipped her hand under his shirt and rubbed his chest. This was the way it was meant to be, he thought, him and Sarah, and the motorcycle humming down the road out in front of them on a bright autumn morning, taking them home to a future he never thought would be, that he had long ago decided would never come, a prayer that would never be answered.

Sarah was trying to say something in his ear as they approached the orchard, but he couldn't hear her over the sound of the wind and the engine. He turned back for an instant to look at her; and she was half smiling with a warm loving look in her eyes. He pulled to a stop at the front porch and turned off the motorcycle.

"Were you trying to say something to me?" he asked.

"Does your mother know you're home?"

"We'll go see her tomorrow."

He got off the bike and headed toward the front door, a gust of wind brought the smell of burning leaves from the north. As he pulled the key from his pocket, he noticed that his hands were shaking.

Inside, Sarah pulled off her stocking cap and threw her coat over a chair. It struck him how apparently at ease she felt in his home. She turned around to face him and took a deep breath, "I could use a drink," she said, "something with alcohol in it."

He wondered if this meant she was having second thoughts about where she was, and what she was doing, and what she was about to do. "I could take you home if you want," he offered.

"Sugar Mo," she smiled, and brushed some loose strands of hair from her face, "I am home."

He did not fully understand at that point, but he liked the sound of it. She pulled off the band from around her ponytail and shook her head, letting her hair fall loose around her shoulders. She walked over to a group of his paintings and ran her finger down the edge of the frame that she had just put on it. He saw his paintings arranged and displayed almost as if they were in a gallery, this was something he had never done, how had this happened in his home? And it dawned on him, finally and completely, and he smiled. Yes, yes, yes, he thought, she was at home.

A floppy-eared puppy of various breeds scampered from the bedroom and came sliding to a halt in front of Moses.

He bent down and stroked its little forehead. "And who is this?" he asked.

"Mutiny," Sarah grinned, "his name is Mutiny."

She poured two glasses of Chardonnay and handed one to Moses, "What shall we drink to this time?" she asked.

"To perfect moments," he touched his glass to hers, "and time standing still."

"Oh, you don't want time standing still," she quipped.

"I don't?"

"No, if it did we would never get to what I have planned for the rest of the day."

"And what is that?"

"In a minute, my wandering young man," she tipped her glass and took a serious drink of her wine. She looked at him and then out the window, in it she saw her reflection, was it really her here, or was it still just a dream? "It seems very strange, Sugar Mo, after all the waiting, after all the nights of fantasy, after all the daydreams . . ."

"It is a dream, my love, a dream come true." Moses Bailey would always remember how she looked that day in that converted barn, in the middle of a cherry orchard on the outskirts of Sutton's Bay, staring out at the autumn afternoon.

She looked from the window over to him, her gray eyes still soft, near weeping. "It's been a long time," she said, "I'm a little shaky."

He stepped over to her, wrapped her in his arms and kissed her on the forehead. "How long has it been since I told you that I love you?"

"Too long." She looked up at him and touched his face with her hands, loving him, and regretting all the time together they had missed. She was unhurried as she unbuttoned his shirt and kissed his chest.

"Well then, for the record," he took her hand and led her over to the bed, sitting down on it before her, looking up into her face, "I love you." He unfastened her denims and slid them from her hips, letting them fall to the floor. She took off her blouse and let it fall on top of them. He helped her off with the rest and she stood before him naked, vulnerable, and totally beautiful.

Her gaze stayed riveted, her eyes to his, but he saw a small smile sneak its way onto her lips. She ran her hand through his hair, her fingertips lightly dancing across his cheek, "I love you, too." It felt so good to be able to confess that to the only one who mattered to hear it.

He lay back on the bed, holding on to her hand, looking up at her, cherishing the moment, almost afraid to let go, afraid that if he did the dream might vanish.

"I seem to remember, if things are going to work out for the best, it's necessary to take these off," she said, and helped him off with his pants with a tug, and climbed onto the bed straddling him with her knees, her dark blond hair cascading down upon his face.

They played and giggled and rolled on the bed like they had done this a hundred times. Moses paused and looked down at her, at the blood pulsing at her throat, at her gray eyes widening as she took all of him, first looking at him and then at the ceiling as she arched her breasts and belly toward him.

She led him into a sensual place where, he would have to admit, he hadn't traveled before. A question sprang into his mind, and then he doubted that she had gone to this place, this paradise, with Doyle either, maybe this was something new for both of them. But there was something, something about the way she was completely at ease with her nakedness as she moved freely and uninhibited underneath him and with him. He touched her with hands that were tender and tentative, and she answered with a mouth that was probing and hungry.

"Give me all of you," she whispered, and he did, and in so doing let go of all the fear. A scream of pleasure caught in her throat as she felt the swell of his pulse, and the crash of the release and she did not know if it was her or him or both, and she smiled because she did not know. With soft, flickering kisses against his neck she said, "It was worth the wait."

"It's easy to say that now," he sighed, "just tell me I'll never have to do it again."

She propped herself up on an elbow. "Sugar Mo, you'll have to wait," she said.

"What? Why?"

"Cause you've worked up a powerful appetite in this girl, and you'll have to wait until after I have something to eat."

"I have so much to learn about you," he said, "like what do you like to eat at times like these."

"There's never been a time like this," she smiled, "but I was thinking about tuna fish sandwiches with lots of onions and potato chips, how's that for quirky?" she asked.

"With or without wine?"

"With of course."

"Just quirky enough."

She leaned over and kissed him, "To the kitchen, you chop the onions, I'll get the tuna." She bounced out of the bed.

"Do we have to get dressed?" he asked, "I love to see you naked."

"That would be wasted effort considering what I have in mind for dessert."

Steve and Dawn had come to call it "The Great Escape," and on the morning in question, Dawn looked through her closet, paging through her uniforms as if they were designer evening wear, decisions, decisions. White, white, and more white, a vision of a wedding gown popped into her head, from where she did not know. She smiled and sang, in fact, she felt like dancing, if only she could, she thought. The sun was bright and cheery as it glowed through the peach and yellow curtains of her apartment. She should be nervous. After all, wasn't she about to risk her whole career on this scheme to grant Moses one last wish? She should have been nervous, she knew that, but for some reason she wasn't. Was it simple naiveté? Was it confidence in that what she was doing was right? Or was it love? A belief that Steve would make everything turn out all right?

The phone rang. "Are you ready? Are you excited?" said Steve's voice on the other end of the line.

"Now don't start with me, I've got to work a whole shift as if it was just another day, don't call me and try to get me all worked up."

"I get worked up every time I think of you."

"All right, enough of that, we have to keep our minds on the mission, as they say."

"Who says that?"

"Are you always this difficult?"

"Just when the pressure's on."

"I've got to go, this would be no day to be late and draw attention to myself."

"See you this afternoon." She heard him click off. How she looked forward to seeing him. She floated out the door, across the porch and out to her car. She adjusted the radio and then pulled her car out into traffic and headed for the nursing home. Her head was swimming with a hundred thoughts, of Moses, of the escape plan, of Steve, and of the future, their future together.

All through the day she kept checking the clock, but the hours seemed to drag. She could see the anticipation in Moses' face every time she passed his room. At long last the count down was inside an hour.

As Dawn passed the main nurses' station near the front entrance Nancy called to her, "Dawn, any plans after work?" Dawn wanted to get one jump ahead, but wondered which direction this conversation was headed. Was Nancy about to ask her to work overtime? Or was she just being a sister? It was so hard to tell with her. Why did she have to pick this day, and this time, to start being civil again? Or was she up to something else, had they been found out already?

"I have to stop at the grocery store on the way home," Dawn lied, "I'm just about out of everything."

"Nancy, I've got to run home," it was Barton's voice as he emerged from his office, "I'll be back in an hour." He looked at Dawn as he spoke, a look of contempt in his eyes. He was headed home? Dawn looked at the clock, and her stomach began to dance with nervous butterflies, as she knew Steve and Barton would be arriving at the house at just about the same time. Warn Steve? Delay Barton? She thought fast and hard.

"Heading home for a nap in the middle of the afternoon, Mr. Hackett?" Dawn spoke off the top of her head, trying to engage him.

"Humph," he grunted, and turned his back to her as he made his way toward the door.

"Does the Board of Directors know you do this kind of thing?" She persisted.

"Dawn!" said Nancy in surprise, "don't forget who's the boss around here. You can only count on the family thing so far."

Barton still had not stopped or turned around. "I don't think Barton thinks of me as family, do you Barton?" she called after him.

"Listen Miss McNally, I'm headed home to pick up some papers for the very Board of Directors you have referred to, if it's any of your affair, and if you'd like to inform them that I've gone after them, please feel free to do so," he was seething, "but do it on your own time." He turned and strutted out, before she could think of a reply to keep him.

Steve drove east along the tree-lined Jefferson Street and slowed and then stopped in front of the brass numbers 665. Barton and Nancy's house stood large, silent, and daunting in the hot afternoon sun. He climbed out of the car and stood facing the house, perspiration covered the key in his palm. He knew right then that he did not have the temperament of a burglar. He looked around the neighborhood nervously, the street, the sidewalk, and the meticulously manicured lawns were all empty. He breathed a sigh of relief and lowered his head lest anyone should be watching from a window.

He followed the paving stones from the driveway, across the rear yard to the back door and let himself in with swift fluid motions. The lack of awkward fumbling surprised him. A golden cocker spaniel came like a bullet through the kitchen, Steve was ready for it to start barking, but instead it started ferociously licking his ankles. "Good puppy," he said as he shuffled toward the phone on the kitchen counter. The kitchen was white on white, white laminated cabinetry over white counter tops, surrounding a white tile floor. The phone sat on a bar height peninsula which jutted out from the wall surround by high stools.

He dialed the emergency services number he had memorized and disguised his voice. "There's a bomb at the Pioneer Manor Nursing Home set to blow in less than an hour." He hung up. Did he really just do that? There were times in his life that seemed as if he was dreaming them or reading them in a book and this suddenly became one of those times.

Just as he had begun this self analysis, the dog let go of his ankle, and began yipping as it made a beeline for the front door. Steve heard the rattle of keys, the hinges creak, and the front door swing open. "Quiet down, quiet." It was Barton's voice. Steve shot a glance at the back door, too far away and too late to think about it. He ducked down behind the snack bar, between two barstools, just as Barton entered the kitchen. Steve tried not to breathe, he heard him open the refrigerator and pull something out of it. It sounded like a glass container as he plunked it on the countertop, inches from Steve's head.

Barton picked up the phone and dialed. "Kathy, baby, it's me." Barton cooed, "can I see you this afternoon? What's that? Well of course I'm married, so are you," Steve could tell the voice on the other end was excited, animated, and not particularly friendly. "Everything will work out, you'll see. No, really, I'll explain everything in a little while. Yes, yes, I know you do. Kisses." Barton hung up the phone, scraped whatever it was off the countertop and stomped off through the house like a man on a mission.

Now was his chance, thought Steve. He tried to imitate some indian he had once seen in a John Wayne movie as he crept silently toward the back door, but the image that kept jumping into his head was that of Peter Pan, who can explain such things? The door gave out a small clack as it closed behind him. He looked through the glass in the door to see if the sound had been noticed by the dog or otherwise, and then hurried around the side of the house opposite the driveway and back out to the street. He tripped on a juniper, landing on one knee. He checked the grass stain on the knee of his pants and kept moving all in the same motion.

Barton saw a flash of motion outside his study window. Damn pigeons again, he thought, if he had a gun he was just in the proper mood to blast them all to kingdom come. No gun, damn it, maybe he should stop and buy one, but no, he had something much more pleasurable planned for that afternoon. While the world thought he was at a meeting with the Board of Directors, he was going to be having a meeting of a completely different kind. Was it too early in the day to have a drink? He did have vodka in the house.

Barton reached for the red labeled bottle and pulled down a glass from the sideboard as Steve pulled away from the curb in his parent's maroon van.

Dawn had punched out and said her usual good-byes to Nancy, One-eyed George, and the girls in the south wing, then ducked into Moses room to wait for the announcement to come over the intercom.

"I don't know how long it's been since I've had an adventure," smiled Moses.

"Well, you're not wiggling your toes in the sand, yet," said Dawn, "we have to get there first."

"I have confidence in you two," winked Moses, "this place is no match for two bright kids like you."

"Attention all staff, attention all staff," it was Nancy's voice booming over the intercom, "we have a condition blue, I repeat, condition blue, this is not a drill, please institute immediate evacuation procedures. All patients should not panic, but calmly follow all instructions of the staff members in their area."

"Time to go," said Moses with the jubilation of a small child, as he jumped into his wheel chair.

Barton would have been proud of the way his staff followed evacuation procedures to the letter, and all of this without so much as a rehearsal or drill. It was obvious that someone had been listening when he had given his lecture.

Dawn lowered her head and steadily wheeled Moses in his chair toward the staff parking lot. From her lowered squint she saw Nancy pass down the intersecting corridor as they approached. She had not even looked their way and Dawn took a deep breath and increased her pace. "Now were cooking," said Moses, "let's put this baby in gear."

Barton coming home had put Steve behind schedule, he tapped on the dashboard trying to quicken the pace, searching the radio for something that would either speed the wheels or slow the time. He tried to make up the lost time, but it would have been easier in his Mustang. He turned onto Riverside Drive, a cloud of smoky exhaust trailing behind him announcing to all the world that he was asking the van to do things it wasn't accustomed to.

Fear struck through him like a flash of lightning when he looked up in his rearview mirror and saw the blue and red flashing bubbles on top of the black and white police cruiser. It was over, he thought, "prison, I wonder if she'll come and visit me in prison?" They hadn't talked about that.

He pulled to the side of the road, stopped the van, and turned it off. He watched in the mirror as the young cop approached, one hand adjusting his dark glasses, the other on the heel of the weapon protruding from the holster on his hip.

"Where's the fire?" asked the officer.

"The what?" Steve responded.

"Do you know how fast you were going?"

Could he be this lucky, just speeding? "Ah, no, too fast?"

"I'd say so, about thirty miles an hour too fast."

"I was just trying to blow some of the carbon out of this old thing."

The officer shook his head, "You don't do that on city streets. License and registration please." Steve pulled the wallet from his pocket, now the jig was up, he was sure, as soon as he called in his name he would find that there was a warrant out for his arrest. Could they know so soon? How? An argument raged in his head as he handed the officer his license and the registration from the glove compartment. He thought of Dawn, pacing the parking lot with Moses in his wheelchair, probably cursing his name. That would just be the topper for the day, prison, and Dawn would hate him.

The officer came back to his window and handed him back his documents along with a speeding ticket, "I just wrote you up for ten over, I was young once myself."

"Thank you, sir." He tried to suppress a smile.

"You can thank me by watching your speed."

"I will, sir, have a good day." He restarted the van, checked the patrol car in his mirror, and puttered back onto the road. Dawn's going to kill me, he thought.

When he pulled into the staff parking lot, Dawn and Moses were nowhere to be seen. He cruised slowly up past the building, his eyes scanning the crowd of staff and patients milling around, but Dawn and Moses were not there. He reached the end of the pavement and turned back toward the street, wondering if he should make another pass or go around to the front of the building. Had something gone wrong? Had one of them misunderstood the plan?

A figure in white stepped out from behind a mammoth oak tree on the edge of the pavement. He stopped the van and looked, and looked again. It was Dawn, and she was not happy. He threw the vehicle in park, and bolted out of his seat and around the front to her.

"Where the hell have you been?" She was struggling with Moses' wheelchair, pushing it through the grass.

Steve took the handles and wheeled it toward the vehicle. "Long story, get the door."

"I told you he'd come," said Moses, "didn't I tell you he'd be here?"

"You doubted me?" asked Steve, looking into her eyes.

How could she admit it when he looked at her with those blue eyes like that? "I doubt if you'll be on time for your own funeral," she snapped.

They lifted Moses into the side door of the van, folded his wheelchair, and threw it in the back. Dawn kept one worried eye on the activity over by the building.

"No cops yet?" asked Steve.

"They're like flies out front," said Moses. "Our plan's working like a charm so far."

"Right," Steve couldn't help but smile, "get in pretty lady, we've got a date for a picnic at the beach." She climbed in and he closed the door after her. "Keep your heads down, both of you, until we get away from here." She ducked down, Moses strained to see all that he could see, and Steve drove calmly, as if they had no particular place to go.

Steve turned the van out onto the highway and headed north, gently increasing the pressure on the accelerator.

"Can I get up now?" asked Dawn from her crouch between the dashboard and the seat.

"Can you be nice?" Steve smiled down at her.

"I'll give you nice," she said, popping up and adjusting her hair with her hand.

They were on their way, talking, joking, and laughing, the three of them, like school children on a field trip. Dawn's heart was racing, she had never done anything like this in her life. She looked at Steve, her smile unsuppressed, surprisingly understanding the prankster within him.

Then, with a quick, sharp, suddenness, they heard a loud pop, and the car lurched frantically to the right.

"Oh shit," Steve grabbed the wheel, became quickly serious, trying to regain control of the van and pulled it to a stop on the shoulder of the road. They sat gasping for breath, as heavy traffic swished past them. The car leaned dramatically downhill toward the shoulder of the road. Steve got out and walked around the car to the passenger side. He threw up his hands and looked to the sky.

Dawn rolled down her window, "What's wrong?"

"Flat tire. Hand me the keys, babe."

It was the first time he had ever used any term of endearment when addressing her and it made her feel soft and warm inside. She suppressed the smile that was trying to force its way to her lips, reached over and pulled the keys from the ignition, and handed them to him. He popped the trunk and she could hear him cursing.

"That sounds bad," said Moses. This was already becoming more of an adventure than he had imagined, and more excitement than he had had in years.

"No spare," said Steve coming back alongside the window.

"Now what?" she asked.

"We flag somebody down and go buy a tire, I guess, except I only have nine dollars left after picking up the picnic."

"That's OK, I'll write a check." Dawn looked beside her in the seat, then looked into the backseat beside Moses.

"Don't look at me," Moses said, "I can't remember the last time they let me have any money."

"Steve, have you seen my purse?"

"Ah, no, now that you mention it, I haven't."

"I forgot my purse," she threw herself back against the seat, "I can't believe it."

Steve turned and slumped against the front fender, he did not want this to happen with Dawn, he felt like such a child, trapped in a situation over which he had no control. What kind of man was he going to make for her if he got himself into situations he couldn't handle? If there was a word for this feeling that went far beyond embarrassment, he did not know the name of it.

A yellow emergency light flashed behind them, the sound of an air brake and the rumble of a diesel engine filled the air. Steve saw a large wrecker parking behind them. He heard the door close and out of the glare stepped a big man with a full, salt and pepper beard, and a blue Detroit Tigers baseball cap on his head with an upturned brim. "Having trouble?"

"We got a flat on the passenger side front," said Steve, hiding his shame.

"Got a spare, kid?" asked the gruff voiced stranger.

"No," Steve simply replied.

"Nobody taught you to check your spare before you go out on the highway?" he chuckled. The sign on the side of the truck read "Sam's Towing', 'Good Samaritan Towing', is the way Sam thought of it. Good Samaritan at a price.

"Did you just stop to laugh at us?" Dawn asked out the window.

"No, ma'am, I just stopped to help," he replied, "that's what I do, help people."

He climbed back up in his rig and pulled it in front of the disabled van, backing up to align it for towing. As he operated the hoist and prepared to lift the van, Steve confessed, "we have no money."

Sam continued with his work. "I'll haul you into the garage and we can work it out there, where you kids from?"

"Evergreen."

"That's not far," said Sam looking Steve square in the eye, "can I trust you?"

"You get us back on the road, I guarantee I'll make it right by you," said Steve.

"I can extend you credit on a tire until Monday," he said.

Sam did not even notice Moses until Dawn and Steve helped him out of the van and boosted him into the cab of the tow truck. "This your Grandpa?" asked Sam.

"Yep," said Moses answering for them.

The three of them arranged themselves in the cab with Sam, and he checked his mirrors and pulled out into traffic.

"Where the three of you headed, anyway?" asked Sam, shifting gears.

"Macatawa," said Steve, "just a picnic on the beach."

"Wonderful day for it," said Sam.

"Yo, Sam," the radio on the dashboard spoke.

Sam picked up the microphone, gave a futile attempt at unraveling the twisted cord with one hand, "go ahead, that you Perkins?"

"Yeah, Sam, just went past your place, that car's parked out in front again."

"You sure?"

"Same Cadillac as last night, same Cadillac as last week."

"That whore." Sam's face turned violet with anger, he downshifted violently and crammed the accelerator to the floor, the truck responding first with a groan, then quickly transcending into a whine.

Steve looked back to see his parents' van swaying back and forth behind the speeding wrecker. Sam snarled, cursing under his breath, and pulled out to pass a station wagon with two Dalmatians barking in the back window.

"Please, Sam, slow down," pleaded Dawn.

The truck and the van flew over a small crest in the road, throwing off sparks as they landed. "That's my mother's van," repeated Steve.

Dawn's face was worried, Steve was growing angry, and Moses grinned.

As Sam reached the outskirts of the little town of Hamilton, he reached across Dawn and opened the glove box, pulling out a revolver. "What's that?" cried Dawn.

"It's a gun," said Moses in amazement.

Sam swung off the highway, turning down a side street, his eyes were intense, his mind focused, blocking out anything and everything his passengers were doing or saying. The silver smoke stack running up the side of the cab spewed exhaust like a fire-breathing dragon as Sam weaved the rig around parked cars as they entered what had been a peaceful, residential neighborhood. The tow truck jumped a curb and took the full measure of two garbage cans standing sentry at the end of a driveway. Sam jammed on the brakes, and the mass of machinery came to a halt with a mixture of squeals and groans in front of a pink cape cod house.

"This is better than an amusement park," smiled Moses.

Sam did not wait for discussion, he checked his gun, threw open the door , and climbed down from the truck. There was the sound of a woman's laughter coming from inside the house. Sam crossed in front of the truck, climbed the front porch steps two at a time, and kicked open the door with a single violent stroke of his meaty leg.

"What's going on in there?" Steve wondered aloud. Suddenly, two shots rang out, and then the glass of the front window of the house burst from a man, who was not Sam, being thrown through it.

"I'm going to kill him!" They could hear Sam yell. The other man stopped on the porch only long enough to pull his pants up from around his ankles. In the darkness and shadows Dawn thought she recognized him, could it be? It looked like Barton.

"Is that guy pulling up his pants that asshole Hackett?" Moses asked.

"You're kidding," said Steve.

"I think it is," confirmed Dawn.

Another shot rang out, coming from inside the house this time, shattering the windshield of the truck.

"Holy shhh. . . ." Began Steve, then, "out, out, everybody out," he threw open the driver's side door, "come on Moses give me your hand." Moses struggled to hurry out of the cab, and Steve had to nearly pick him up and carry him. "Can you stand here for a minute?" Steve asked Moses.

Moses nodded and took a deep breath, his smile was gone.

Sam climbed through the broken house window and let loose another shot; this one splattered the side mirror of the van.

"Quick into that car," commanded Steve. He threw open the back door of a navy blue Cadillac, and Dawn scampered in; he lifted Moses inside, and climbed in after him. "Lock the doors."

The other man ran frantically to the Cadillac, and the three of them could see clearly now, it was indeed Barton, his face flushed and terrified, "Get out of my car, unlock the door, get out of my car," he screamed. He began banging on the window with his fists.

Dawn let out a shriek as a head popped up in the front seat. It was the head of a young black man with dreadlocks; his face bore the expression of a man who had been disturbed in his work. In his hands were wires coming from under the dashboard, he finished making the connections with a last twist of the wires. A small spark flashed, and the engine cranked to life. The young man threw the car into gear and stomped on the accelerator, just as Sam caught up with Barton who was desperately banging on the window. Steve looked back to see Sam throw aside his gun and lay into Baton with his bare fists.

"Thank you, sir," Dawn said to the young black man behind the wheel. He did not reply immediately. "We are so lucky you happened to be there just now, thank you so much."

"Dawn," said Moses. "Dawn?"

"What?"

"He's a car thief. Am I right sir?"

"Oh," her breath seeped out of her and she sank down in the seat.

"Sir, if you could just be so kind as to pull over at the next corner and let us out, we'll be no further trouble to you," said Steve.

"The problem with that is the three of you just witnessed me stealing this here car, I'm not used to having no witnesses, sounds like a bad idea to me," he replied with a grimace.

They rode along in silence; they could sense the wheels turning in the young black man's mind.

"Well what are you going to do with us?" Dawn asked finally. "Kill us? Sell us on the white slave market?"

He rolled his eyes, now the girl was into it, he thought.

"I'm guessing our car thief here is a specialist," said Moses, "what he does is steal cars, and he does it very well, I'm guessing. I don't think murder is part of his repertoire, am I right, sir?"

"I ain't no killer."

"Well there is a solution," said Moses. He studied the young man's eyes.

"How's that?"

"Give us the car."

"What?" He was incredulous, "I stole it, it's my car."

"Pull over, and you get out, and go get yourself another car, how long does it take for you? Ten minutes? Five?" Moses reasoned, "If we end up with the car, how can we testify that you stole it? We're the ones who will have the stolen property." He drove along silently; Moses could see the idea sinking in.

He pulled over on the shoulder of the road, a factory parking lot opposite. He opened the door and stepped out. "Merry Christmas," he said, and slammed the door. They watched him cross the road, his tool bag in hand, and disappear through a hedge before Steve climbed into the driver's seat.

"To the beach," said Moses, he was smiling again.

"In a stolen car?" Asked Dawn

"Borrowed," said Steve, giving her a sideways glance, "we'll give it back."

"I hate to think of what will happen to you if you get caught in it," she said.

"We'll just leave it at the beach, with all the problems that Barton is having right now, he'll be glad just to get it back in one piece," said Moses.

"We could bring the car back to Sam and exchange it for my parent's van." said Steve, "that way Sam can deal with Mr. Barton Hackett."

"If Sam didn't kill him already," said Dawn.

"Whatever we're going to do, let's do it after the sunset," said Moses, "or better yet, in the morning?"

"You're planning to make a night of it?" asked Dawn.

"I'm a royal pain in the ass, aren't I?" Moses smiled, "am I asking too much?"

"Like Steve said, this is your night," she said, "We didn't go through all of this just to disappoint you."

"Do you mean it?" asked the old man frailly.

"Of course we mean it," said Steve, looking at Dawn with eyes of appreciation.

"We need more wine," said Moses.

"You want me to spend my last nine dollars?" asked Steve.

"Yes," Dawn and Moses answered in unison, smiling at each other.

"It's going to be a special evening," said Moses, becoming unexpectedly serious, "we need some sacramental wine."

Steve wondered about Moses' choice of words, but drove on in silence.

FOURTEEN

Father Cavanaugh's house stood across the street from the Catholic Church in Sutton's Bay. Sarah sat in his kitchen, where she had visited with him often during her lonely days of waiting, the brown clay tile had the look of durability and the slab of oak that had been shaped into the table was large and sturdy.

Sarah had been raised catholic and it had been natural for her to seek out the priest during her time of tribulation. Sometimes over his morning coffee at the Bayside Grill, but more often at that very kitchen table, she had shared her feelings of failure over her divorce, and her tremendous sense of insecurity at gambling her entire future on someone she had not known would even ever come home, let alone accept her back into his life. And it was with no small amount of disappointment that Sarah learned Father Cavanaugh could not perform their wedding ceremony.

"Father Cavanaugh, I don't understand it," said Sarah, "if it wasn't for you, I don't think I would have made it through all those month's alone, it would only be natural for you to be the one to marry us."

He looked at her with wrinkles of anguish in his forehead, and compassion in his eyes. "We've become good friends, Sarah, you and I, and I hope to make a friend of Moses too, but it's not up to me, it's not just between friends, the Church does not recognize your divorce from Doyle, and Moses isn't a member of the faith," he shook his head, "I'm sorry there's nothing I can do." Although he could not endorse her divorce from Doyle, Father Cavanaugh certainly understood it.

"It's just not fair," she protested, "it's hard to think of getting married to Moses without you there."

"Oh, I'll be there," Father Cavanaugh winked, "I wouldn't miss the biggest party that Sutton's Bay has had in a decade, I just can't participate in the ceremony."

"Sounds crazy to me," Sarah said wistfully, running her hands across the table.

"It is crazy," he confirmed, "I can give you my best wishes as your friend, but I just can't give you my blessing as your priest."

For Moses it was of little consequence, other than the disappointment the news brought to Sarah, which he had taken as a personal affront. For he took anything which disappointed Sarah as a personal affront. As a young man it was love, his love of Sarah, which was Moses' only religion.

Together they visited the Methodist church in Northport where Moses had gone as a child, and where Ida was still a member. But there was something there that Sarah found uncomfortable and foreboding, whether it was in the eye of Pastor Fisher or the old arching timbers of the church she did not know.

Finally, almost by the process of elimination, they settled on having a Presbyterian minister from Traverse City perform the ceremony at Sutton's Bay's public park along the shore with all of their friends and family gathered for the celebration.

Sarah's mother had come to town two weeks before the event to help with preparations, and of course, Ida was never short on advice. They had decided on doing this outside and the pressure was on to pull it off while the last breaths of summer remained.

The leaves were in full color as the day approached. The pine trees stood in marked contrast to all the shades of crimson, gold and orange adorning the surrounding countryside. The grass leading down to the beach was still a plush green.

Bill and the crew from the Bayside Grill were taking care of the food, much to Sarah's relief. And Mr. McKinney had lined up a three-piece combo, who regularly played the Traverse City night spots from Memorial Day to Labor Day, to add some music to the occasion.

Marge had thought the frenzy that Sarah went through when picking out her dress for her high society wedding to Doyle was nothing short of ridiculous, but it was common place when compared to the agony Sarah put herself through for her wedding to Moses. If things, and especially her dress weren't going to be perfect, somebody would probably have to die to pay the price. Lucky for Moses, the dress shopping was something that mother and daughter went off to Traverse City to take care of on their own.

The night before the wedding Moses sat in 'Slap Shot', his legs draped over the stern, and watched Sarah cooking dinner. His tousled hair fell across one eye, and his white tee shirt and denim pants each bore a smudge of blue paint from his afternoons work. Sarah put a lid on the pot where the stew was simmering, walked through the living room, and climbed into the boat beside him. She wore everything well, and that evening as he watched her move through the house in a lavender jump suit, it was no different, whatever she wore made him want to see her naked.

"We're about to set sail together for the rest of our lives," she said, gently giving him a kiss on the cheek.

"Are you scared?" he asked.

"No, I'm whatever the opposite of scared is." She smiled, "I've never been so sure of any decision in my whole life."

"I'm glad you said it, because it's like that for me too. It's like I've been married to you my whole life, and tomorrow's just the time that we've picked to let everybody else know about it."

She placed her hand on top of his as he idly held the tiller, "Are you going to teach me to sail?" she asked.

"I want to share everything with you," he smiled, "everything that I know, everything that I've felt, everything that I've ever dreamed, everything that I am."

"Doyle almost treated me like a child," a touch of sorrow edged her voice, "he wanted me to be seen but not heard."

"I want to explore everything that makes you who you are, I want to know your opinion on everything and anything, I want to talk for hours on end, late into the night and learn all there is to know about you."

"And then what?" she asked. She nuzzled her cheek into his chest and slipped a hand under his shirt.

He unbuttoned her top two buttons, and slid a hand inside her clothes, caressing her breast. "You are mine, aren't you?" he asked.

"Every inch of me." She unbuttoned the rest of her jumpsuit and slipped it off her legs, standing before him naked and silent in the boat.

He watched her without moving or saying anything for a long while, then tenderly reached for her and brought her to him.

They made love in the boat, there in the living room, and the waves of passion swept over them, and carried them away. The stew simmered, and then went dry, but there would be other stews. The moon crept up over a distant hill and shone through the prism of a cherry tree, through the side window, blanketing the two lovers in moon glow as they lay naked in each others arms on the floor of the boat.

When the morning sun had replaced the moon, Moses whispered, "It's tomorrow Mrs. Bailey."

"That's not official until this afternoon," she sighed.

"Do you need it to be official to feel it?"

"No, no I don't." She smiled and burrowed back into his side, returning to her dream.

The morning was bright, scattered white, puffy clouds leisurely strolled across the sky, but stayed out of the way of the sun, which announced its presence with all the strength of a mid-summer's day. When Marge arrived with the wedding dress, Sarah was dancing around the house in Moses white tee shirt, her breasts bouncing the blue smudge.

"I think we have to interrupt this wedded bliss for the wedding," said Marge.

"Where's Daddy?" asked Sarah.

"He's looking after the set up of the bar with Mr. McKinney."

Moses walked from the bedroom naked, and lifted the lid of the cookie jar and peered in.

"Oh, Sugar Mo," called Sarah smiling.

"What, my love?" He looked over to Sarah and suddenly recognized that they were not alone. "Geez," he clamored, reaching for a dishtowel to cover himself, "somebody could tell a fella he's got company."

"Isn't anything I haven't seen before," said Marge.

"But it's been a long time since you've seen anything as fine as that, admit it, Mom," said Sarah.

"I'll do no such thing," said Marge, "your father still turns my crank, I think he gets better with age."

"Are you talking about technique or looks?" asked Sarah.

"I think I better find somewhere to go," said Moses, "this is more girl talk than I really want to hear."

"It's just as well," said Marge, "it's time for your bride to start getting ready anyway, and you know you can't see her in her wedding dress."

Holding the dishtowel over his private parts he walked over to Sarah and gave her a kiss, "I'll take my stuff and go out the back." He backed out of the room. "See you at the wedding."

Marge had shown a mother's patience during the week of shopping and fitting that she had endured with Sarah in Traverse City. Sarah had tried on nearly every dress in town and then once she had decided on one, she required so many alterations to be done to it that it was a totally unique design from what it had been originally. Marge held it now while Sarah slipped it on, and buttoned the twenty-six satin-covered fasteners that ran up the back. It was a white combination of satin and lace.

"A bride doesn't usually wear white, the second time around," Marge had said during their shopping trip.

"It's the first time around for Moses," Sarah had responded, "and as long as I'm the woman in his life, he isn't going to get short changed in any way."

Marge hadn't said anything further about the color of the wedding dress. Now she looked at her daughter in the tight-fitting bodice, and long sleeves all of lace, rising from a full, flowing satin skirt and train. The lace stopped at the top of her breasts, revealing just a hint of cleavage below her mother's pearls, and beautifully sculpted bare shoulders. "You're a beautiful bride," said Marge.

They stood before a full-length looking glass that Moses had borrowed from Mabel Twilley. In it they saw the reflection of a bride with her golden hair twisted high on her head, smooth skin of velvet, and full lips of cherry red carrying a smile of happiness known only by those who are in the middle of a dream coming true.

"For the first time in my life, I really feel beautiful," said Sarah. She squeezed her mother's hand, "thanks for being here, Mom, and thanks for sharing this with me."

"Where else would I be?"

Sarah pressed her hand to her racing heart and looked around the simple home they had made together, where her clothes would nestle into drawers beside his in the pine chest of drawers and Ida's hand-me-down wardrobe closet, where she would spend her days in the smell of oil paint and tobacco, and where they would share the four-poster bed forevermore.

"My lady, your carriage awaits," said Harry coming into the living room, "my princess, look at you," smiling at his daughter in appreciation

"It's time, Sarah," said Marge.

Sarah's face was aglow with a sublime radiance. Time for wishes and dreams to come true, time to join her life to his, Sarah thought, and her exhilaration amplified.

Ike and Mabel Twilley owned and worked the cherry orchard that surrounded Moses Bailey's home. It was Ike who, believing in the talent of the young artist, had sold Moses the barn for his studio for a payment of three paintings per year.

Moses knocked at Ike Twilley's back door, Ike's wife Mabel answered. She had flour on the front of her blue and white checked apron and her hands had remnants of cookie dough. She smiled broadly at the sight of Moses, dressed in a sweater and dungarees, his new suit in a bag slung over his shoulder.

"Today's the big day, eh?" she said, pushing open the screen door.

"The biggest."

"You've got yourself quite a girl there."

"I know," said Moses, "she's the most beautiful girl I've ever met, and sometimes I can't believe that I'm so lucky that she fell in love with me."

"Oh, she's a cutie all right," said Mabel, "but I was talking about what's she's got on the inside. It took some guts to move to this little town where she didn't know a soul, take up a job she had never done, waiting for a man she didn't know would ever show."

"Her beauty runs deep, there's no denying it. What's unbelievable, is that she did it all for me."

"I've known you since you were knee high, coming down here from Northport to pick cherries to pay for supplies to build that little boat of yours, and you've always sold yourself short, like you didn't have a thing to offer the world, while all the while every girl in the county was going to bed praying that you'd just notice them."

"Mabel, you're making me blush."

"You're modest to a fault, Moses Bailey." Mabel went back to the kitchen counter to finish filling the cookie sheet, "pour yourself a cup of coffee, Ike will be in any minute."

"The bride and her mother have kind of taken over my house, I thought I'd get ready here if it was all right."

"I don't think a man's ever ready to get married," said Ike, entering the kitchen. His suntanned face flashed a smile of white teeth under his silver mustache, crinkling the crow's feet around his eyes.

"Not every man is like you, Ike Twilley," said Mabel without looking up from her work, "some men eventually figure out why God made two sexes."

Moses smiled to himself and finished pouring his coffee. "Coffee, Ike?"

"I'll take a cup if the ice in here hasn't gotten to it." He moved up behind Mabel and gave her rump a pinch.

Mabel thrust her hips toward the kitchen cabinets, "Ike," she squealed, "don't give the boy any bad ideas, it's his wedding day."

"I'm sure the boy has enough ideas of his own," Ike chuckled.

Automobiles lined the grassy edges of the sandy access drive, as friends and family of Moses and Sarah milled in and around the red and white striped canvas canopies in the park. Bill and his crew from the Bayside Grill had prepared the food. Bill also kept a watchful eye on the ample supply of drink that Harry had provided, bringing two cases of his favorite whiskey along with him from Chicago.

Reverend Baraga was thin-faced and thin-lipped, with a few strands of thin hair slicked back over his thin skull. His eyes peered out through thin slits behind thin-rimmed glasses. Reverend Baraga was thin. He stood with Moses between the trunks of two inter-twined birch trees that were to be used to form a wedding alcove. Surrounding each trunk were bouquets of wild flowers, behind them, the waves of Grand Traverse Bay lapped gently at the shore.

"You got the ring, Mr. McKinney?" Moses asked nervously of his best man.

"We got the ring, and we got the preacher, all we need is the bride."

"What time is it?" Moses asked nervously.

"She's only five minutes late," Reverend Baraga comforted, "I can't remember the last time I've had a bride who was on time."

"Do you think she's changed her mind?" Moses said.

"I think you're more nervous than I've ever seen you," said Mr. McKinney. "You're calm and collected in a tied hockey game, with thirty seconds left and the championship on the line, but your girl is five minutes late and you're in a tizzy."

"I think they call it love," joked Reverend Baraga.

"Relax," said McKinney, "the horse and carriage I rented for her just takes a little while to get here."

"Thank you for that," said Moses turning to his best man, "I think that was just the perfect touch. I so want this day to be everything that Sarah has dreamed of."

A shiny black carriage, pulled by a pure white horse turned the corner from St. Joseph Avenue and down the approach to the park. It pulled to a stop and the door popped open and out stepped Harry who helped Marge down. Inside, Sarah caught and held a deep breath, trying to steady her nerves. She shut her eyes for an instant and listened to the sweet music winding up from the park below. But neither her forced breathing exercise, nor the soothing music did anything to calm the trembling in her stomach.

She pressed a hand to her waist, and then as Moses watched intently, Sarah emerged from the carriage and descended down to the red velvet runner that had been laid across the grass.

He had been waiting for a glimpse of his bride, and their eyes met. She was breathtaking in her white lace gown with her mother's pearls draped around her delicate neck. Moses forgot to breathe. He never knew that a woman could be so beautiful, so beautiful that he would have to remind his heart to beat. Their gazes locked across the field of green, and the guests lifted their faces in anticipation, but for a time that had no length they were conscious of nothing but each other.

"Breathe, Moses, breathe," whispered McKinney from behind him. Moses took a deep breath. In his brand new tailed jacket, tuxedo shirt, and pleated pants, he was the focus of attention of all the girls of marriageable age, and even some of those who were beyond.

They continued to stare at each other, their throats dry, their stomachs dancing, their pulses sprinting, etching the moment across their hearts for all time. At last, the murmur of the gathering infiltrated into their solitary union and Moses smiled, and Sarah's smile answered.

Harry escorted his daughter down the red velvet to the wedding alcove, as the music played. She took her place beside Moses and they joined hands. Moses momentarily closed his eyes as he felt her fingers intertwine with his.

"Who gives this woman?" asked Reverend Baraga.

"Her mother and I do," said Harry.

Sarah felt a smile grow within her, she was scarcely aware of the crowd of family and friends as she felt only Moses' strong hand encompassing hers. Reverend Baraga spoke of undying love while Moses gently rubbed his thumb against hers.

Then they turned to face each other, holding hands for everyone to see. His cheeks reddened, his palms damp, and Sarah realized that she was not the only one with fragile nerves.

His voice was deeper than usual, and she noticed a slight trembling in it, as he spoke his vows, "I, Moses Bailey, take you Sarah . . ." But his eyes, intense and locked upon hers, never wavered.

Inside she felt her heart swelling, and wondered if she would be able to speak when it came her turn.

"Until death us do part," Moses finished with a love rising within him so real and intense, it was as if the inspiration for a thousand paintings had descended upon him simultaneously. As he held firmly to her hand, he listened to her voice, soft and quivering. In the corner of her eye, he saw the glimmer of tears, and his heart exploded open in celebration. He knew he was loved, and in that instant found a belief in miracles. What else could explain the wonder of it all?

Mr. McKinney handed Moses the ring. With Reverend Baraga smiling on, Moses' shaking hands slid the circle of gold onto her delicate finger. She swallowed hard as she watched in wonder as it slid over her knuckle, realizing that it bound them together forevermore. Their hands met, their gazes intertwined, and in their hearts their union was preserved until death and beyond.

Reverend Baraga pronounced them man and wife, and the kiss that followed was so impassioned, so intense, that you could hear more than one matronly gasp coming from the gallery. When the kiss ended, Moses lifted his face just enough to fall into her soft gray eyes once more. Their breathing became one breath, and not a spec, not an iota, not a jot, of the significance of the moment was lost on them. Husband and wife, as God had intended.

Finally, he stood up straight and squeezed her hand, a broad smile breaking onto his face like a cresting wave. She fluttered her eyelids as she regained her composure in realization that the world did in fact contain more people than just her and Moses. She smiled, releasing the guests from the enchantment in which they had been captured, and several women, Ida included, picked up their hankies to wipe away the dew that had formed at their eyes.

"I love you," he said, the words feeling totally inadequate.

"Half as much, Sugar Mo, half as much," she said, and kissed him once more, wrapping her arms around him as if she would never let him go.

"Half as much?" he whispered in wonder.

"Half as much as I love you." She laughed.

The music spilled over the park, joyous and exultant, and the voices of their friends and family rose in volume along with the music. In seconds, they were swept away by a crowd of well-wishers, and separated for most of the afternoon, only catching a fleeting kiss or a tender glance for the rest of the day.

Bill brought forth the wedding feast, and served it buffet style. Harry and Ike manned the bar, children teased the seagulls with peanuts and pretzels, dancing began on the wooden floor of the picnic shelter, and the sound of joy rose from the gathering at the shore.

There were so many guests for Sarah to meet, and old acquaintances for Moses to revisit, that the demands of the throng barely allowed them a wedding dance.

Moses grasped Sarah's arm as they left the dance floor, and pulled her briefly behind a gigantic oak and surrounded her with his arms, and spent most of a minute simply gazing into her luminous gray eyes. Then, just as he touched his lips to hers, they were discovered and whisked away back onto the dance floor by Roy and Fran, who ran the general store.

"There's plenty of time for that," said Fran, putting her right hand into Moses' left, "now it's time to dance with the old fat ladies." She threw back her head and let go of a roar of laughter. Moses whirled her out onto the dance floor, looking back with yearning at Sarah, who was smiling at him over the top of Roy's bald head, which crowned his stumpy frame.

An hour and a half later they touched hands in front of the buffet table, but barely had time to exchange glances before Jacob Baker, the town physician, interrupted with a toast.

"To the prettiest girl in Sutton's Bay," he said, lifting his glass, "that is to say the second prettiest girl in Sutton's Bay," he amended looking at Agnes, his wife, "and the man she decided to bestow the honor of being her husband, Moses Bailey." The crowd gathered around the table, and those at the bar nearby laughed at his inebriated formality.

The musicians took their last break and headed for the bar, and in the sudden silence Moses leaned back against a birch tree, took his pack of Lucky Strikes from his inside jacket pocket and lit one. He inhaled deeply, and then let the smoke role out through his nose. A wave of contentment spilled over him as he looked at his wife across the expanse of green being the perfect hostess to their guests. It was the inner satisfaction he had only known before when he completed a painting, knowing he had done his best work, or as a child when he had finished brushing on the last coat of lacquer onto the boat he had built, and stood back almost in disbelief at what he had accomplished. It was a feeling very akin to scoring the winning goal in the last seconds of a crucial game, but somehow more lasting. He smiled and was able to enjoy one more puff before the moment was interrupted by Mabel Twilley's concern that he get one of her famous cookies before they were all gone.

As the day of celebration moved into evening, and the Chinese lanterns which were hung from the canvas canopies and the eaves of the picnic shelter glowed into the descending dusk, Moses could see the weariness creep over Sarah's face.

He caught her attention and mouthed, "Are you ready?"

She nodded and then smiled.

He stepped over to his mother, who was refilling her glass with champagne punch, and whispered in her ear, "We're going," and gave her a kiss on the cheek. She turned to him and smiled.

Sarah waved to her father across the lawn of green and blew him a kiss; her mother was instantly at her side and embraced her with a tear of joy in the corner of her eye. "You were right," Marge said quietly, "this is the first time."

Moses strode over to Sarah, cradled her face gently in his hands, and kissed her forehead. "I want to be alone with you," he said. She smiled softly in agreement, but said nothing, her heart in her throat. He took her hand and led her through the crowd, nodding and smiling a final time to the guests he encountered, but persisting toward his waiting motorcycle. He jumped on it and it sprang to life with a roar. "My lady," he said, extending his hand in invitation.

"She's going on her honeymoon on that motorcycle in her wedding dress?" Ida asked in disbelief, forever the practical one.

"I don't think she'd have it any other way," said Marge, smiling, her hands clasped to her chest.

Sarah gathered the train of her dress in her left hand, placed her white patent leather high heel on the footrest of the Harley, and swung herself onto the seat behind him. By this time, most of the male guests were well inebriated, and whistles and hoots went up from the throng as she revealed her long slender legs in her white stockings, as she sat straddling the motorcycle seat. She sandwiched the excess of material of her dress between her stomach and his lower back, threw her arms around his waist, and pressed her cheek between his shoulder blades, closing her eyes.

Moses grinned as he felt her breasts pressing into his back, and her hands fondling his stomach. He released the clutch and cranked the accelerator as the crowd showered them with rice and waved good-bye. They sped out of the park, turned onto St. Joseph Avenue, and vanished over the hill.

"Alone at last," she sighed, a smile of contentment blanketing her face, "let our togetherness begin."

It was well past noon when Moses Bailey woke on his first day as a married man, and he knew from the instant that he opened his eyes that he could never again imagine anything other than being married, married to Sarah, physically, spiritually, and emotionally, married always in all ways, forevermore.

He heard the shower running on the other side of the wall next to the bed, heard Sarah singing her favorite song off key, and looked across the room at her white wedding gown lying over an expensively upholstered chair by the window. He smiled and curled an arm under the pillow at his head, and for the first time, looked about the suite he had rented for them at the Twin Gables, a bed and breakfast in

Leland, realizing with an amused surprise that when Sarah was in the room, he saw nothing else.

The wallpaper was heavily textured, with an appearance of fabric, in a design of scrolls and scallops in shades of magenta and pink. The carved headboard of the bed and the matching dresser and bedside table were all of richly polished mahogany. Two chairs with satiny, striped upholstery, occupied the space created by a bay window that stuck its nose out into a shaded courtyard.

Leland lay on the opposite side of the Leelanau peninsula from Sutton's Bay and nestled into the Lake Michigan shore where it provided refuge and a homeport for a small fishing fleet. Moses could see the wooden docks that lined the inlet from the west window of his room. The boats were all out, but the docks hummed with activity in anticipation of their return. He had made the twenty-two mile trek after the wedding with Sarah clinging tightly on the back of the motorcycle, and both were glad they hadn't decide to go twenty-three, barely able to restrain their passion for that short distance.

Sarah emerged from the bathroom wrapped in fluffy pink towel, her hair wet and dangling, her shoulders suntanned and soft, her smile joyous, and her gray eyes totally captivating. Moses was again oblivious to his surroundings.

She jumped back into bed and curled into his side, "what are we going to do today, Mr. Bailey."

He chuckled and caressed her shoulder.

"Besides that," she giggled and kissed his cheek.

"The path down to the beach is right across the street, and this time of year we should have it all to ourselves."

"You say that like you've been here before." Her face took on a pout of disappointment.

"I've never stayed here before, this will always be our place. But I have been to the beach, you have to remember we're still in my stomping grounds."

"You do get around, Sugar Mo."

"Past tense, Mrs. Bailey, past tense, the only getting around I'm going to do any more is getting around you." He buried his face in the small of her neck, kissed her skin, and inhaled the smell of her.

Her towel fell open as if it had a mind of its own, or more precisely, as if moved by the force of their single-minded intention. She dripped with anticipation as his lips danced upon her nakedness. And they let their bodies join together once more in answer to their rising urgency, which they found could be momentarily pacified, but never exhausted.

No one had ever explained to him why they called it Indian Summer, but it had always been his favorite time of the year. The summer temperatures lingered on, but became all the more precious as the turning colors of the leaves warned of what was to come. Each day of summer weather might be the last, giving way without notice to the blustery winds of autumn.

The sky held the early shades of evening when they finally emerged from their room. They took the flowered bedspread from their bed, bought a bottle of wine from a grinning merchant wearing three days worth of white bristles on his chin, and made their way over the path of sand, through the beach grass, and down to the water's edge. The sand was soft and clean, the water calmly lapping against the shore, and the beach was empty.

Moses spread out the blanket, and flopped down on his knees upon it. He opened the wine and realized they would have to drink from the bottle, as they had brought no glasses. He was about to remark on how sensual it seemed to share wine from the bottle with each other, when he looked up and totally forgot what he was going to say.

Sarah stood before him naked, her skin radiant in the sun. "Why do you look so shocked?" she asked. "This is what you had in mind, wasn't it?"

His mouth formed a soft smile. "Only in my dreams," he said. And forever in his memory. Forevermore, there would be no time of year that could compare with Indian Summer, and no time of day like sunset.

She knelt on the blanket, and he parked the wine bottle in the sand without looking away from her. She opened her mouth to his and felt the hot, flickering, exploration of his tongue fanning the flames of passion into a roaring inferno once again. She quickly ran her hands down his buttons, freeing them in quick succession, and then his pants as well.

He fell backward into the sand and she fell on top of him, and he wrapped her in his arms. Her nipples were rigid and pressed into his chest, and he smiled at the feeling. She saw his smile and pressed herself to him all the more. "Is there a way we can make today last forever?" he asked.

"Carve it in your memory, Sugar Mo," she kissed his neck, " carve it in your memory and it will be with you always." She reached down and took hold of him, lowering herself on to him, closing her eyes and softly moaning as she felt his yearning swell within her. She arched her back and lifted her face to the sky, riding her urgency to a quick, throbbing conclusion. His bliss soon followed, and she momentarily reopened her eyes, looking down at him with a wide grin, before collapsing back on top of him.

When she had rolled away to catch her breath, he turned over on his stomach and dug into his shirt pocket for a cigarette.

"Let's go feel the water," she said.

"You go, I'll smoke."

She spanked him once on his white buttocks and sprang to her feet. He lit his cigarette and released a white cloud to the sky. He leaned back on his elbows watching her saunter down to the waters edge. The sculpture of her cheek as it descended to her neck, the curve of her breasts, and the way her belly indented between her hip bones in invitation, caused a stirring within him that he knew would be with him for the rest of his days.

Sunsets, Moses concluded, were like women, each one unique, and each one in their own way beautiful. And he marveled again at Sarah standing naked and unashamed on the shore, the sun setting on the horizon behind her, showering her in lights of red, orange, pink and purple, and wondered why he had been blessed with the most beautiful one of all.

Steve pulled the blue Cadillac into the sand parking lot of the Party Harbor convenience store, climbed from the car, and then stuck his head back in the window and said, "Name your poison, Moses."

"Chardonnay, if that's OK," said Moses.

"I think that there's something significant about that," said Dawn, as Steve headed into the store.

"Yes," replied Moses without further explanation, a distant look in his eye.

To their delight, when the trio arrived at the beach, Steve discovered a couple of blankets in the trunk of the Cadillac.

"My hero," said Dawn.

"I can't have my lady sitting in the sand." And that is exactly how he thought of her, 'his lady', and there wasn't a dragon he wouldn't slay for her.

Steve opened the back door of the car for Moses, and Moses pulled himself from the middle of the seat to the doorframe. Steve reached in and put an arm under Moses knees and the other behind his back to lift him out.

Moses stiffened out his arm. "I'd like to try and walk," he said.

"We'll do it," said Steve, "just grab my arm."

He stuck out his bent arm in front of Moses, and Moses grabbed it and hoisted himself out of the car and onto his feet.

"Well, so much for the hard part, your on your feet, now you just have to put one in front of the other till we get where we're going."

Moses was like a toddler taking his first steps, clinging to Steve's arm for balance and support, but step-by-step, they made their way through the sand down to the water's edge.

The sun was big, round and orange and still up off the horizon, it had yet to turn the sky purple and pink or set the shimmering water on fire. Dawn spread out one of the blankets and Moses lowered himself onto it with a grateful sigh. He pulled off his shoes and then his socks, and pushed his toes into the cool sand underneath the warm surface. He picked up a handful of sand and watched with delight as the granules ran through the cracks between his fingers, flooding him with memories of summers gone.

"I can never repay you for what you have done for me," said Moses, looking out at the water, the sun and the sky, "but I could share with you a secret of the universe."

Steve laughed. "We are your humble students, oh wise one."

Moses leaned back on his elbows, and as he did, years seemed to fall from his face. "Heaven is like a day at the beach." The goldish yellow sphere in the sky was burning so bright he could not look at it directly.

"Were you an artist or did you write fortune cookies?" Dawn teased.

Moses smiled up at the sky for a minute and then another, before he replied. "When the day finally comes when you find out I'm right, just remember who told you."

"I'll never forget it," Dawn reached over and squeezed his hand.

Steve opened the wine and poured into the paper cups he had brought.

"I'll drink from the bottle, if you don't mind," said Moses, "with my hands it's a lot easier for me to handle."

"Anything you want, Moses," said Dawn patting his arm, "this is your trip."

Moses looked quietly out across the lake, "It's been hard," he said softly, almost in a whisper, "living with eyes that fail you, living with legs that can no longer bear your weight. It's been heartbreaking to be a painter whose hands can no longer hold a brush. But the hardest thing of all," he gulped as if holding back tears by sheer force of will, "has been living all these years in a world where there is no Sarah."

Dawn could hear the yearning in his voice, and see the heartache on his face, and tears began to well up in her own eyes for this little old man she had grown to love. "You never found anyone else?" she asked. "In all those years, you never found anyone else?"

"No, I've never been any good at pretending, and that's what life with anyone else would have been, pretending. I was lucky enough to find my one true love, some people never do."

"Is that what you've learned," asked Steve looking first at Moses and then to Dawn, "that there is just one true love for everyone?"

"Are there more than two halves to a whole?"

Steve sat down next to Moses on the blanket and put an arm around Moses' shoulders. Moses watched the water lapping against the shore. Dawn dried her tears with Steve's handkerchief.

"What I'd really like," said Moses turning to Dawn, "and I know it probably sounds selfish after all the two of you have done for me, but I'd like to watch this show alone and just spend time with my own thoughts. It's a big beach, why don't the two of you go over that dune over there and pretend like you like each other." He pointed to the north and smiled.

"I don't know about that Moses," said Dawn.

"Whether you like each other?" asked Moses, smiling.

"No, seriously" she said donning her nurse's tone, "what if you need us?"

"Look at the sun hanging there big and orange in the sky, the sunset's not more than an hour away, I'm sitting here on a blanket in the sand, what am I going to do, fall off the beach?"

"I don't know."

"Dawn, you were right before," said Steve, "this is his trip." Steve looked down at Moses and thought about the inevitability of age, this was a reflection of what was to come in his own life. The realization was at once terrifying and sobering. But then in the next instant the fear evaporated in the knowledge that he could face everything the future would bring if he were sharing it with the right partner. And then he admitted the truth to himself, there was no avoiding it, or hiding from it, the right partner was standing right in front of him.

"I'll be fine," said Moses, as they rose to stand beside him, "but I'm keeping the wine."

"This glass is all I need," said Dawn, lifting her paper cup.

"This girl is all I need," said Steve, taking up Dawn's hand and lacing his fingers through hers. She looked at him and their eyes met, and for a moment it seemed as if the whole world had stood still.

Finally, she broke off the gaze and looked to Moses, "Are you sure you'll be all right?"

"What are you going to do if someone comes along and tells you that you have to leave?" asked Steve.

"I'll tell them to go to hell," Moses said firmly.

"I don't suppose we'll be so far away that we can't hear that," said Dawn.

"Why don't you stop being a nurse for ten seconds," said Moses, "and be who you really are?"

"And who might that be?" she asked.

"A girl in love," smiled Moses. He returned his gaze to the horizon as Steve and Dawn walked down the beach hand in hand, the other blanket slung over Steve's shoulder, Dawn sipping from her paper cup and then putting it to Steve's lips. There was something about sharing wine from the same cup that made them both smile.

The sun descended turning the sky pink and then purple and the water to shimmering gold. The huge orange circle in the sky turned red as its bottom touched the water. And the golden, glistening path across the water widened as if welcoming Moses home. The sun glowed on his face, and gently settled into the water in the distance. A half circle now deep red with violet around the edges, then a quarter circle, and then finally sploosh, it disappeared. The sun had set, the day was done, and the world was still, except for the gentle rustling of the waves, caught in that magical moment between day and night.

FIFTEEN

As the summer of 1952 passed and slipped into fall, Moses watched over Sarah like a protective mother hen. Moses had missed the birth of his first child, Nathaniel, because there was nothing he could do about it. But there would be nothing short of another world war that would keep him from Sarah's side this time around. And as autumn turned to winter and 1952 became 1953, with the impending day approaching, he would barely let her out of his sight.

Nathaniel Bailey was nine years old and could barely contain his excitement at the prospect of having a little brother or sister. In his heart he carried the unspoken desire that it would be a brother, as he didn't really know quite what to make of this other gender, he was only aware that they were somehow different.

Sarah sat in a big easy chair in the living room beside the sailboat watching the snow come down outside the window. Some things had not changed a bit in the ensuing years. Nathaniel sat on his knees in front of her, his arms outstretched, his ear against her ripe belly. "He's in there, really?" he asked.

"Really and truly," said Sarah stroking his blond hair.

Moses looked over at them from the kitchen sink where he was doing the dishes. Mutiny, still floppy-eared, but no longer a puppy, strolled across the room from the sailboat to his favorite napping place in the center of the rug under the kitchen table. Norman Rockwell could not have painted a nicer scene, thought Moses. He thought about the room in the loft that he had finished for Nathaniel. If the new little one were a boy there would be nothing wrong with the two boys sharing the room, but what if they had a little girl? Would they have to think about leaving the cherry orchard? Or could they get by with just adding on?

"Good thing you bought milk and bread yesterday," said Sarah, watching the big flakes of snow, "I don't think anyone's going anywhere today."

"Roy and Fran probably closed the store early anyway, they probably didn't get much business in weather like this."

"If they opened at all. It's been snowing like this since last night, it was like someone turned on the snow switch around seven o'clock last night and forgot how to turn it off."

"Well, that's why they invented the word blizzard, to describe weather like this, right Nat?"

"Did you see the snowman Dad and I made this morning, Mom?" Nathaniel asked.

"Sure did," she smiled, "if I didn't know better, I'd say you two were quite the artists."

"Aw, Mom, that's not art, what Dad does with his paint is art."

"The way you live your life can be art," she said. "But wasn't that my best ski hat that your man was wearing?"

"It'll dry, Mom," said Moses, "or else our favorite girl will be getting a new one for Valentine's Day, isn't that right Nat?"

"I thought we already bought her one at Mr. Reedy's?" Nathaniel said, and then blushed, and covered his mouth with his little hands. Sarah and Moses both laughed and she pulled the little boy to her and kissed his head.

The afternoon gently folded into evening and found Moses trying to make a little headway on his latest painting, Sarah in her chair reading, and Nathaniel playing with his favorite toy truck at her feet.

"Ow," Sarah cried, wincing, her hands grabbing her belly tight, "something's not right."

"What's wrong, Mom?" asked Nathaniel.

"The baby's kicking like I've never felt before, like it's going wild." She grimaced and breathed sharply at another stab of pain.

Moses was at her side in an instant, bending on a knee, concern and worry written on his face.

"Ooh," she winced again, "it's too early, it's a month too early."

"What?" said Moses, "has it started?"

"I think so," she said, "help me lie down, maybe things will calm down."

He picked her up in his arms and carried her toward the bed. "Nathaniel, can you call Doctor Baker? His number is by the phone, just get him on the line and I'll talk to him."

"It's probably just false labor," she said, in a last desperate attempt to be optimistic, "I hate to pester Dr. Baker on a Saturday."

"It's just a phone call," Moses said and then glanced back toward the chair where she had been sitting, and then gasped.

Moses laid Sarah on the bed, and propped up her head with a pillow. Her face was furrowed and showing signs of perspiration around the edges. "It's not right, it's just not right," she said, doing her best to suppress a cry, her face suddenly as white as the bed sheets.

"Everything will be fine," he tried to sound reassuring, but wasn't sure he was doing too good a job of it.

"Dad, Dr. Baker." Nathaniel stood holding out the phone, his eyes fastened on his mother.

"Jacob, it's Moses. I think Sarah's gone into labor, and something's wrong," he looked again at the chair where she had been sitting, "there's blood, quite a lot of it."

Nathaniel followed his father's eyes to the chair, "Oh, oh, oh," was all he could manage, pointing breathlessly.

"Are you sure, Moses?" asked Jacob Baker, "are you sure it's not just her water that's broken?"

"Would it be bright red, Jacob?"

"No, no it wouldn't," he could hear the sudden urgency in Jacob's voice, "how much blood Moses?"

"How much?" Moses irritation began to rise in his voice, "What do you mean how much? How would I measure such a thing?"

"I mean is it a little spotting or is there more?"

"There's more than a little spotting, Jacob, a lot more."

"I'm calling for an ambulance, and I'm on my way."

"You'll have to park out on the road and walk in," said Moses, "the drive has a four foot drift in it."

Moses hung up the phone and looked at Nathaniel, the little boy's face was twisted in agony as he stared at his mother on the bed. In his little hands he clung to a wooden carving of a hippopotamus that Mr. McKinney had given them after hearing that Sarah was pregnant. "Tart" Nathaniel called it. Mr. McKinney had explained to him how Taurt was the ancient Egyptian goddess of childbirth, portrayed by a female hippopotamus standing upright, with large pendulous human breasts. Nathaniel had found some comfort in Mr. McKinney's reassurance that the little hippo would look after his mother, but now he wondered if the thing really knew its job.

"Nat," said Moses, trying to find a distraction for the little one, "go out and try to shovel a path for Dr. Baker."

"Oh, God," cried Sarah, clutching Moses arm with all her strength, her nails digging into his skin. Her eyes were beginning to look glassy, her breathing heavy and labored. Nathaniel finished buttoning his coat, looked back at his mother, and went out the door, tears streaming down his face.

Dr. Jacob Baker, had graduated from the University of Michigan in 1932, and turned his back on the lure of a rich practice in a suburb of Detroit, opting instead to return to where he was born. And for a long time after he set up his family practice, he was the only doctor in Leelanau County.

He put the phone back in its cradle and ran a hand through his prematurely gray head of hair. His wife put her hand on his arm, a concerned look on her face. "What is it?" she asked, she had heard his call to the ambulance, "you have to go out in this blizzard, don't you?"

"It's Mrs. Bailey, she's in trouble."

Agnes Baker was practiced at seeing the real message in the eyes behind the horn-rimmed bifocals, and that night they were more than a little worried. "She's gone into premature labor?" she asked.

"No, it would be bad enough to have a premature delivery in the middle of a snow storm like this, but I'm afraid it's much worse than that."

"How could that be Jacob? She's a healthy young woman, what are you saying."

"God only knows why these things happen, Agnes, I'm just hoping against hope that I'm wrong. It sounds like it's an abruption of the placenta."

"Where the placenta pulls away from the wall of the uterus?"

"Yes, in the hospital we would do an emergency cesarean section, but out there in the middle of that orchard, that baby will die because it no longer gets what it needs, and the mother will bleed to death." He threw on his coat, checked the contents of his black bag and snapped the clasp, "If I'm right, there's not a thing that me or the ambulance from Traverse City will be able to do, Moses will lose his wife and his baby before either of us get there."

"Is there anything I can do, Jacob?" she pleaded as he opened the door.

"Just pray that I'm wrong, Agnes, just pray."

Nathaniel worked furiously out in the brutal wind, fighting the driving snow. He would scoop as much in his shovel as his small arms could lift, and then fling it downwind with all his might. The only sound he heard was the howling of the wind, and the screaming cry of his mother inside the house. His tears were frozen on his cheeks, he paused for breath and looked up at the snowdrift that was taller than he was, "son of a bitch," said the little man, and he attacked it once more.

"Oh God," Sarah screamed, she was totally drenched in sweat, "make it stop, Sugar Mo, make it stop." The pain from her abdomen was excruciating. She was squeezing his right hand with the grip of a vice, her nails had broken through the skin, but the blood on the bed was not his, and the blood was everywhere.

He could see the vein in her throat throbbing with a violent pulse. With his free hand, he wiped her pale face with a washcloth, "the doctor's on his way, my lady, everything is going to be all right." He looked at all the blood and his heart sank, as something inside him knew that he was lying.

"Call Father Cavanaugh," Sarah was nearly breathless, "I want Father Cavanaugh."

"Anything, Sarah, anything you want, you just hold on, the doctor's on his way."

With a suddenness that scared him, Sarah released the grip on his arm. Her eyes were closed and her breathing became shallow and unforced. The racing throb in her neck slowed to where he could barely detect it. He stood beside the bed and rapped on the window, motioning for Nathaniel to come inside.

"I've got a lot more to do, Dad," said Nathaniel hurrying through the door, then stopping still in his tracks as he saw the tears on his father's face."

Moses searched for the words, his voice catching in his throat, "I think your mother is leaving us, Nat, come over here and give her a kiss good-bye."

"Leaving us?" But why? Where is she going?" Nathaniel threw his coat to the floor and flew to his mother's side.

"She's going to live with the angels," answered his father.

Nathaniel threw himself onto her, wrapping her in his arms, burying his face in her chest, "Don't go, Mom, stay with us," He glanced at his father, "Dad," his voice was panicked, "she won't answer me. Mom, Mom, I love you." He began to weep, his sobbing uncontrollable.

Moses gently stroked his son's back, not noticing the tears streaming down his own cheeks. "She's gone, son."

Jacob Baker tied his wool scarf around his face and trudged through the snow up the drive through the orchard. At the house he found Moses and Nathaniel sitting on the bed beside Sarah's body, their heads bowed together. He confirmed what they already knew, and then Jacob called Ike Twilley, and told him what had happened. He asked if Ike would come over and plow the drive with his tractor so they could get Sarah's body to the funeral home. Ike recovered from the initial shock of the news, and then promised to come right down. Mabel Twilley promised to come down too, and help put the house back in order as best she could.

Moses called Father Cavanaugh, but was speechless when the priest answered the phone. Jacob took the phone from Moses, recounted the story to the priest, and then heard a long silence at the other end of the line.

Mabel Twilley had made coffee in the Bailey kitchen, and Ike sipped on a cup trying to recapture some of the warmth after completing his plowing chores in the blustering cold.

Outside on the porch, Nathaniel clung to Moses, his arms around his neck, his legs wrapped around his father's waist, like a baby cub hanging onto its mother, as they watched the car carrying Sarah's body disappear down the drive. Jacob Baker stood beside them, his hand on Moses' back.

"I thought we were going to have a baby?" said Nathaniel, whimpering.

"The baby has gone with your mother," said Jacob. "We'll have to wait until we get to heaven to see him."

"The baby was a boy?" Moses wondered.

"Did mother want to go?" asked Nathaniel, openly crying, clinging to his father's neck with all his might.

"No," said Moses, "there wasn't any place in the world your mother would rather be than right here being Nathaniel Bailey's mother."

"Then why?"

"I don't know," was all Moses could manage, barely able to stand the pain of his own heart breaking.

Marge and Harry bought chains for the tires of their Buick and came to Sutton's Bay through the winter storm for their daughter's funeral, but Moses wasn't much of a host, in fact, he wasn't much of anything. What worried Ida Bailey was if her son could pull himself together enough to be a father.

The wind was cold and biting as it swept over the peninsula as they all made their way to the church for the funeral service. Marge and Harry stood with hands folded, tears in their eyes, Ida Bailey stood next to them watching her son and the little Nathaniel. The Catholic Church was somber, Jacob and Agnes Baker, Ike and Mabel

Twilley, and Gerald McKinney all stood in the pews absorbed in their own quiet thoughts.

Father Cavanaugh spoke, fighting back tears of his own by shear force of will. Moses had not felt the wind as he walked to the church, and now he was barely aware of his son's little hand in his own. He did not hear a word the priest said, but wondered instead, if he would be able to wake from this nightmare, or if he would be captured in this dream forever. When the service was over, he did not know it. Someone he did not acknowledge as Gerald McKinney led him back to the black Cadillac and helped him into the back seat.

Bill had closed the restaurant for a reception after the funeral. Nathaniel visited with Grandma Marge and Grandpa Harry, while Ida tried to get Moses to eat something. "You've got to eat, Sarah would want you to," she said.

"I'm not hungry, ma."

"How about one of Bill's fried cinnamon rolls, you always loved Bill's fried cinnamon rolls."

"I'm still stuck on a completely different question."

"What would that be?"

"If I want to go on living without her."

"You don't have a choice about that, don't be ridiculous," said Ida, "I know you better than anyone in the world, you're not that selfish."

"What do you mean? Selfish?"

"Look over there at that little boy."

He sat with his head between his hands, "Look damn it, I said look," she was intense, but trying not to yell at him.

He lifted his head and watched Nathaniel standing beside his Grandfather.

"I know you're not selfish enough to deprive that little boy of his father after he already lost his mother, are you?"

He lowered his head back between his hands.

"Are you?" she repeated.

He raised his head back up and looked at the boy, and at that moment Nathaniel turned to look at him, and when their gaze met he recognized Sarah in the boy's soft gray eyes.

He sighed, a small sob escaping, then choked out a muffled, "No."

Dawn and Steve watched the sunset as they strolled down the beach, his right hand entwined with her left. Steve looked at the pink of the sky as it reflected in Dawn's soft brown eyes and knew that he could spend a lifetime watching the world being reflected in those eyes.

"I think he was really happy," said Dawn.

"So that's two men you've made happy today," Steve said.

"It was your idea."

"It wouldn't have been possible without you."

When the last traces of the day had vanished over the horizon, the moonlight sparkled across the cresting water as the waves gently tumbled into the sand. The smell of the water was fresh, crisp and clean, and the sound was soothing as it swished and rushed down the shoreline. You could almost hear Leslie Gore singing, "When I'm walking with you, hand in hand by the shore," except for Steve and Dawn it would have had to be a different singer from a different generation.

In the moonlight, Dawn's white uniform shimmered as if it were made of satin. She had worn the one she had shortened for length; she had worn it just for him. It clung provocatively to her, the neckline displaying enough cleavage to have Steve's imagination racing. She had never thought she would ever be brave enough to wear such a short dress, and had feared all day at work that her sister would say something to her about it, but tonight, basking in the admiration of his eyes, it all seemed perfectly natural.

Steve thought the moon reflecting in her hair gave her an almost mystical halo. He turned to her, his eyes twinkling like the stars in the sky above, and slowly placed his hands on her hips. She shuddered and looked at him with a questioning gaze as his hands came to rest on her deformity, but his expression did not change, there was no sign of the revulsion she was expecting from that moment. To Steve it was not a deformity, it was just Dawn, a misalignment perhaps, but no less endearing than a crooked smile. He felt her warmth coming through to his fingertips from underneath her dress.

"It doesn't bother you?" she asked.

"What?"

"The way I am?"

"I love the way you are." He said. "God let you go through life with an imperfection, and it's lucky for me he did."

"Lucky? How in the world can you say that? Do you know how miserable life has been like this?"

"I didn't say lucky for you," he pressed a finger to her lips, "I said lucky for me. If you were perfect, you would have been so busy with other men in your life, that you would have never even noticed me and I would have never had a chance with you. The way I look at it, I'm here with you tonight, because you have that imperfection." She tilted up her face and he looked longingly into her eyes. "Lucky for me."

His hand moved to her cheek and then back to her lips, his hand tenderly tracing their outline. In response, she dropped her shoes in the sand and clasped her hands in back of his neck.

Softly he took her head in his hands and then lowered his head to place kisses first upon her forehead, then her cheek. His lips brushed her temple, and then finally, her lips. His mouth was warm, tender, and inviting, the sensation of his lips upon hers, electric.

His arms surrounded her, and she felt her nipples respond as her breasts pressed against his chest. As she was locked in this embrace, she was suddenly overcome by the feeling that she never wanted this moment to end.

"I'm afraid I'm not going to be very good at this," she said timidly; glad that he could not see her face reddening in the darkness.

He cradled her chin in his hand, lifting it to look her squarely in the eyes. "You have no reason to apologize." Her eyes were locked upon his, "Are you afraid?" he asked, wondering if she wasn't always going to carry a fear of men with her because of what she had been through.

"No," she said, but he saw hesitation in her eyes.

"Would you admit it to me if you were?"

"I have no reason to be afraid, I love you," but her voice was tentative, and her eyes stayed on his as if unable to let go.

Her mouth was soft, warm, and open as they shared kisses and hugs in the moonlight, their hands moving, exploring, exciting each other. Slowly, deliberately, he unbuttoned her uniform, button by button, then he eagerly explored the flesh beneath her unbuttoned uniform with his fingertips, skimming his hand lightly over the surface of the skin of her collarbone, her neck, her breasts, and then down to her stomach.

"Wait," she gasped.

All the fears and apprehensions from his knowledge of what Barton had done to her, raced through him. "We don't have to do anything you don't want to do, that you don't feel comfortable about," he tried to reassure her.

"It's not that," she said, " I want to be here, I want to be with you, but I have to warn you before we go any further." All the dread of that moment, imagined and otherwise, that she had lived with for so many years welled up within her and then spilled upon the surface.

"Warn me?"

"I don't want you to faint at the sight of me, because I'm crooked."

His eyebrows bunched up in confusion, "you're what?"

"My hips, I'm deformed, that's why I limp, one's higher than the other, I'm crooked."

"Well, if we're making confessions, I guess I've got to admit something too," he said.

"What?" she asked tenderly.

"When I'm around you," he started slowly.

"Yes, go on."

"And I see the curve of your calves, and catch a glimpse of your thighs," he paused.

"Yes, and?"

"And I touch your bare skin," he stopped and smiled at her.

"Yes?"

"I get a bit bent myself."

She laughed and gave him a mock punch. And with the laughter, the anxiety and self-consciousness melted away. Strangely, she was not in the least inhibited any longer about his touch, but rather, she silently wondered why it had taken him so long. Smoothly, he guided the dress down her arms, until it fell to the sand around her ankles; she helped him remove her bra and panties of matching white lace, revealing her nakedness underneath. She looked up to his face to see him smiling in appreciation. She had fantasized of this moment when she had dressed that morning, but somehow, she never thought her fantasy would come true.

Dawn whispered a confession to Steve, "I was afraid I'd live my life alone, that I'd always be unloved."

His finger softly trembled as it moved down the side of her neck, across her shoulder, and then down to treasure the fullness of her breast.

"Dawn, is it evil for me to confess that I want you?" He kissed her, "I want to be so good for you."

"There's nothing evil about it, it's good already."

"Tell me what you're feeling."

"I love the feel of your hands on me, it makes me feel . . ." she gasped as a wave of passion overcame her, "for the first time in my life, I feel whole. You're the only one who has ever made me feel beautiful."

"Dawn, look at you," he said admiringly, "how could you ever doubt it?" He took a cold, erect nipple into his mouth and warmed it with his tongue. Her eyes closed and she forgot whether she was breathing in or out at that particular moment. A feeling of inner warmth like she had never known before rushed through her. And as he took the other breast into his mouth, all the apprehension, nervousness and fear, and all the ugliness of her memories both immediate and longstanding, vanished in the moonlight.

His lips locked upon hers and his tongue flickered hot and flashing into her welcoming mouth. A need she didn't even know was in her pushed her hands first to his belt buckle and then to the zipper of his pants, exposing the full extent of his yearning for her. He bent and slipped an arm under her knees, wrapping her up in his arms, holding her tight against his chest. He carried her a few steps down the beach and then knelt, laying her down on a blanket in the soft sand.

As she lay back to take a full look at his face, she saw him devouring her with his eyes. Her hands moved from his face down the front of his chest, unbuttoning his shirt.

He looked down at the beauty of her face in the moonlight, and asked himself if he were the luckiest man in the world or merely dreaming. He knelt over her, again finding her lips with his, his fingers tracing the outline of her breasts, then down across her stomach, and then down. He murmured as he explored her rising hipbone, and then gasped, "oh my," as he discovered her wetness.

Tears came to her eyes, and she choked on the words, "I never knew it could be like this, I mean, I imagined how it would be, but I never guessed it could be so . . ." she could not find a word that was grand enough to describe the immense emotions she was feeling, and kissed him instead.

His lips followed the course charted by his fingers, and she openly moved her legs as she felt his kiss upon her inner thigh and then his tongue exploring her. She arched her pelvis toward his face and ran her fingers through his thick hair, as his mouth tasted her with a reverence he otherwise reserved for communion.

His tongue aroused a flaming passion within her, his right hand softly gripping her breast, his left hand underneath her, delighting in the curve of her buttocks. She surrendered to the juices that ran uncontrollably inside her as his lips worked their sweet torture up her stomach, across her breasts, and back to her mouth.

"You like that?"

"Very much," she said, "when I go to bed at night, I see your hands, and think about them touching me."

"You pictured my hands?"

"Yes," she confessed and closed her eyes.

"And what were they doing?" he whispered, "this?" His hand found her and she shuttered.

"Yes," she gasped, "oh Steve, yes."

"Touch me," he told her, "don't be afraid, I'm all yours."

Her fingers were timid, and he took her hand to teach her the way. With her first stroke she heard his breath grow short. He rolled against her, then slowly drawing away, teasing her with the promise of fulfillment to come.

She could wait no longer and finally commanded, "I want you inside me." His tongue explored her mouth and then she felt his fullness sliding into her wetness like it was the missing piece of a puzzle. She wrapped her legs around him like she would never let him go.

His body joined hers with serenity and grace, when all she had been expecting was awkwardness and embarrassment, and she was at last filled, body and soul, and though the physical part of her virginity had been previously stolen, she now gave up the rest willingly, gladly.

His head was buried in the small of her neck smelling her intoxicating perfume, and could not see the broad smile upon her face. Slowly they rocked together, cherishing the oneness that at last they had found. Their spirits took flight together, dancing into the night.

In unison, the two of them rolled over on the blanket, then she rose up, arching her back in joyous exaltation, lifting her face to the starry sky, moving on top of him with an urgency like she had never felt before.

He looked up at her in naked appreciation as she closed her eyes. He caressed her breasts and she trembled, biting her bottom lip to keep from screaming with delight as a tidal wave inside her swept her away and she crashed down upon him once more, pressing her breasts against his chest as the convulsions pulsed within her.

"Are you all right?" he whispered.

"Better than all right," she smiled.

"Your hip?"

She had forgotten all about her hip, "it's not complaining a bit," she replied. She put her head to his chest, and burrowed against him, closing her eyes, feeling as if she were about to burst with emotion.

His arms wrapped around her, his face pressed to her ear. "I love you," he whispered. His hands slowly slid down her back as another convulsion made her shiver, his hands coming to rest on her hips.

Just as the waves of pleasure inside her began to ebb, again she felt the urgency and the passion of his thrusts and then his explosion, giving to her something so intense, so personally hers, so connected, that she knew in the depths of her heart that he had never shared this with anyone until this moment.

Finally, she was able to catch her breath, and with her head lying against his chest, she sighed, "I love you too."

"I think I've loved you from the moment I first saw you," he was smiling, and then grew very solemn, "and maybe even before that."

"I love you," it was said and it would never be unsaid.

"Forever," she whispered into his neck.

"Forever and ever."

Moses' face was still warm from the sunset, a smile of joy fixed upon it at the feel of the sand beneath him, and the touch of it in his hands. He took a sip of wine and watched the stars come out, remembering a night, many years before, when the stars also seemed so bright, the sky so clear.

He had come home to Sutton's Bay on leave from the war to visit Sarah and his newborn baby, the year was 1943. The afternoon had been cloudy, with spits of rain off and on, and a harsh wind constant and unforgiving out of the north.

"You're not thinking about taking that boat out in this weather are you?" Sarah had asked, her face pinched up in a frown.

"Besides thoughts of you and the baby, it's the one thought that has gotten me through the terrors of this war," Moses had said, and indeed, he had been dreaming and daydreaming about it. He had missed sailing every bit as much as he had missed his painting.

When evening had arrived, he knew that sailing would have been better left for another day, but he was determined, "stubborn," his mother had called it when he was a child, so out into the water he headed.

The waters of Grand Traverse Bay were raging, rolling in off Lake Michigan unfettered, pushed by a gale force wind blasting directly out of the north. The clouds had blown off, but the wind was unrelenting. That was what had made the clear skies and the stars so unusual that night. A wind like that usually came in at the front of an approaching storm, after the skies had clouded in warning, but not that night. It was a mysterious wind on a cold starry night.

His joy at returning home, and the thrill of feeling his boat harnessing the fury of the wind was short lived. He had just come about and was tying off the line once more when a blast of wind so fierce and so powerful snuck up on him with such surprise that he could not react. He did not know if he had been caught up in a waterspout or just a blast of wind, but the next thing he knew, his twelve-foot boat was on its side, the sail in the water and Moses in the churning surf beside it. He had capsized and there was no way in that turbulent water that he was going to right his faithful 'Slap Shot'. Each cresting breaker brought another mouthful of water as he struggled. He pushed his wet hair back and watched the floundering boat, it was a piece of his life, a piece of him, but he would have to abandon it if he were to survive.

He searched the horizon for some sign of help, but there was none. He was too close to shore to be in the shipping lanes of the commercial vessels, and no pleasure craft in their right mind would be out on a night like that. He would have to swim for shore, and just hope, hope and pray, that somehow his boat would survive the night and that he could find it in the light of day.

He had picked out an object on the shoreline to be the focus of his swim and tried to kick away from the boat, but he did not move. He kicked again and paddled his arms, but there was something wrapped around his leg. Panic filled him, another green wave crashed over him. And as the water enfolded him, he was sure he was going to drown. He spit out another mouthful of the bay and reached down. It was the bowline, he could tell by the touch of it, but he could not free himself of it. A tumultuous swell of water swept over him and the boat rolled and pulled him under with it. The water was green and angry, and it would be the last thing in this life he would see. He was going to die, he had been certain of it. Sarah's face had flashed in his mind, and he had been instantly filled with regret, for he was about to die without being able to say good-bye to Sarah, his Sarah, the love of his life. And that was the last he could remember, until the stars.

The next memory was almost unconnected to what had gone before. The stars had been clear and bright; and he had looked up at them without comprehending what had happened, stared at them, with a half-open eye. He had been sprawled on the shore half-drown, somehow spewed out by the violent water, his face crushed into the wet sand, barely conscious, unable to move. How he had gotten there, he had never been able to figure out, then or anytime since.

That's the condition in which she had found him, lying nearly lifeless, washed up on the wet sand of Donovan's Point. How she had found him, why she had looked there, he had never quite understood, but she did. And she had leaned over him, and put her lips to his, and breathed life back into him.

He had never forgotten the look of the stars on that night, a night very much like this, thought Moses, no matter how many years had passed. On this night, though, the wind was calm and gentle. Good thing, he thought, for these old bones could not stand another storm.

But Moses' placid contentment was short-lived. The empty wine bottle dropped into the sand as he grabbed his chest in answer to a swift, sharp, stabbing pain. Was it his heart? He wondered. First his hands, then his legs, then his eyes. Now his heart? The pain stabbed again. He grimaced, a small groan escaping from his mouth. Then he noticed that the brightest star on the horizon seemed to be getting closer. Was he having a heart attack? His breathing became labored. That star, he thought, is still getting closer. The pain, his face wrinkled in agony as his hands clutched his chest. Should he call out for Steve and Dawn?

Then he tried to call out, but the pain made his voice catch in his throat. He had thought for months that the end was nigh, and it wasn't that he minded that it had finally arrived, but the ache in his chest was unbearable.

"Oh, God," finally came his cry with what breath was left in him. He closed his eyes and struggled to breathe, straining for one more breath. When he reopened them, the bright star was all he could see. The starlight showered down around him, enveloping him in its glow. And all the memories that had made up his life, all the tears and laughter, all the joy and sorrow, returned to him once more.

And just as suddenly as it had come, the pain vanished, and a calm he hadn't felt in many years replaced it. A gentle hand took his, and he felt a kiss upon his cheek. Then a tender voice, and his spirit exalted in recognition of it, whispered in his ear, "I've been waiting for you, Sugar Mo."

Steve and Dawn stood hand in hand beside the grave as the flesh and bones, which Moses Bailey had left behind, were unceremoniously lowered into the ground. The day was hot, the cemetery grass was dry, and on the warm breeze was the faint, freshwater smell of Lake Michigan in the distance. White, puffy clouds drifted in front of the sun, and in the midst of the gathering of headstones, three old pine trees majestically shot upward toward the heavens.

Barton Hackett was in attendance in his official capacity as representative of the nursing home. There was no one else there to notice the mess that had become of his face. In addition to the burn and bruises that Steve had inflicted upon him and the abrasions and welts that Sam had administered, was a new swollen lump that Nancy had added with her frying pan. Barton gently lifted his finger to it, and then pulled it away cursing, wincing in pain.

A tear streaked down Dawn's cheek as she embraced the knowledge of how much she would miss Moses, and Steve felt a twinge of anger at how little acknowledgement was being paid to the old man's passing.

"Barton," said Steve, "can't these guys wait for the minister?"

There was a look of disdain on Barton's face, "If you feel you have to talk to me, you can address me as Mr. Hackett."

"Barton, why can't they wait?" Dawn asked, repeating the question.

"There's not going to be a minister," Barton said, obviously irritated.

"Don't you think somebody should say a few words at a burial like this?" asked Dawn.

"Why?" retorted Barton, "it won't make him any less dead."

"It would be useless to try and explain it," said Steve, "to a man who has no soul."

Dawn looked at Steve and felt as though the boy who had arrived at Pioneer Manor a few short weeks before had also been laid to rest, and had left a new man standing beside her.

"I want to go back," she said.

"Go back?" questioned Steve, confusion written on his face.

"I want to go back to the beach and watch the sun go down. It just seems like the right way to end the day that Moses Bailey is buried."

The yellow backhoe coughed its own cloud of diesel exhaust and methodically went about its business refilling the hole it had dug only hours before.

"Do you believe in forever?" Dawn asked Steve.

Steve stared ahead pensively, and did not answer her right away, watching another bucket of dirt spill into the grave. "I never really thought about it until I met Moses," he finally said, "and I don't think I really believed in love until I met you."

She looked at Steve's face, "Doesn't it seem that if you believe in one, you believe in the other?"

He lifted his face and turned toward her and his gaze locked onto her eyes, "I believe I'll love you forever," he said. And she smiled.

They turned and walked toward the car, still hand in hand, and as they left, the clouds parted and the sun shone down once more.

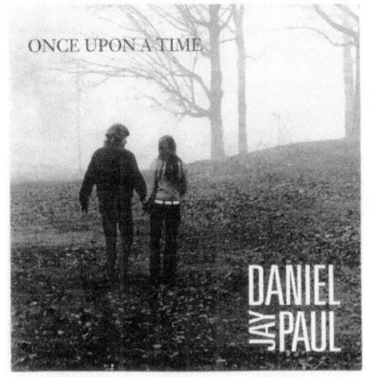